Think of the Earth

Thou art a dreaming thing,
A fever of thyself: think of the earth.

JOHN KEATS

Think of the Earth

Bertram Brooker

Introduction, Notes, and Bibliography
by Glenn Willmott

Brown Bear Press

Think of the Earth
by Bertram Brooker
Introduction, Notes, and Bibliography by Glenn Willmott

Brown Bear Press acknowledges the financial support of the Government of Canada through the Book Publishing Industry Development Programme for our publishing activities through Canadian Scholars' Press.

Canadian Cataloguing in Publication Data

Brooker, Bertram, 1888-1955
Think of the earth

ISBN 1-894184-00-9

I. Willmott, Glenn, 1963– . II. Title.

PS8503.R63T5 2000 C813'.52 C00-932239-6
PR9199.3.B6966T5 2000

First published in 2000 by Brown Bear Press
180 Bloor Street West, Suite 1202
Toronto, Ontario M5S 2V6

Brown Bear Press was founded with the express purpose of bringing great Canadian literature back into print. Please send any suggestions for reprinting to the attention of the Publisher.

Publisher: Ruth Bradley-St-Cyr
Marketing Manager: Susan Cuk
Production Editor and Proofreading: Linda Bissinger
Cover and interior design: Gordon Robertson

00 01 02 03 04 05 06 6 5 4 3 2 1

Printed and bound in Canada

To Raymond Mullens

without whose encouragement and help this book would never have been finished

BERTRAM BROOKER

Acknowledgements

This edition has been made possible in part through the generous support of a Research Grant from the Social Sciences and Humanities Council of Canada. This writer would also like to thank Ruth Bradley-St-Cyr, Publisher of Brown Bear Press, whose love of Canadian literature inspired the project from beginning to end; to Stephen Ross of the Graduate Program in English at Queen's University, for his cheerfully tireless research assistance; to Yaël Schlick of the English Department, for invaluable critical suggestions during the revision process; and to the Brooker family, and especially John Brooker, who generously responded to our myriad needs, and provided the excellent 1936 copy of the novel upon which this edition is based.

Glenn Willmott
Kingston, Ontario
October 2000

CONTENTS

Acknowledgements vi
Introduction ix

PART ONE: FRIDAY

1 The Town 3
2 The Printshop 17
3 Tavistock 27
4 The Lawyer's Office 41
5 Linklater 47
6 The Canon 55
7 Laura 63
8 The Encounter 73
9 The World's Sorrows 83
10 The Secret 93

PART TWO: SATURDAY

1 The Bunk Car 109
2 Gawthorp 119
3 Questions 131

4 Jukes 141
5 The Lake 149
6 The Drive Home 161
7 Togetherness 173
8 The Comforter 183

PART THREE: SUNDAY

1 Laura Awakens 197
2 Struggle 205
3 Surrender 213
4 Love 227
5 Faith 247
6 Transfiguration 261
7 The Miracle 273
8 Illumination 281

Notes 291
Selected Bibliography 297

Introduction

"That corpse you planted last year in your garden,
"Has it begun to sprout? Will it bloom this year?
"Or has the sudden frost disturbed its bed?
"Oh keep the Dog far hence, that's friend to men,
"Or with his nails he'll dig it up again!
"You! hypocrite lecteur!—mon semblable,—mon frère!"

– T.S. Eliot, *The Waste Land*

At the turn of the century, the modern age seemed to hold such promise. Yet, in the wake of a world war, when Eliot published these lines, this promise seemed to come at a mephistophelian cost, a cost from which none escaped responsibility. That "you" accused of burying its corpse as the seed of selfish ends, that "you" suddenly turns out to be us: you, hypocritical reader, you too are implicated here. An obscure crime seems to have been committed, of which none of us is innocent.

That, too, is the premise of this novel about a man obsessed by the desire to embody, to make manifest, and thus symbolically to justify, the barbarism—as Brooker's contemporary, the German-Jewish writer Walter Benjamin put it—that goes hand in hand with civilized history. To justify this history is to struggle with the question: must the violence of war, the oppression of working classes, and the colonization of ethnic and gender differences, belong to the "unity" of our civilization? Do our most personal, daily lives, yours and mine, depend upon it? Is not every corner of our lives, from the food and clothing we buy, to the automobiles or airplanes we use, made possible by a global industrial machinery, its ambivalent politics, its structural poverty, and its catastrophic ecology? In such an interdependent world, is Canada any different?

This novel, written two decades after the totalizing violence of the First World War, during the escalating labour conflicts and sufferings of the Great Depression, looks back to the world at the turn of the modern century as the emergence of the scene of a vast crime—an ongoing immiseration of worldwide proportions, in which all may recognize their complicity and their guilt. Even in peaceable Canada, in a small Prairie town far from centres of global power in wealth and politics, the fateful structures of immigrant exploitation, aboriginal oppression, imperialist warfare, and a ruthlessly mobile, capitalist rationalization haunt the life of the community. But it is the uncanny apprehension, not merely of the invasion of global injustice into every corner of the world, but of a newly agonizing, global complicity, of every person and community with the miseries of others—what we must buy into, in order to live—that makes this historical novel so peculiarly contemporary to us at the century's end. The novel also stages a familiar Canadian dilemma in a unique way. What is Canada? Does it represent a way of living with modernity that is, or may be, different?

The purpose of this introduction is not to answer these questions, but to supply a beginning framework and contexts useful for understanding the way these questions get asked in the novel (my own reading of the novel is forthcoming in my book, *Unreal*

Country: Modernity and the Canadian Novel in English). Nor can I hope to do justice to the full range and richness of the novel's intertexts, but only aim to provide here, together with my notes, enough commentary to help the reader appreciate the novel's critical and literary values today. I will begin with a discussion of the author himself—his life, his activities, and interests. I'll then turn to the novel, to sketch out its general theme, to indicate some intertexts with which it is in dialogue, and to hint at an appreciation of its style.

Bertram Brooker

In an unpublished autobiographical novel completed after *Think of the Earth*, Brooker paints a portrait of childhood in impoverished urban England, the grey air redolent of the pub and the fish and chips shop, and roaring with passing trains. The child protagonist is born six months following the miscarriage of a female twin, marking him as somehow "queer." Feeling "in a vague sort of way, that he oughtn't to have been born . . . that he belongs, somehow, with his dead sister," he tells us he is destined to feel incomplete, and to search for some kind of primal, ideal completion in the world and others around him. Whether this is literally true, or a writer's metaphor, it shows just how profound was Brooker's sense of otherness as constitutive of self, and of unresolved differences as constitutive of life, as well as the insatiable desire to keep searching them out, to see them whole. This unusual sense would mark all of his art.

Brooker was born in Croydon, just south of London, in 1888. His father was a train despatcher, and from a young age Brooker worked odd jobs to help support the family, leaving school at the age of 12 to work for a dairy. By this time he was also singing in a church choir, and the experience of music would remain extremely important in his later painting and writing. In 1905, when Brooker was seventeen, his family immigrated to Canada, making their destination Portage la Prairie, Manitoba. He and his father found work in the building of the new Grand Trunk Pacific railroad—just as this novel's protagonist will do. In the choir of the Anglican church, Brooker met Mary Aurilla Porter, whom he married in 1913. His Canadian career henceforth is fascinating and diverse. He co-owned a cinema in Neepawa, and sold filmscripts to Vitagraph. He wrote free-lance journalism for newspapers in the West and in Ontario, notably "The Seven Arts" column for the Toronto *Globe* which was syndicated across the country. He went into advertising. In the mid-1920s he became editor and publisher of *Marketing* in Toronto, then in 1929 copy and art director for J.J. Gibbons advertising agency. In 1937 he moved to MacLaren Advertising, where he had risen to vice-president by the time of his death in 1955. Under the pseudonym Richard Surrey, he published two groundbreaking books on forms of writing and visual design in advertising, replete with literary and artistic examples and references, whose poetic and aesthetic analyses of advertising prefigure the approach and insights of Marshall McLuhan's *The Mechanical Bride: Folklore of Industrial Man* (1951), the polemical optimism of his *Culture is Our Business* (1970), and the birth of cultural studies.

Brooker was a prolific and versatile artist, writing essays, poetry, plays, and fiction, and from the 1920s onward, drawing and painting as well. He was a member of the Arts and Letter Club, where he met the Group of Seven, and where Arthur Lismer sponsored his first exhibition of paintings in 1927. Later he became actively involved in P.E.N. Canada. Initially strongly influenced by the modernist aesthetics, mystical philosophy, and Canadian nationalism of Lawren Harris and F.B. Housser, he became known both as a pioneer abstractionist in Canada, associated with the Group, and as a commentator on the arts in

Canada in influential publications of the day. Today he is best known for this intense involvement in modern Canadian art, a helpful overview of which may be found in Dennis Reid's book for the National Gallery of Canada. Brooker's literary contribution is no less important. He published poetry and a short story in *Canadian Forum*, wrote numerous plays, including avant-garde dramas brought to stage by the expressionist Herman Voaden, and wrote three published novels, of which *Think of the Earth* won the first Governor General's award for fiction in 1936. The second novel is *The Tangled Miracle*, a crime thriller, written under a pseudonym, about the death of a mystical cult leader. The third novel, *The Robber*, is about a revolutionary leader in the Holy Land whose career parallels and contrasts that of Jesus, his contemporary and rival as an icon of subversion; this is his best-crafted novel, and some consider it his finest. The foremost scholar of this wider scope of Brooker's drama and fiction is Sherrill Grace: balanced, insightful, and detailed, her work provides an excellent account of its interpretive problems and contexts. Other fundamental literary resources are Birk Sproxton's edition of Brooker's poetry, and Jennifer Oille Sinclair's special issue of *Provincial Essays* devoted to "Bertram Brooker and Emergent Modernism."

It is not easy to represent the range and ferment of Brooker's literary, philosophical, political, and artistic interests. His wide-ranging engagement in diverse arts reflects the highly individualistic, experimental, and often anti-conventional approach to society and art of William Blake. In his illuminated book, *The Marriage of Heaven and Hell* (1793), Blake strove to transcend conventional concepts of good and evil, prefiguring the moral concerns of this novel. In an autobiographical fragment of 1937, he says that the existentialist philosopher Friedrich Nietzsche also made a profound, early impact on him. Certainly the commitment to a world "beyond good and evil" is evident as early as his cinema days in Neepawa. In an article published in *The Photoplay Author* in 1913, he foresees a cinema that will "supercede our churches," and should provide a drama that is "neither tragedy or comedy—the world has had enough of morals, it wants inspiration"; in an unpublished play of 1912, *Cassandra*, the heroine is writing a book similar to *Thus Spoke Zarathustra* (1885), Nietzsche's most popular account of his "transvaluation of all values" such as good and evil (qtd. and discussed by Anton Wagner 42, 46). This corrosively historicist and existentialist philosophy was a consistent thread in Brooker's work, which he wove together, however paradoxically, with various traditions of idealism in Christian discourse, modern mysticism, nationalism, and social politics. Such idealism was never a starting point, like his Nietzschean dicta, but the form of an impulse, a desire, to totalize and make sense of his world even so. In this quest he explored classics in philosophy—e.g. Arthur Schopenhauer, Voltaire, David Hume, Francis Bacon, Aristotle—and in literature—e.g. Fyodor Dostoevsky, Leo Tolstoy, Walt Whitman, the English romantics, J.W. von Goethe, John Milton, William Shakespeare, the Bible (especially Job). He also read modern writers—e.g. Alfred North Whitehead, G.K. Chesterton, Henry Adams, T.S. Eliot, Aldous Huxley, George Bernard Shaw, Vasili Kandinski, Joseph Conrad, Maurice Maeterlink, Norbert Wiener—and was interested in Canadian writers such as Martha Ostenso and Morley Callaghan (a powerful portrait of whom he painted in 1932). Indeed there is a striking reference to Callaghan's work in Brooker's unpublished "Self-Portrait: An Experiment in Autobiography" of 1937, a year after the publication of *Think of the Earth*. In trying to tell us about his own early interest in mystical dialectics, subsequently countered by a rejection of unifying theories of the world, he finds a parallel in Callaghan's novel (presumably *Such Is My Beloved*, 1934) about "a man who wanted to be the St Thomas Aquinas of his time" and goes mad. Brooker says he identifies with this man, but without going mad. The same story, of the same tendential madness, is told by *Think of the Earth*.

It must lastly be mentioned that Brooker brought his intellectual concerns to the realm of social politics. Perhaps because of the "filthiness, viciousness and woe" of the English "slums" in which he grew up (qtd. in Wagner, 44), Brooker was always sympathetic to working-class suffering and its points of view. There are significant working-class characters and groups in most of his fiction (e.g. his short story published in *Canadian Forum*, reprinted by Donna Phillips). In many of his drafts and plans for unfinished novels, class struggle and strike action are central to the plot; a railway-workers' strike is the climax of an earlier outline of *Think of the Earth*. No doubt his witnessing of the Winnipeg General Strike in 1919, in which he was a specially appointed constable, affected him deeply, for in general, he was sympathetic to the revolutionary spirit of class struggle as akin to the revolutionary role of the artist in society. For this very reason, however, he was wary of Communism and Marxism to the extent that these orthodoxies presented a unified and moralized vision of history and the world which was counter to his own sense of it as creatively unpredictable, conflicted and heterogeneous (for a statement contemporary with *Think of the Earth*, see Brooker's Introduction to his *Yearbook of the Arts in Canada 1936).*

Think of the Earth

In order to talk about this novel's concerns, but without giving anything away, its peculiar plot may be summarized as follows. A stranger comes to town, and partly because of his odd ideas, partly because he associates with persons marginal to acceptable society, he gains a reputation for eccentricity. When it appears that he thinks himself a potential messiah, and is anticipating some kind of miraculous murder, he is judged to be mad and dangerous. For this murder, a subplot is elaborated, which involves the betrayal of a Métis man and his search for restitution. Another subplot is the developing love between the stranger and the daughter of an Anglican cleric, who is also wooed by the aggressive son of a wealthy land speculator. Arguably, because of the discursive rather than narrative importance of the mystery surrounding the stranger and his feared violence, what I have called the two subplots are better understood as a bifurcated main plot, in which our supposed protagonist is not necessarily central. In the following thematic discussion, therefore, the focus on this protagonist's ideas is the result of adhering to the novel's most direct and simplified expression of its concerns, and does not represent the crucial functions of other characters and elements.

The novel's theme is posed in the form of a theological problem. However, it would be a mistake to see the novel as necessarily Christian or even religious—except in an unconventionally broad sense. Theology is present in this novel to provide an imagery for the idea and the ideal of totality, which is to say, what Brooker expected to be a popularly accessible language in which to talk about the abstraction of metaphysical order in the day-to-day appearance of a fragmented world. The problem can be divided into the following steps: (a) Crime no longer appears exceptional, but somehow intrinsic to our world, which reproduces "misery" in every corner of life, for conquered races and oppressed classes everywhere. This is where Joseph Conrad's influence is most felt. Poplar Plains is like Marlow's Africa, a place where modernity has collapsed together its own legitimating signs of good and evil, of darkness and light. (b) How is such a world, in which there is no getting *outside* of crime, tolerable?

Indeed, how is the traditional morality of good and evil meaningful? (c) Perhaps we need a symbolic martyr, like Christ, to represent this condition to us, and by so doing, to transcend it, offering a new and more adequate, *transvalued* morality. The desire to represent a new kind of world is not only theological: it is a problem for art. Here is where the promises and problems facing William Blake's revolutionary poet, John Keats' sympathetic poet, and Walt Whitman's democratic poet are explicitly invoked as intertexts. (d) But a Christ that has not committed a crime, cannot be an adequate symbol for this world and its suffering—that is, not only the suffering of immiseration, but the suffering of the criminal, of the condition of complicity that appears inescapable; what new form of Christ is called for? (e) The protagonist finds his answer somewhat in the way Nietzsche did—in himself! He will embody a new, truer morality, one that is "beyond good and evil," but he would also suffer some universally symbolic event that will reveal the truth of this morality—that "there is no evil," hence no crime—to the world.

The protagonist's messianism, therefore, is not simply an eccentric mania, a character flaw to be overcome for a happy ending. It arises from this deeper thematic problem, which transcends the protagonist and affects the novel itself as a literary form. It is the problem of representing in the unity of a symbolic act, a symbolic hero, or a symbolic form such as the novel, the shifting, heterogenous welter of modern life—a life that refuses to be pinned down, categorized, or delimited, which is to say, falsely unified in its differences, falsely arrested in its evolutions. The protagonist wants to "represent" just such a chameleonic world, a world in which existence precedes essence, a world of creativity and contradiction. It is a world in which good and evil, and indeed the very order of things and their God, are indeterminate products of ongoing human creation and struggle. Would not a single symbol, or image, or text, by definition be impossible?

Hence the protagonist's central problem in the novel, which is also that of the novel itself: wanting—indeed, urgently needing, to compensate his sense of self and sanity for the horrors given to his perceptions and feelings in the world—to express and reveal this new and peculiarly modern vision, but at the same time unable to "rest" with any one image of it, any one symbolic action, any one form of redemption or restitution (and certainly none proceeding narrowly from his own uniqueness, his own will). He wishes to abandon himself to a larger totality that is *unrepresentable*, and become its *sign*. To "think of the earth" means always to turn back from such a sign, to a world that escapes it.

It is important to understand this general problem of representation, as distinct from the problem of morality, because only the former gets resolved at the novel's end (and implicitly through the novel's form). We may be expecting, like all the townspeople who try to pigeonhole our hero as merely "mad," that the novel's narrative closure will see him "cured." But he holds to all the same premises with which he began, and only changes his understanding of how to "see" them and to represent them in himself to others. He is not cured of his apparently asocial and "dangerous" amorality. Rather, as a result of witnessing the actual and theatrical realizations of his desired "crime," he learns how the world and himself are to be read; he learns to adapt to a darkly glimpsed, symbolic order. Symbolization of that modern world in which the self is enmeshed—the possibility or impossibility of such representation, as well as its tolerability or forbiddenness, once moral symbols appear obsolete—turns out to be the central theme of the novel.

The political dimension of this problem of symbolization is prophetic for us today. The reader will discover that Brooker at once represents his Prairie town with loving regional detail, historical as well as social, and reveals the region's structural position in a nation and a world system that have created it and partly determine its fate. We must ask, is Poplar Plains an allegory of a particular region, the West, an allegory of a larger nation, Canada, or an allegory of a postnational society, whose migrants and markets cannot be understood apart from a global situation? Does Poplar Plains have a Western identity, apart from Canada; or a Canadian identity, apart from modernity itself? The novel both seeks to understand its local world by trying to imagine its whole space and time (with character types and events representing various ideologies and historical interests and developments, coming together at a crucial, transitional date), and by undermining this view of the whole by questioning its inclusive adequacy and asking us to look again at unintegrated details and differences (to think of the earth). In feeling the problem of "unity" to be exemplified on the Canadian frontier, which is to say in Canada as a frontier, as a nation peristently in the making (or the unmaking), Brooker's novel is remarkably prescient.

Finally, what I have attempted to lay out as a thematic problem affecting the symbolic status of the protagonist and of the setting, is inevitably a problem for the symbolic coherence of the novel itself. In one sense, Brooker's solution is a realist one. He will strive to represent in realist detail, a peripheral community's entanglement in the injustices of modern social development, preferably at a moment of transition that will throw this development into relief (hence the historical perspective supplied by the aged cleric, the setting of the action in the opening decade of the new century, and the building of the new railway which brings new immigrant populations as well as new industrial activities and relations into what had been an agricultural, and before that colonial trading, settlement). But in another sense, the problem is more difficult, and realism is not enough. The novel seeks not only to depict this dark modernity, but to make sense of it, to discover its logic, its own structure of feeling and ideal justification. This requires romance. The protagonist seeks a way of embodying this sense in a universal sign: a murder that will paradoxically be the sign of the rationalization or justification of that inescapable murder—hence its "innocence"—which he sees as the driving truth of the modern world. The plot is driven by the promise of an ideal change, either in the protagonist or metonymically in his world. The world is swept up in this promise; no person or particle escapes. It cannot simply *be*, it must *mean*, and further, according to the logic of romance, it must portend the fulfillment or the failure of this promise. But the logic of romance is already the logic of good and evil, in another form, which this novel wants to transcend. The novel's closure seems to declare, as does its title, a retreat to a simple realism. But the order of things that is affirmed is not so simple, pregnant as it is with the values of Nietzschean creativity, and of a "love" which draws the self into and across the indeterminate web of particular differences of existence, their sensualities and conflicts. It is worth remembering that this web includes the novel's audience. However fraught the style and structure of the novel, therefore, it does not alienate itself from the popular audience of its time, and rather has a stake in playing to it. While disfigured by the formal problems of modernist writing, therefore, it avoids inventing new generic conventions, or pursuing the specialized audience of high modernism.

Think of the Earth does not clearly resolve the thematic or stylistic problems it sets for itself, just as it does not entirely escape the prejudices of symbols and languages (e.g. Native, Christian, sexual, existentialist, romantic) of its time and place. But its very irresolution takes a particularly Canadian and prophetically contemporary form. Its unstable compression of desires for unity and difference, of desires for signs of belonging and for skepticism towards them, belongs to our national history.

Think of the Earth

I

Friday

ONE

The Town

I

HE BRUSHED the flat thatch of hair from his forehead with a slow sweep of his hand, and stood up, turning his back on the litter of notes he had been scribbling all afternoon. Even here, among his books in the little library, there was an outdoor look about him. He had lived much in the sun. His skin had been permanently browned and toughened during the early days out there as a missionary among the Indians. His face was seamed now with a network of wrinkles like a withered apple. There was something of the backwoodsman, too, in his slow awkwardness, and the uncertain, hesitant drawl of his speech. Without his clerical collar no stranger would have taken him for a minister, yet Canon Macaulay was better known than the bishop from end to end of Manitoba.

He had come there from the East by steamboat down the Red River to Winnipeg, and by canoe to this very spot which was now the centre of his deanery, where he had built a log church with his own hands on the shore of the lake for a congregation of breeds and Indians, who had settled in a scattered village there not many years before.

He had been there thirty years and the place had changed beyond belief. The town of Poplar Plains had grown up in the meantime, and now a second railroad was coming through. Jim Conover's farm had been torn up with steam shovels, and turned into a huge gravel pit, employing a couple of hundred Galicians. North of the tracks, on the bare prairie, the Galicians were building themselves a village of tar-papered shacks. Out west of town a frame roundhouse had been flung up. They were excavating with scrapers at the end of Anne Street for a station that was to be built of Manitoba limestone. The town council had decided to put down granolithic sidewalks. A new bank was going up; and the member for Lakeside had told Dr. Bundy that the plans for the new wing at the Home for Incurables had finally passed the cabinet.

This year of 1907 was the best the community had seen since the boom of '82. There was an air of hustling expectancy everywhere—everywhere, perhaps, except at St. Stephen's rectory, where Canon Macaulay, with his ageing wife, and a daughter, Laura, lived near the edge of poverty on his tiny stipend.

The Canon lamented the changes that were taking place in the town. He had been there long enough to have his memories of the old village grow glamorous with the passing of time. Mrs. Macaulay, on the other hand, had never recovered from the shock of transplantation to the "wilds." It had dazed her, and she had gone about ever since in a sort of trance, seldom leaving the house except to walk across the lawn to the church and back again, mingling among the parishioners like a sleep-walker. Her increasing deafness made her more than ever a recluse. Most of her time was spent upstairs, doing needlework for unfortunates poorer than themselves.

There had been talk of keeping Laura in the East and giving her proper tuition so that she might become a concert pianist; but lack of money had made it impossible. She was back in town for good, giving lessons in a little room across the hall; a small, slender girl with eager eyes and an elusive smile which betrayed the inward ecstasies she fed on in the quiet house.

2

The Canon swung round again to his desk. With a deliberate sweep of his two hands he scooped the litter of papers together. He stood still, frowning, shuffling the edges of the slips of paper until they were even. He shook his head dejectedly and reached for the mounted buffalo-hoof he used for a paper-weight. He placed the hoof squarely on top of the papers, standing there pressing on it and shaking his head.

He should never have started a sermon with another man's thought. The idea was fantastic—paradoxical. He should leave such notions alone. These rebellious youngsters were always trying to bait somebody with hard sayings. He shouldn't have allowed himself to be disturbed.

And yet he could hear Tavistock's voice very distinctly, mouthing that phrase with his precise English accent: "The Comforter will come to reprove the world of sin and righteousness and judgment."

The problem of good and evil was old enough, but this was a new slant on it. Nobody had ever quoted that phrase at him before. And it puzzled him.

He leaned against the desk, twisting one leg around the other. "Confound these youngsters," he grumbled to himself. "They seize on something like this and make a mountain of it—"

But he knew he was being unjust. This Englishman he had run into the other night was no ordinary quibbler. He was no ordinary man. There was something strange about him—something unusually forceful. There was a penetrating quality in his voice, for one thing, and a very dramatic way of talking—almost as though he were playing a role on the stage and knew all his speeches in advance.

"Yes, yes," the Canon complained to himself, impatiently, "but why can't I answer him? I've thought of nothing else for a couple of days now. He seems to have got under my skin. And yet I can get nothing down but a lot of gabble—a lot of dry old doctrine. Somehow or other he made this thing a matter of life and death. What's the matter with me that I can't answer him in his own terms? I must be getting old-fashioned. I haven't any sense of the dramatic. I'm an old fogey. I'm getting old."

He felt like calling Laura in to fling a string of questions at her. "What are my sermons like, darling? Are they ever dramatic? Do they soak into your mind? D'you think they change anyone's life?"

But he knew what his pulpit manner was like. He wasn't magnetic, like this Englishman. And all he spouted was old doctrine.

"I'm getting old," he said ruefully, straightening his legs and shuffling across the worn carpet to the study door.

He went through the curtained doorway into the hall, and there was Laura in the music-room, as they called it now, standing behind a diminutive, fair-haired girl, who sat very upright on the piano stool, striking at the notes timidly with one finger.

At the hall-rack he stopped to fit tightly down on his head the round black hat that made him look a little more like a parson. Standing there, he glanced again at Laura. She, like everything else, was growing up. The pleated white blouse she wore had a close-fitting neck of lace that came tightly up under her chin. It gave her a dressed-up look, he thought, like the pictures of royalty in the English illustrated papers which he picked up occasionally at the magistrate's house, when he went on Saturday nights to play cribbage. She was a woman already and would perhaps be leaving them soon. Young Harry Anderson had come back from Winnipeg to teach singing in the town, and she might marry him one of these days. There would be no young voice through the house, then. Only Jessica and himself moving slowly in and out of the rooms and on the stairs—the two of them left there with perhaps twenty years to live—and the house echoing around them.

"Are you going with the notices?" Laura said, suddenly turning and seeing him there.

He nodded his round hat at her, and she half-called again: "Did you think of going for the mail, too?"

With a gruff, double grunt in his throat he assented, and when she parted her lips at him, the travesty of a beard, not so big as a half-dollar, in the deep cleft of his chin, twisted a little sideways as his face crumpled into a familiar, intimate grimace.

3

He went out on to the verandah, his fingers lingering on the knob of the door as he closed it, his squat head bobbing under the clerical hat as he went down the steps and out of the shade of the dusty lilacs into dazzling sunshine.

The spring had been late and the sun was making up for lost time, baking the black prairie roads until they were patterned with cracks like old china, and blistering the paint on the frame buildings of the town as it poured down, day after day, in an unbroken spell of "harvesting" weather.

The Canon paused with his hand on the hot post of the gate to sniff the leafy smell of the garden. He belonged to the plains and the bush. The stamp of the backwoods clung to him in spite of his black clothes, his round collar, and the silver cross on his watch-chain. He lifted his seared, parched face into the sunshine, inhaling deeply the hot, earthy air. There was no hurry.

He was only going to the *Monitor* office—his usual Friday afternoon errand.

Glancing for a moment at the upper windows, he started along the raised wooden sidewalk toward the avenue. His black eyes, very wide apart under thick, slanting eyebrows, concerned themselves with the sights of the street, travelling across the scorched grass of the boulevard and the dusty black road to the walls of the Methodist Church with its three windows arching thinly too close to the roof—then back, across the road again, to ascend slowly and intimately the peaked front of his own little church, until his glance reached the generously projecting eaves and the slim steeple holding aloft a cross.

Almost stifling in his face was the heat flung out by the blistered walls of the Manitoba Hotel, a square wooden box of a building which stood at the corner, the yard running back along Charlotte Street with dilapidated outhouses behind, and a high board fence which cut off the stable from the fringe of lawn surrounding the church. Stale fumes of beer and a low roar of voices were belched at the Canon as he passed the slitted swing doors of the bar.

He reached the corner, walking leisurely, with his hands behind him, and looked up the avenue. It was wide enough to dwarf the tin fronts of stores on the opposite side.

He glanced first westward, beyond the last few dwindling shacks and the sprawling lumber yard, to the poplar bluff that hid the horizon and blotted out all but the white gables of Judge Boak's old house, gleaming in a blur of green.

Eastward, the rutted dust of the avenue cut the town widely in half. Turning that way the Canon faced the two familiar stunted rows of tin and wooden shop-fronts, with room enough between the two sidewalks for a dozen buggies to drive abreast.

In the old days he had seen trotting races up and down there, before the track was built at the new Exhibition Grounds. He remembered the first year they had held the winter races on the avenue, a year when the snow came early and was too deep and loose on the lake for them to make the usual ice-track there. The snow was hard-packed in the centre of the wide avenue that winter, and piled up in front of the stores, making a bank that was higher in places than people's heads on the sidewalk.

His backward-turning mind swung quickly into the present as somebody called out, "'Ware there, Canon!" from above his head. Stone for the new bank was littered in his way, and looking up he saw a big block circling slowly in the air as it rose on a tackle to the pediment over the columned doorway. Fred Adams, clinging to the masonry with one hand, was steadying the rope with the other.

"Wouldn't do your head no good—this wouldn't," Fred Adams bawled down at him.

"You're right, it wouldn't," the Canon said, a smile breaking over his face as he recognized one of his vestrymen.

While his head was thrown back he studied the block of stone, noting the shine of the sun on its side and the veined pattern running through it.

"You don't tell me it's marble," he called up at the mason.

"Sure it's marble—what else?" Adams shouted down, grinning broadly at the screwed-up face squinting against the sunlight with a flabbergasted air.

"God bless my soul!" the Canon murmured, dropping his chin and moving slowly on. "Marble! Marble in Poplar Plains!"

4

He went musingly on, pondering the changes that were coming over the place. It would never be the same again, and he would never get used to it. His mind would always be harking back to the old days, when they all knew each other and called each other by their first names. Precious few of them there were then, in squatters' cabins along the lake-shore, listening at night to the drums of the Crees and watching the glow of their fires around the bend where the Home stood now.

He had reached the corner of Anne Street, and was halfway across, but the old blue water-cart, with Toby Cottrell perched half-asleep on top, was turning on to the avenue. The Canon scrambled back on the sidewalk to avoid the spurting water.

Toby's cart was a relic of older days, and the smell of the sprinkled dust made him think of times when there were not even wooden sidewalks anywhere, but just a few planks thrown down along the paths. Yet here he was on a broad cement sidewalk, the newest innovation in the town, glaring whitely in the sun.

The coming of the new railroad had caused a slight boom in real estate. People who had been holding property for years were making money on it. The wives of bankers, lawyers, real estate men and a few politicians were beginning to put on airs. There were "society" weddings every now and then these last few years, and the English church, on such occasions, would be banked with flowers. Eight or nine choir-boys would be there with the organist to sing "The Voice that breathed o'er Eden," and the Canon, at the steps of the tiny chancel, in cassock, surplice, stole and hood, surrounded by women in billowing gowns and bare arms—with the perfume of hothouse flowers, brought in from Winnipeg, sweetly assailing his nostrils—would utter the lines of the marriage ceremony in a voice that was changing too, influenced by the finery and the new manners of his parishioners. His eyelids fluttered more than usual when they all crowded into the vestry, and the little girls he had christened and prepared for confirmation stood around him—grown women now—frivolous, scented, in soft-coloured silks, looking down into his ageing eyes as though he were a sort of tradesman who dispensed religion and marriage certificates.

On these occasions he became very conscious of the flat thatch of hair hanging stiffly over his forehead. His squat, wizened face, the discoloured, dark moustache that dropped over his ungainly mouth, his neck scored with deep wrinkles, had all been coarsened by roughing it so many years. While others prospered he was still unable to afford a horse and buggy, and was forced to visit his parishioners on foot, in all sorts of weather, reaching distant parts of his deanery in somebody's wagon or going out with a section gang on a hand-car, sitting on a spike-keg between the rising and falling handles.

In the winter, when it was often thirty or forty below zero, and blizzards blew across the prairie, piling great drifts across the roads, it was a heart-breaking task to drive miles into the country in a borrowed cutter to read the funeral service over the body of some worn-out old farmer who perhaps had never entered his church; or plod through the snow on foot to the outskirts of the town, to the shack of some old Indian he had known since his earliest days, to speak words of comfort in broken Cree. And perhaps, before leaving, he would find a rusty buck-saw, and cut a few sticks of cord-wood for the dazed old squaw, crouched beside the bed, helpless and wailing.

All along the lake there were cabins, and even a tepee or two still, which few white men, other than himself, had ever entered. They knew him well in these huts, for it was along this bank that he had built his first church with his own hands, his hammer ringing out over the water in the days when the bush grew down to its edge. The Indians coming in to the fort would sit around on old willow roots, listening to his talk, grunting and nodding and smoking their long pipes.

5

A familiar voice hailing him brought the Canon out of his reverie. Dr. Bundy, head of the Home for Incurables, was sitting in a very new-looking buggy, drawn up close to the walk. He was the closest friend the Macaulays had in the town, a heavy, blond man whose face was almost hidden by thick yellow-grey whiskers and a sharp-pointed beard.

"Good land, you *are* all slicked up, Sturge," the Canon said, surveying the newly washed rig, the glistening red spokes, the whip upright in its holder, with a brand new lash tied to the stock, and the glossy flanks of Minnie, a favourite roan mare the doctor had driven for years.

"Yes, we're pretty snappy in our old age," the doctor chuckled, looking down his beard into the Canon's twinkling black eyes.

"I was hoping I would see you before Sunday," Macaulay said, lowering his voice and resting one foot on the step of the buggy. "I was talking to the Relief Committee yesterday about old Dave Linklater. You know where he is—down there."

Dr. Bundy nodded and grunted simultaneously.

"You haven't seen him lately, I guess."

"No."

The Canon screwed up his face and looked significantly into Dr. Bundy's serious slate-blue eyes. "He's a candidate for you, Sturge, I'm afraid."

"Is that so—is *that* so?" said the doctor, shaking his big unwieldy head slowly from side to side.

"He's got two granddaughters, you know—little wisps of things that ought to be looked after. Instead of that, they're looking after *him*. He's in bad shape, Sturge. Just a living skeleton, and raving—cursing one minute and quoting scripture the next."

The Canon clicked his tongue two or three times against the

roof of his mouth, and wagged his head apprehensively. "I tell you, I was shocked. One of the youngsters is sick, too—the older one. Nothing serious, I guess, but still . . . Laura is going over after supper with something, just to keep them going. I believe the town will be sending Fred Philp to-day or to-morrow—"right away," they said—to see what can be done. The old man ought to be up at the Home, Sturge. That's a sure thing."

A short, professional grunt sounded in the doctor's throat. "Not dangerous, is he?"

"I don't know. I don't think so. It's religious mania—and pretty far gone."

The Canon paused and wiped two fingers across his straggling moustache.

"I dropped in there the other night, and there was a man called Tavistock—an Englishman—he's the timekeeper out at the railroad, and a bit of a fanatic himself, from what I could gather. He told me that Julie Robillard has been keeping 'em alive the last month or so. She runs across there with something every day."

The doctor grunted again, less professionally. "Well, well," he said, thoughtfully, a slight smile curling his thick moustache. "Old Julie turning Good Samaritan, eh?"

The Canon's head began bobbing in a quick series of nods. "She's running a straight boarding-house, apparently. Pitts stays there—you know? — the old fellow at the *Monitor* — and two or three men from the brickyard. This man Tavistock knows all about them, apparently. He's a queer chap—he—"

The Canon took his foot from the step and leaned closer to the buggy. He was conscious of the passers-by behind him. More than once, while they had been talking, he had noticed the doctor's downward glance caught by a nod as somebody went past. They were familiar figures in the town—old-timers, both of them. People hushed their chatter as they went by, ready to nod or speak if either of them should glance their way.

"You haven't run across this fellow Tavistock, have you?" the Canon asked, wrinkling his nose to look up into the light.

The doctor was about to reply, but instead he raised his hand and echoed a "good day" uttered by someone passing on the walk. The Canon felt a hand laid on his shoulder, and turned to find a red, bloated, familiar face looking at him with a half-diffident, half-cynical smile.

"Well—Clem Anderson!" he exclaimed, turning about to look the new-comer up and down. "Just back from Edmonton, aren't you?"

"Yes, sir," snapped Anderson, in a flat, blatant voice. "Thought I'd just butt in to tell you, Canon, you'll soon have one less crook in this town to worry about. I'm sellin' up—everything—lock, stock, and barrel."

"Land alive!—you don't tell me!" Canon Macaulay stepped back a stride and looked up over his shoulder at Bundy. "What do you know about that, Sturge?"

"Moving up to Edmonton, Clem, eh?" the doctor said, in a tone that aimed at being cordial.

"Yup!" Anderson replied, dragging the cigar from his mouth and puffing smoke over his head. "It's a hoodooed town, this is, and I'm through with it. It's cost me plenty, believe me. But right now is a darned good time to clean up."

He stuck the cigar back into the corner of his mouth and sucked it in, teetering to and fro on his toes and heels with an arrogant swagger. "Things is boomin' for a bit, just now," he grinned, "and yours truly is goin' to get *his* while the goin' is good. But you watch her slide again. This bloody boom—excuse me, Canon—it's just a flash in the pan. She'll slide again—sure as God made little apples! When they close down them pits out there—you'll see."

He thrust out his jaw, so that the cigar performed a half-circle in the air and remained tilted at a rakish angle, while he glanced insolently from one to the other. "Let 'em stay here as likes it," he blared loudly, in his professional auctioneer's voice, swerving his eyes into their corners to see if he was being overheard. "I'm off!"

He thrust his hands in his pockets and moved away, jingling the silver in his pockets.

Bundy, leaning down from the buggy seat, whispered in the Canon's ear: "I'll bet young Harry will be as tickled as anybody to see him go."

"Yes, I guess so," the Canon nodded meaningly. "They haven't had a notion in common since the boy came back from Winnipeg. But, you know, Sturge," he said, putting his foot up on the rest again, "it bothers me to see Laura going around with him . . . even . . ."

"Oof!" grunted Bundy, blowing out his breath. "She doesn't care two straws for him. Why, that's as plain as the nose in your face, man. No, no. She's not a kid any more, Malcolm. No, no. There's nothing to worry about *there.*" He leaned over and touched the Canon's shoulder lightly. "I sometimes wonder, though, who there is in town—or likely to come here—good enough to tie her shoe-strings."

The Canon's face crumpled into a smile of embarrassed pride. He took his foot from the step and stood looking down at his scuffed shoes to hide the shamefaced affection that suddenly flashed in his black, slanting eyes.

"I must get along, Malcolm," Bundy said, straightening himself in the seat and gathering up the lines that had slipped down over Minnie's flank.

The Canon stepped back from the wheel. "Good-bye, Sturge," he said. "Come in Sunday, sure."

"Yes, I will," cried Bundy vigorously.

Holding up his hand in a sort of salute, he clicked his teeth at Minnie and drove off.

6

The Canon went on along the avenue, his hands behind his back again, his head bobbing. The people passing him were perspiring and puffing, and kept their eyes half closed against the glare; but the sun did not bother him. He had lived under it for thirty years out there. He nodded absent-mindedly to those he knew, his thoughts dragged into the present to say a word or two to Ed Ryan, standing under his awning, and to Nick Greenslade, pitching an armful of bundles into the back of his democrat; but soon relapsing into the past again by way of some memory that these faces recalled—a christening, a funeral, or perhaps a time when he had gone to the town hall to get relief for them when times were bad.

He reached the corner where the Bellevue stood. Its wooden balcony overhung the sidewalk, throwing a strip of shadow in which two or three squaws in bright-coloured blankets were crouched, with an old dog lying panting beside them.

The cool, sour smell of the bar floated out at him through the screen-doors as he turned the corner, lingering in the air as he passed the stables and a vacant lot behind. There was the *Monitor* office, with its yellow, brick-veneered front and the sign in Old English letters over the smudgy windows.

The sound of hammers from the blacksmith's shop across the way rang cheerfully in his ears as he went up the three warped and sloping steps to the open door.

TWO

The Printshop

I

THE CANON walked through into the back shop, fanning himself with his round hat, and puffing a little now that his walk was over. It was press day and there was nobody in the front office, which was simply a few feet of space screened off by a wooden partition, open at the top, so that the noise and smells of the shop were all through the building.

Old Pitts was carrying up paper from the basement, his bald head shiny with perspiration and his cheeks inflating and collapsing like a cornet-player's with every step he took under the heavy load of newsprint. In a corner by the back window a red-headed youth with a squinting eye was setting up type. Dick Gawthorp, owner and editor of the *Monitor*, was limping around the press, clamping down the front and back pages of the paper. His upright, winged collar framed a drowsy, massive face in which the heavy brows and broad nose stood out conspicuously. His grey eyes had a tired, short-sighted look from handling type and reading proof since he was a youngster.

He gave a final twist of the key in the last quoin that needed tightening, and drew his head out from under the cylinders.

Then he limped forward, rubbing his inky hands.

The Canon was nodding to Pitts, who had clambered up on the platform with his load and was getting ready to feed the press.

While he felt in his pocket for the notices, the Canon greeted Gawthorp with a remark about the heat and the way the threshing was going, the picture forming in his mind of broad, stooked fields and the blower sending a cloud of broken straw into the air.

"You bet your life," said Gawthorp thoughtfully. "Another week of this, Canon, and she'll be a bumper—sure."

"Yes," agreed the Canon, unfolding his crumpled notices, "things look pretty good, Dick."

"You bet they do," the editor said, wagging his heavy, drowsy head on one side. "The best crop since ninety-nine, they all say; and most every person around here well ahead with threshing. Joe Tulloch says they're just about through out Oakland way."

He took the scrap of paper the Canon handed him, and spread it out on the stone top of a make-up table, to be sure that everything was readable; bending over it with puckered eyes.

"The sheriff passed out this morning," he said, without looking. "I guess you heard."

"No." A double noise in the Canon's throat conveyed a resigned acceptance of things. "Is *that* so?" he added thoughtfully, standing there nodding, his eyes glazed in memory. "God bless us, Dick, there soon won't be any of the old landmarks left," he mused, twisting one foot around the other and resting his elbow on the table. "I wouldn't wonder if Dave Linklater's the next," he went on. "I was just talking to Sturge Bundy about getting him into the Home."

The Canon plucked at the few hairs of his beard, looking sideways at the floor, and recalling his first sight of Dave Linklater, in his prime, at a breed wedding, fully twenty-five years back, or maybe more. Dave had just come back from the mines in California then, dead broke.

"A man who's had the gold bug all his life," the Canon said aloud, "and there he is—dying in want, and raving about laying up treasure in heaven. I didn't know how badly fixed they were till a couple of days ago. They've been mighty close to starving."

Old Pitts, sprawling across the stack of paper he had hoisted up, fastened his big watery eyes on the Canon. "Julie's been helpin' out a bit over there at Dave's place, y'know," he said in a husky voice. "She an' old Dave are daggers drawn, half the time, but she's been a regular Sister of Mercy, just the same."

"So I've heard," the Canon nodded, looking up into the little Englishman's twitching face with ready recognition of Julie's generosity.

He looked at Pitts, but he was thinking of Julie—an enormously rotund, ageing French half-breed woman, who had once been notorious in the town, and was still a town character. Everybody called her Julie, or Aunt Julie, even in her presence, and she accepted the familiarity as though it were some sort of homage to her pitiful fame.

"There's a man called Tavistock who's been helping them, too," the Canon said suddenly. "I met him down there the other night. He says he used to know you in Johannesburg."

Pitts blinked his eyes and glanced sideways at Gawthorp, who was resting his back against the shelf of the cutting machine.

"I've known him for years," said Pitts. The husky voice came out of his slack mouth reminiscently. "Eight or nine years at least, sir," he added. With his mouth wide open and his face set in a solemn stare that comically resembled a goldfish, gulping at the side of its bowl, he remained silent, lost in old memories.

2

"In Jo'burg, sir," Pitts presently exploded, with a sudden shaking of his head, as though he had come up from under water; "in Jo'burg, I *lived* with him, you might say. He was an actor in a repertoire company that got stranded out there. I used to play in the orchestra in the same theatre. He's what we call a 'toff,' over home, sir. A regular toff—y'know what I mean?—born with a silver spoon in his mouth. But—it's funny—he never cottoned to his own kind. He was the leading man, and he *could* have been a reg'lar matinee idol. But, no. He didn't seem to care who he hung around with. God knows, he couldn't have been particular, or he wouldn't have spent so much time at my place." His face collapsed into a curious grimace as he raised his shoulders slowly in an obsequious shrug. "A gentleman—he is—if ever there was one. A prince, sir. But, maybe a little *you* know—kind of queer."

"He's been that way some time, then," the Canon breathed out, his lower lip twisting thoughtfully under his moustache.

"What's queer about him?" demanded Gawthorp. "I've run into him a few times, and I never noticed anything out-of-the-way about him."

He was thinking particularly of the time when that Irishman had died of t.b. He had gone out to the pits to get an item about it for his paper, and Tavistock had given him all the information that could be gleaned from the few papers in the dead man's valise. It was Tavistock who had nursed the man, running to the cook-car for ice and salt when the hæmorrhages came on, and bunking in there with him at nights, looking after him like a regular trained nurse, the fellows said. He had written a letter home, too, to the man's relatives in County Kildare. Half of it he had taken down when the fellow had a sort of spurt of talking and wishing, just before he died. He was wishing he was back there in

Ireland. He knew he was going to die, and he would have liked to die there. Tavistock had taken down what he said, and wrote the rest himself after the fellow had closed his eyes.

Gawthorp leaned back against the cutter and thought of that day. The undertaker hadn't got there, and he had gone into the bunk-car with Tavistock to look at the body. He remembered the tall Englishman standing quietly beside the bunk. His head was on one side as though he were leaning against something in the air. His eyes seemed to fade back into his head. Gawthorp remembered very distinctly what he had said. It had struck him at the time. He said: When I look at the dead, I seem to be surer than ever that there isn't any death."

It had struck him at the time, but he hadn't thought it "queer." It was just that the fellow was sort of thoughtful. And he didn't mind talking about religion. He wasn't ashamed of it, the way a lot of fellows are. He had said other things, but Gawthorp couldn't remember them now. He could only remember that he had taken to him, and that the second time he saw him—somewhere in the town—he had felt he had known him a long time.

"He figures things out for himself," Gawthorp said aloud, looking across at Pitts. "He's got notions of his own. There was a fellow like him down in Brantford when I was a youngster. He used to read the Bible a lot, and he'd talk your head off about religion. Never went to church, that I know of, but it was as good as a sermon—what he used to get off. I can listen to a fellow like that for hours."

Pitts raised a stumpy finger in front of his face. "So can I," he said, "and I *have* listened to him—till all hours of the morning. My wife understood more of it than I did. She was in the company, too. They talked plays half the time, but we used to get gassing about all sorts of things—*you* know—about tragedy—murder—*that* sort of business. He's a broody chap, you know. He's had something on his mind ever since I've known him. My wife knew that. She said to me more than once: 'He'll do something crazy one of these days, you see if he doesn't.' I guess you'd call him a reformer. Ain't that what you call 'em?"

The Canon's moustache curved upward in a slow, thoughtful smile. "Yes," he agreed. "I suppose that's just what he is."

"I'll tell you," Pitts stuttered, in a hesitating manner. He got down from the platform and came around the end of the press, stumbling over its projecting base and almost running at the Canon, with his head down, as he recovered himself from tripping. "I've never said this to anyone," he said, glancing first at Gawthorp and then at Canon Macaulay, and arching his unshaven upper lip with an air of mystery, "but here's what I mean, sir."

3

He addressed himself to the Canon, for it was plain that Gawthorp, still propped in the same position against the cutter, was half lost in a day-dream, swerving his tired eyes occasionally in Pitts' direction, but allowing his glance to drift away again across the besmudged walls to the open door, where a circus poster, pasted crookedly on the side of a shed across the lane, caught and held his eye.

Pitts smoothed a grimy white apron over his bulging paunch. "I've seen Englishmen in all sorts of tight corners," he said "Educated chaps—good family, and all that—and there's always something kind of solitary about 'em. You know what I mean?—a bit distant. And he *is* that. But there's something else. It's hard to put your finger on it, but he strikes me like a chap who is living a sort of life—something—Gosh! I don't know . . ."

He raised his finger and held it perfectly still, as though its stillness and the upheld vertical thrust of it, very close to the Canon's face, somehow denoted the kind of life he meant.

The Canon, accustomed to this delight in mysteriousness which Pitts so often indulged, was not as usual amused by it. His tangled black brows drew slowly together as he stared at the old man with the utmost seriousness.

"You mean," he said, his voice coming deeply out of the piling thought about this stranger who had curiously disturbed him, "you mean he's devoted to some idea. You might say he's *dedicated* to it."

"That's it! The very word for it!" declared Pitts, his round eyes expressing solemn gratitude for such an explanation.

"Yes," the Canon added, with less certainty. "That's what I felt the other night—he acts as though he were hiding a secret." He paused, but burst out again the next instant: "Yes—yes—I get that—but what is he *doing?* How does he pick out the people he *does* mix with? How did he get to know Linklater, for instance."

Pitts, standing close to the Canon and rubbing his hands together eagerly, scarcely waited for him to pause. "Well, Canon," he said, "it's funny—you see I hadn't the faintest notion he was in this country even—let alone this town. It was Julie. Julie came home from Linklater's one night and said something about a chap—I've forgotten what she said, now, but she sort of described him—a stranger, anyway—a chap who was always out boating at nights and passed the place often. The kids play around in the water all the time—and this chap started taking them for rides in his boat. And then, I guess, he must have run across old Dave, and found they were pretty near starving. So he's been helping 'em—you see—taking them stuff. One night, when I was over there having a chin with old Dave—*who* should walk in but Tavistock. Well, sir, you could have knocked me down with a feather."

He stopped and looked at the Canon challengingly, as though expecting him to blow at him and bowl him over.

The Canon had been listening impatiently, fingering the

silver cross on his watch-chain and sucking at the corner of his mouth.

"And now he's going away again," he said, as though the man's strangeness somehow angered him. "He's leaving the railroad, isn't he?"

"I don't know, sir," said Pitts. "He hasn't said anything to me about it, but then I haven't seen him much just lately."

The Canon almost glared at the old man. "Well, he was very indefinite—guarded—about it, but I certainly gathered he was quitting. He didn't say he had anywhere else to go, except . . ."

He paused, trying to recall the impression the man had made on him. He had a feeling that Tavistock was at the point of throwing everything to the winds. He sounded like a man who was sick of life—disgusted with the world. Another mind twisted by a queer sort of atheism into a blind alley! "Why do so many of these gifted fellows fizzle out?" the Canon asked himself. He had known fellows like him at college—brilliant fellows—who could preach circles around everybody else in their year. But how few of them stuck? A lot of men of that type were never ordained. This man was perhaps more greatly gifted than anyone he had in mind. A fine-looking man—a fine presence—magnetic! A deep, penetrating voice. A splendid talker. He stirred you. There was almost a hint of greatness in the way he spoke—the ringing conviction—the prophetic fervour in his voice. Somewhere—in the right place—he would be an outstanding man, if he could bring himself down to earth, instead of frittering away his gifts in abstruse speculations! What a pity!—a man like that throwing his life away—hiding his light under a bushel. "Let your light so shine before men—" the Canon began to mutter, but checked himself.

"What made him come to this country?" he asked Pitts, with unusual abruptness.

"That I can't tell you, sir." The old man shook his head slowly from side to side. "He don't seem to care where he is, or how he earns a living. He just seems to live for this—this here business he has on his mind all the time. He says he'll never do any more acting. You'd think he'd always hated the stage, to hear him talk. But I guess he just got a sickener of it over there in Jo'burg."

Pitts would have liked to go on talking, but the Canon, with his brows tightly knit so that they met in a bulging twist over his blunt nose, was obviously lost in thought.

The heat in the dingy shop seemed to settle down like fumes over the three men, standing there close together, looking different ways, with no impulse to speak or move a finger.

The bus rumbling past from the station, and the cries of the driver as he pulled the horses into the yard of the Bellevue, aroused Gawthorp. The bubble of silence which enveloped them broke, as he dragged his lame leg forward, and said: "Well, I guess I'll have to get busy."

The Canon grunted, nodded and started toward the door, squeezing his body sideways between the type-cases as he made his way out.

THREE

Tavistock

I

LATE IN THE AFTERNOON, having made his regular round of the pits, Tavistock went back to the bunk car he shared with Louis Roff, the interpreter. It had been his home since the spring—a bunk with a valise under it—the car standing in the same place all summer in a string of broken-down box-cars with little windows cut in their sides, a foot of stove-pipe sticking out of each roof, and an unpainted ladder spiked beside each door.

This line of boarding-cars, which housed the foremen, engineers, mechanics and office staff, stood on the west bank, almost at the brink of the "big pit." On that side there were scores of crooked tracks overgrown with grass and weeds, scorched brown by the burning sunshine. It was a wilderness of rusting steel and rotten ties where old dump-cars were "spotted" for repairs.

The pits were almost exhausted, and all this flimsy trackage would soon be pulled up. They were down to clay in most sections of the "big pit," which was now almost a mile long. Looking down from the bank it resembled a dried-up riverbed in which everything appeared dwarfed. The slow-moving trains of dump-cars looked like long red worms crawling toward the main slope.

The steam shovels, thrusting their jaws into the sliding gravel, seemed no bigger than clockwork beetles. The Galicians working on either side of the trains were mere dots, as insignificant as gnats.

Black prairie dust, blowing from the stubble-fields of neighbouring farms, beat grittily into Tavistock's face as he reached the top of the slope and crossed the tracks, striding along with bent head, his high shoulders swinging easily.

Gregory, the boss foreman, standing in the doorway of Otis Webb's car, leaning back out of the sun, saw the lanky Englishman coming.

"Here's the duke," he said, over his shoulder, to Webb, who was at the window watching the action of one of the shovels in the second pit.

Webb was the engineer in charge of ballasting—a hard-boiled, experienced railroader who had been brought up from Montana. He always grinned sourly when Gregory referred to Tavistock as "the duke."

The foreman hadn't taken to Tavistock at first. When he saw him in the pits calling out the men's numbers with a pronounced English accent, he had taken it for granted that Tavistock was too "toney" to make a railroader. But once or twice in the evenings they had run into each other in the dark, wandering at the pit's edge for a breath of air before turning in, and the foreman had modified his opinion.

"He's high and mighty, all right," he confided to Webb some time later, "but I'll be damned if there ain't something gosh-awful human—somehow—underneath. Why, he's like a kid, in some ways. Talks to you like a kid would. Did y'ever talk to him? All about God and stuff like that—just like a Sunday school kid."

After another talk with Tavistock he said to Webb: "That time-keeper feller's got something on his mind—do you know it? He don't come out plump and plain with it—but he's expectin' some big news. I wouldn't wonder if he's waitin' for some duke to kick out. I've seen guys—supposed to be dukes—on the stage, that couldn't hold a candle to him for lookin' blue-blooded."

After that Gregory had always called him "the duke," even to his face. When he passed him in the pits or took a seat anywhere near him at meal-times in the dining-car, he would look sideways at him, his eyes cocked humorously upward, and say: "Well, how's the duke?"

2

Gregory leaned into the glare long enough to spit out a mouthful of tobacco juice, aiming carefully to hit the end of a tie. Sucking up the brown dribble on his lower lip, he jerked his head back into the shade.

"Looks like he's going to town," he said lazily, over his shoulder, to the engineer.

"He is," said Webb, scraping absent-mindedly at the day's growth of stubble on his chin. "He wanted to knock off early to see a lawyer about something. You knew he was quittin'."

"Sure. Tomorrow—ain't it?"

"Yup. I've got a new guy comin' out from Winnipeg in the mornin'. I hope he'll be a damn sight different. That feller gives me the creeps. You'd think he'd killed his own mother, the way he goes around."

Gregory, leaning out to watch Tavistock's progress along the main track, made an elaborate meaningless grimace at the Chinese cook, who at that moment appeared in the doorway of the cook-car opposite. He spat again, rolled his chew over his tongue, and said: "He ain't such a bad guy. I never seen a gentler feller, any place. You'd think he was a reg'lar nurse the way he looked after that bloody Wasnyk when he got hurt there that time. And what was that Irishman's name?—the feller that took the hæmorrhage all of a sudden. Look at the way he sat up with him, when the God damn hospital even was scared to take him. Bunked in there for three nights with him, b'Jesus, till he died."

He lurched sideways with his shoulder propped against the door and looked at the thick hair curling at the back of Webb's neck. "That guy's had a bellyful o' grief, if you ask me. And, I guess that's what makes him kind o' gentle—kind o' womanish. What gets me, though, is the way he goes round without a hat! God! Imagine goin' 'round without a hat—in *this* sun!"

He leaned out again and watched Tavistock striding bare-headed along the high dump until he passed out of sight behind the water-tank.

3

It was a mile and a half to town along the main track. The new rails shone with a hard blue glitter. The fresh gravel all along the high grade reflected the pouring light and heat of the blistering sun. On either side of the track the wheat fields extended to the far-off horizon. Clouds of broken straw, belched into the air by a noisy threshing outfit on a near-by farm, powdered the sky with drifting gold.

But Tavistock saw nothing of the scene around him. He strode along with eager, impetuous pace. He did not see even the ties he was treading, white and new as they were, with adze-marks still shining, and the resin oozing out of them in the heat.

He was a man about thirty, very tall, and with wide, straight shoulders which swung easily as he walked. His bare head was slender and flattened at the back, but his face widened in a remarkable way at the temples and sloped sharply to a narrow, jutting chin. His eyes were unusually large, greyish-brown in colour, shot with green. They were extremely mobile and betrayed the slightest change in his thoughts. His wide mouth was set very low in his face, the lips full, but drawn at the corners.

He was wearing a khaki shirt without a necktie, corduroy breeches, and high-laced boots half-way up his shins. A brown Norfolk jacket was slung over his shoulder. His boots and clothes were powdered with fine yellow dust from the pits.

He trod the ties with long, urgent strides. To-morrow he was leaving the pits, and perhaps would quit the town. He was excited. Every now and again he flung a glance back over his shoulder at the dwindling tank and the rows of standing cars.

"This place has hindered me," he said to himself.

He threw back his shoulders and drew in a deep breath. His eyelids drooped as the slower rhythm of his breathing seemed to clear his mind of pressing thoughts. He began to feel free of the place—free to dream again. For days there had been a cleared, uncluttered space growing in his mind. It was a space he could enter, shutting himself in from the world. He seemed to be standing at the brink of a limitless, pale gulf. As he became accustomed to the strange sensation, the space took the form of a sphere. He looked into its depths with a profound curiosity, as though recognizing the description of a promised land. Its vast emptiness, its purity, its shining transparency fascinated him. He felt himself drawn into it, treading its unsubstantial blueness timidly. He thought of Peter walking on the water. It was like the inside of an enormous shell, murmurous with unimagined possibilities. He felt himself in the presence of invisible powers, capable of performing any miracle.

An immense thankfulness poured through him like a warm rain. This was the place—the state—he had sought, day after day, year after year. The last vestige of anxiety was washed from his mind. The miracle he had waited for so patiently was trembling in the air above him.

"It is possible!" rang out a voice, reverberating around him like a tolled bell.

The voice brought him out of his day-dream. He knew the words. They were Faust's. He was accustomed to this trick of his memory, jolting him with old phrases he had forgotten, as though spoken by a voice in his ear.

He dramatized everything that happened to him. It was a strain in his nature. "I was an actor before I was born," he had often told himself. He responded intuitively to tragedy. He entered into it, becoming a sufferer himself. He had imagined himself bearing the extremest woes.

His father and mother dying, within a few months of each other, when he was very young, had deepened the childish melancholy which even earlier had sometimes sent him into hiding to cry his heart out—over nothing. But his aunt, who then brought him up, had influenced him most. He remembered well the funereal atmosphere of that house in Bedfordshire. His aunt, his father's sister, was a childless titled lady, who nursed her own bereavement and made the house a shrine to the memory of her husband. The Irish-Spanish strain in the family seemed to come alive again in her. He had often heard her say: "We Tavistocks are fated."

He had loved her. The Maunders—his mother's side and even his mother herself—were all cold, belligerent, grey-eyed—"a staring lot," his aunt had called them. But she was warm-natured, impulsive and, like himself, easily moved to tears. He remembered how she wept when he went up to Cambridge.

Her influence followed him even there. "Behold, this dreamer cometh," his classmates said among themselves, seeing him strolling down "the backs" toward the river, his head bent, his shoulders lax, as though behind a bier. "The melancholy Dane," they had called him.

Everything, it seemed, had thrust him toward the stage to

mouth tragic poetry. He had often stood at his window, looking down at Milton's mulberry tree in the garden of Christ's College, rehearsing Hamlet's lines, feeling Hamlet's voice behind his own! He had often slipped away, up the stone-flagged stairs, closing the heavy panelled door of his room behind him, shutting himself in and going to the mullioned windows to stand there brooding—questioning—*questing!*

Sometimes, across the bank of the muddy Cam, he had fancied he could see shapes moving under the trees, floating toward him, mingling their ghostly voices with the voices in his mind. Ancient voices! The bitter questioning of Job! The vexed soul of the psalmist crying out to his God! All these men—then, as now—crying out, questioning, seeking, demanding an answer to the puzzle of existence. Lear! Hamlet! Their words sounded in his ears like his own voice. "Why is there evil in the world?—What is the meaning of death?—What is beyond it?—Can man ever return to the state of innocence he lost in Eden?"

Sometimes the wailings of Blake's strange, mythical characters hinted at answers more puzzling than his questions. Sometimes, in the chapel, Bach's organ music, or a motet of Palestrina, would lift him into a mood of acceptance. All his doubts would crumble, and then he would walk for hours in the rain, oblivious of everything around him. The voices would no longer question. They would be singing songs of joy.

This habit of inward listening had grown on him—through his brief career on the London stage, beginning with a walking-on part in Irving's production of *The Inferno*—through the years of touring in the provinces and in Africa—and was now firmly fixed. He could not remember a time when his mind had been free of voices—questions—yearnings—urgings to act—to do something—at one stroke—that would open the eyes of the world. He had met a number of men who felt as he did. They had become preachers or writers. But here he was, past thirty now—

still waiting for the one stroke—still expecting a miracle.

For a long time he hadn't known what sort of miracle it might be, but now the nature of his act was clear to him—terrifyingly clear. The moment, too, seemed to be drawing nearer. This transparent, shell-like space in his mind was murmurous with miracles.

Only a few more steps were needed to achieve the final isolation his destiny demanded. To-day he was going to dispose of this legacy which had come unexpectedly after years of delay. To-morrow he would quit the camp. Perhaps, in a few days, he would be in the mountains. . . .

4

He fixed his gaze on the huge sunlit clouds piled in the sky. They stood like mountains above the few spires and chimneys which were all that could be seen of the town over intervening tree-tops.

The track swung southward. He passed the signal tower where the two railroads crossed. The bush ended, and over the shining tin roofs of the Galicians' shacks the three grain elevators came into view, one behind the other, towering above everything else in the town. Their tall red sides caught the full light of the western-moving sun.

Something about their shape and height impressed Tavistock for the first time. He had been there since spring, but he had given no thought to where he was. He had gone about the pits and through the town with his eyes turned inward. The three elevators, suddenly striking his attention, reminded him of how little he had looked around.

On the north side of the track the Galicians had built uneven rows of tiny, tar-papered shacks, with wretched gardens behind them in which heavy women moved languidly in the heat, talking to each other across vacant lots, or dragging half-clad children out of mischief. Every day, in the pits, he called out the numbers of the undersized, surly-looking men who lived in this jumble of tin and tar-paper. He had seen them at night, in their black shirts and overalls, hoeing at the back of these patchwork hutches.

Did they suffer? he wondered. Did they brood? Did they believe in the God they worshipped in the queer church, whose curved zinc cupola, dwarfed to mushroom size by the towering elevators, shone too glitteringly to be looked at? Did it ever occur to them that they, and all men, had strayed from an Eden of innocence—man's natural state—and were fallen now into a mire of doubt and despair?

He came to the first road crossing, and there were the white, slanting planks of the cattle-guard between the rails to be trod over carefully. He turned south along the road.

On this side of the track the older part of the town presented a planned and better-kept appearance. The white gables of Judge Boak's old house leaned out of the poplars ahead of him. The house had long been closed up and wore that sinister air which associates itself with boarded-up windows. Beyond the chokecherry trees, which encircled the overgrown lawns like a hedge, began the sedate parallel rows of cheerfully painted wooden houses, each with its verandah at the front, where women sat rocking in the evenings, and a pump at the back, with an occasional neat lattice fence running back to the lane.

Every street and lane in the town was laid out in perfectly straight lines, intersecting each other at identical distances. Houses closely packed together within each of these severely rectangular blocks were carefully placed so that their fronts were at the same distance from the sidewalks. Everything stood plumb and square.

Did these people never yearn for the unexpected—the sudden thrilling ascents and descents which are to be found equally in nature and in the soul? Could there be heights of aspiration or profound depths of yearning in these stark lives, bent by need and greed over the grim monotony of the land? His mind revolted at the picture of men moving like slaves over the flat, square fields, their heads bent, their eyes never lifted from interminable furrows.

He had reached the avenue, taking his usual short-cut across a vacant lot behind the lumber yard. A heavy team, beset by flies, plodded toward him, flicking their tails and throwing their heads back savagely, showing their long yellow teeth. An old farmer was nodding in the spring-seat of the wagon. Tavistock looked wonderingly at the lean face, empty of expression.

5

Since he had come to the prairies his sense of the impending miracle had grown weaker, and he had begun to wonder whether these new surroundings—the flatness of the country, the hard, hustling life of the people, the uninspiring flimsiness of the straggling town—had influenced him, even though he had scarcely looked around.

He had decided to move on to the Rockies. He had heard them described. The vastness and height of the imagined scene had become mingled with the loftiness of his aspirations. He believed that there, at the foot of some towering peak, the final inspiration—the high impulse he had so long awaited—might come to him.

On these plains only the skies had inspired him. The heavy summer clouds often piled up into marvellous aerial scenes, like stage-sets awaiting the enactment of colossal pageants. He remembered particularly a day when a succession of long flat clouds, like grey slabs of stone, mounted like steps above the blue gloom of a far-away thunderstorm. He had longed for power to stride up, treading the air, and discovering in some hidden height the final secret of everything. Starry nights had stirred him, too, calling to mind a line about "the whiteness and height of stars" which had lately returned repeatedly in his thoughts. But there was nothing else here to lift his mind to the sublimities. At home, in England, he had always been moved by music, but here there was no music. Sometimes he went to the English church solely to hear old familiar chants and hymns, even though the choir dragged them out unbearably.

Once, in all the time he had been in the town, he had heard the piano played with real feeling. One night he had stopped to listen outside a little dark house near the church, standing in the shadow of a lilac bush so as not to be observed. Somebody was playing one of Bach's Preludes and Fugues. The weaving of solemn, intricate melodies was unmistakable. When the fugue closed, resolving into the major, he was consumed with curiosity to know who would be playing with such feeling and command of the keyboard in a tiny out-of-the-way town.

He walked past, his eyes fastened on the windows, expecting to see, perhaps, an old man—the Anglican organist, probably. But instead, in dim candlelight, a girl's head, a perfect dark oval, was framed against the gleaming page on the music-rest. Her shoulders sloped in a way he seemed to know. She swung around on the stool, and as soon as he saw her profile, sharply outlined against the steady flame of the candle, he knew it was the girl he had seen often on the lake, and sometimes in church, whose eager eyes and full lips, often parted breathlessly, had unexpectedly disturbed him.

It had been unexpected because he had believed himself, at last, wholly detached and passionless. Love had more than once swept him aside from his lonely chosen path, anchoring him to earth for a while, and delaying the achievement of his purpose. But his dream had been stronger than reality. Each time he had relinquished the lesser rapture. It was to break such a spell that he had left Africa. "I am like Goethe," he had often told himself. "I run away from women."

He had run away from that woman in Johannesburg for half a dozen reasons. For one thing he had never felt a moment's love for her, yet she fascinated him strangely. She played minor roles in the stock company out there. When he first saw her, at a rehearsal one day, he had thought immediately of Beardsley. She had a cruel, voluptuous face. She might easily have inspired Beardsley's drawings for Wilde's *Salome*.

For some unaccountable reason she had married Pitts. He had never understood it, but after performances he had often gone back to their place to talk. She was almost frantically ambitious. He remembered her understudying the role of Lady Macbeth. The cold vehemence of her nature poured itself into the part. The memory of her whisper—"Give me the daggers"—could chill his blood even now.

It was finding Pitts here in Poplar Plains that had made him think of Clara again. What a shock it had been to see him—so aged—so broken down! They had both drifted to this spot, drawn by the work the new railroad provided. It was natural enough, and yet it seemed to him that Pitts had been sent there—a ghost out of his past—to remind him, with his whitened hair and rheumy eyes, of how long he had delayed the act his mind had contemplated all these years.

Clara had somehow stiffened his resolve, but in the end he had not been able to look at her without a shudder. Thinking of her brought to mind his final memory of Johannesburg—of how he had stood on the station platform, looking at the wild sky. The sun was setting behind a stormy pile of clouds drifting like smoke through the sky, and as the train pulled out between mountainous mine-dumps the last glow of the sunken sun splashed the great heaps of slag with blood-colour. It made him think of an inferno from which he had escaped at last.

Women had always hindered him. "But I have put them behind me, now," he told himself, even though the dark oval head of the girl at the piano hung vividly in his memory as he uttered the thought. "I shall never meet her," he said, thinking of an evening on the lake when the man she was with had turned the canoe about and her face was suddenly gilded with the last, flaming rays of the sun. "I shall never meet her," he repeated. "In a day or two, as soon as this legacy business is fixed up, I shall go to the mountains."

He began to picture the grandeur and loneliness of the mountains, rearing them up in his mind, in the cleared, blue space which he seemed to be able to conjure into existence, now, whenever he willed.

His eyes glowed. People passing him on the crowded sidewalk, as he approached the heart of the town, turned to look back at him. Even here he strode along blindly. Even while he gazed about absently, looking for the name of "Fetterly" somewhere—on a sign or a window—he felt himself endowed with a superhuman power—he felt the power *within* himself, for the first time—and he heard again the reverberation of Faust's voice, a bell-like sound ringing through his thoughts—"It is *possible!*"

FOUR

The Lawyer's Office

I

THE CROWN PROSECUTOR for the Poplar Plains district was a sharp-featured, ageing lawyer named Fetterly. In his office, behind a huge flat-topped desk, half covered with documents, he looked coldly formidable. Miss Sadler, coming in to say that Mr. Tavistock was waiting outside, carefully avoided the shock of meeting Mr. Fetterly's glance. He did not look up, but after a moment or two Miss Sadler felt she could interpret the almost imperceptible movement of his bent head as the equivalent of a nod. She retreated noiselessly to the outer office.

The stranger who had just given her his name had lingered near the front window and was gazing abstractedly over the faded curtain into the street. His long legs, straddled wide apart, seemed so deliberately and permanently set, and the slant of his head, as though listening to something, was so exactly poised, that she hesitated to disturb his reverie. She stood behind him, biting nervously at the pen-holder in her ink-stained fingers.

This opportunity to observe him, without being noticed, excited her and produced a slow flush on her pasty cheeks. His appearance, when she had looked up to find his eyes bent on her, had caused her a quick, startled breath. He was not merely unfamiliar, but strange. Miss Sadler had never seen so sad a face, nor so far-away a look in a man's eyes.

He turned, as though drawn by the presence of someone who knew what was in his mind. There was a gentle, expectant smile on his face, and when she said: "Mr. Fetterly will see you," she saw the smile fade, and guessed that absent-mindedly he had turned to her, expecting other words—another voice, perhaps. "He has lost somebody," she said to herself, as he strode past her into the prosecutor's office.

2

Mr. Fetterly, who never wasted anything, spent no more than a moment in glancing at his visitor. His small, cold eyes made a quick inventory in the manner of a bill offering a reward for a criminal: "About 35, tall, pale complexion, long dark hair, wearing brown Norfolk coat, corduroy breeches, speaks with English accent."

Reducing his greeting to the curtest minimum, he read aloud a letter from a famous firm of lawyers in London, telling of the conclusion of the suit in Chancery which had stretched over so many years. The heir, sitting perfectly still, displayed a lack of interest that seemed, to Mr. Fetterly, to smack of insolence. To maintain his own dignity he felt forced to enlarge upon the importance of the suit, doing his utmost to impress Tavistock with the remarkable history of his own family. He cited the names of well-known judges and lawyers whose names had been connected with the litigation over the Maunder estate for nearly a quarter of a century. He had been looking all this up in his law books, but Tavistock was apparently so little interested in the money involved that Mr. Fetterly grew uncomfortable. His flow of words tumbled unheard into the vacancy of silence and detachment in which the visitor was wrapped.

Mr. Fetterly's voice seemed to lose its power to cross the desk, and yet he kept on, his discomfiture increasing with every word, the more so because from time to time Tavistock cast at him a sudden glance, charged with intense curiosity, which had nothing whatever to do with the estate or its settlement.

At last Mr. Fetterly could babble no longer. Pulling himself together with an effort, he rose from his chair, stepped back toward the window, and brought his peroration to a close.

"I'm afraid I'm less interested in this than you seem to be," he heard Tavistock saying. His English accent sounded strange in the room after the lawyer's nasal twang. "My parents died when I was a youngster, and I've been knocking about in all sorts of places ever since." He paused and looked steadily at Mr. Fetterly. "And as for the money," he added, a little awkwardly, "I shan't need money."

As he uttered these last words his mind seemed to revert to the subject of his former reverie, and his glance became fixed on the pattern of the carpet spreading under the desk.

"You're not refusing this legacy, surely," said the prosecutor, controlling his surprise.

"Well—I don't know. I don't want it, you see," said the other simply.

Mr. Fetterly screwed up his eyes and assumed his professional manner when examining a witness. "What?" he exclaimed. "Are you telling me that seriously? Most of us find money very useful. But, if . . ." He waved his hand in the air as much as to say, "You are *not* a witness, of course, and I can't press you."

"I really came in," said Tavistock, "just to clear things up. We never know—do we?—what is likely to happen? I suppose, if I died to-morrow—this money would revert to the estate."

"Yes," said Mr. Fetterly, "it would."

3

Tavistock squared his chair to the desk. "I'd better make a will," he said. He thought a moment and went on abruptly: "There is an old man living down by the lake—old Linklater."

"Dave Linklater?"

"Yes. He lives there with two granddaughters. They are almost destitute, and the old chap can't live much longer. The girls' names are . . ."

He stopped suddenly and seemed to forget himself in a new concern that glowed deeply in his eyes as he looked questioningly at the lawyer. "Those little girls," he said slowly. "Would this money spoil them, do you think? Will they suffer more *with* it—or without it?"

"Suffer!" exclaimed Mr. Fetterly, as though the word was utterly unfamiliar.

Tavistock leaned across the desk. "Do you know anything about suffering?" he demanded, as though he had become the cross-examiner. "You're a lawyer. You deal with the most unfortunate people—criminals—murderers. Do you know anything about the suffering of people who are told they are criminals?"

"The *suffering* of criminals?" said Mr. Fetterly, with the puzzled air of a man repeating something in a foreign language.

"Yes," said Tavistock, looking fixedly at the lawyer's spare face as though wondering what went on behind his small, cold eyes. "You must have had unusual opportunities to observe the effect of punishment—and remorse—on prisoners you've had to deal with."

Mr. Fetterly sensed a decided fanaticism in Tavistock's tone which perhaps accounted for his morose appearance.

"If you're making a study of this sort of thing," he said, "I'd advise you to talk to Sturge Bundy, the head of the Home for Incurables here. He has some pretty theories."

"Never mind him. I am asking *you*," said Tavistock, with growing impatience. "What is *your* view of suffering? Do you know what a murderer suffers? Can anyone—without committing a crime—realize the suffering—the remorse—the horror of guilt—that follows it in a criminal's mind? Do you think it is possible for us—you or me—to experience that suffering, without *ourselves* committing a murder?"

Mr. Fetterly looked at Tavistock as though he suspected him of being out of his mind, but in the burning eyes there was a light of compassion so contagious that his manner immediately softened.

"I think not," he said, swallowing hastily.

"You think we can't?"

"I think we can't."

"Criminals, in prison, frequently pray, I suppose," said Tavistock bitterly.

"Yes, they do."

"They pray to a God who never committed a crime—a God who cannot suffer *with them*." A sharper gleam appeared in Tavistock's eyes as he placed extraordinary emphasis on the last two words.

Mr. Fetterly said: "You are not orthodox, I see."

"You *see! What* do you see?" A look of indescribable weariness passed over the Englishman's face. "It is the orthodox God I am talking about. The orthodox God never committed a crime."

"But we are told," said the prosecutor oratorically, "that he sent his son to take away the sins of the world."

"You're like all the rest," Tavistock exclaimed. "You say—I

see! But *what* do you see? *What* do you suffer?" He sprang up and strode rapidly to the door.

"Where are you going?" exclaimed the prosecutor.

"You'll see me again. You're the prosecutor here, aren't you?" said Tavistock, in a calmer tone, pausing in the doorway. And when Fetterly nodded he repeated: "You'll see me again," and turned to go.

"But you wanted me to draft a will," Mr. Fetterly said, taking a step or two around his desk.

Tavistock moved his lips over one another silently, and half closed his eyes. "Draw it up," he said thoughtfully. "Leave everything I have . . . no!"

He turned his back on the lawyer and took two strides away from him.

"Never mind!" he cried, over his shoulder. "Let it go—for now."

He walked rapidly through the outer office and stepped into the sunlight pouring down on the awnings all along the avenue. On the glaring new sidewalk he stood still a moment to take a great breath.

FIVE

Linklater

I

LINKLATER'S HOUSE stood by itself on the lake-shore, surrounded by a garden overgrown with a tangle of blueberry bushes, young poplar shoots and pig-weed as tall as a man. It was a two-story box of a house with a peak roof. When it was first built by Linklater's son-in-law, and neatly painted green and white, with the trees around it and the flowers close to the narrow verandah, and the lake almost at the back door, it had presented a tidy and comfortable appearance.

All that was changed now, for the son-in-law had run away with the wife of a contractor while Linklater had been prospecting up north. The old man had come back in time to be at his daughter's bedside when she died, leaving the two orphaned children to his care.

Almost at once he had closed off the upper portion of the house, boarding up the stairway, perhaps because his daughter had died up there, or because the roof leaked, or because he was now too feeble to climb; for the exposure to cold and damp on his last trip north had cramped him with rheumatism and caused him to shake with a kind of ague.

Later on he had knocked out the wooden partition between the two lower rooms, using it for firewood during a winter when it was hard for him to get around outside. There was now one long room from the front to the back of the narrow house, with a woodshed behind, constructed of waste slabs from the mill. Between the house and the reedy shore of the lake was a boathouse, sinking into the water, and beside it a flat-bottomed boat lay half-submerged in mud and pebbles.

The white and green paint had long ago faded, blistered or peeled off, and the floor of the verandah in the front of the house was sunken and decayed. Boys had broken all the upper windows. Some were broken below, too, and had been patched with newspapers. All about the place was the musty smell of worm-eaten wood, rain-soaked rags, and dying weeds.

Inside there was little furniture. Most of it had been sold. There remained two beds, and in the middle of the room the round top of a dining-table—the centre leg of which had been broken or disposed of somehow—unevenly supported now by four sticks of cord-wood. There were two or three rickety old chairs, a sofa with the horsehair bursting out of it at the sides, a stove, an old washstand, a trunk, and a few boxes piled in a corner.

2

The front door stood open as Canon Macaulay and Fred Philp went through the tangled garden. Raised voices, reverberating hollowly against the walls, as in an empty house, came through the door as they stepped up on the crumbling verandah.

The Canon had run across Philp in the Post Office and had persuaded him to come at once, on his way home, to investigate the pitiful conditions at the old prospector's house.

"Leave me alone! Do you hear?" old Dave was croaking in a

cracked, high-pitched voice. "Get down on your knees, Jack. You've been a sinful man."

The old man was squatting in a low arm-chair that was almost falling to pieces. He was obviously ill, starved, feeble. His parched skin drooped from the bones of his face like threadbare silk. What remained of his hair hung in long, dirty, yellow-grey wisps almost on to his shoulders. He wore an old cardigan full of holes, and a pair of greasy trousers that had once been blue. On his feet were odd carpet slippers, one much older than the other and tied across his instep with string. Out of a gaping hole stuck three of his toes, which shook continually, as did his whole body, with a kind of palsy.

"He'll be comin' in clouds—do you hear?" came in a mumble from the gaping mouth.

Jack Jukes, a breed who made a living by selling bush whisky to interdicts and Indians, was standing by the old man's chair. He wore the shoddy black clothes, moccasins and red neckerchief which the Treaty Indians of the neighbourhood had affected years before. His skin was so permanently tanned and wrinkled that he was often mistaken for a full-blooded Cree. He spoke very brokenly, too, for his home as a boy had been a tepee in the Cree settlement east of town.

In his youth he had acted as guide to parties of incoming settlers and hunters, but latterly he had managed to acquire a few acres which he called a farm, where he lived in an old log cabin within a stone's throw of the village of his tribe. The produce of his garden—for it was scarcely more than that—together with the whisky trade he carried on, kept him alive.

Looking up and recognizing the two men in the doorway, the breed glared at them dully, and went on, without even a nod, growling under his breath: "Anderson boy—him got new scheme. All the time scheme. Close mor'gage on me now. Me lose farm."

"What's the trouble, Jukes?" demanded Canon Macaulay, stepping across the sill and approaching the breed with his blunt head thrust forward enquiringly.

Fred Philp had taken off his hat and stood just inside the door nervously twirling the brim in his fingers.

"Fools and blind!" shouted Linklater, raising a quivering finger high over his head.

"Me come see old man," snarled Jukes, over his shoulder, at the Canon. "Me and him partners."

Linklater sat forward and spat out the word "Fools!" again with even greater emphasis.

Jukes tapped his forehead. "Him go crazy—die soon," he muttered, his brows drawn angrily down over smouldering eyes. "What becomes money—hoom?"

"What money?" said Canon Macaulay.

"Me and Anderson stake him—go north—prospect—up there—Rainy Lake. Three partners—see? Him hide money some place. Him go crazy—hide money. Maybe die. What becomes?—hoom?"

"He struck it rich, did he?" asked the Canon, looking from one to the other.

"Him stake claim," the breed growled, swinging his head to and fro rhythmically in a fever of impatience. "Stake claim—work it some—take nuggets—go Winnipeg."

"Celebrate?" asked the Canon.

"Maybe celebrate," Jukes nodded. "Go Winnipeg—find woman. Him know that woman long time—twenty year, maybe. Go same place and find her—but her not same this time. Live by her own self this time—sing hymns—pray plenty. What you call that?—hoom?"

"You mean she'd been saved, I guess," said the Canon, his lip twisting under his moustache in a wry smile.

"Yup!" the breed exploded. "Dave saved, too. Sing hymns—

pray plenty—just like now. Him stay there long time—then his papoose—she get sick."

The Canon, his hands behind his back, his brow knotted in the attempt to untangle the breed's story, remembered the daughter, Millie. He recalled the talk in the town when her husband ran off with the other woman. She had died very soon after.

"Millie get sick," Jukes went on, in the same monotonous, growling tone. "She die soon if not hurry up. They send Winnipeg—that woman's place—find old Dave—him come home."

As though reminded of a refrain, by hearing its first note, the old man, who had sunk into a daze, began muttering: "For in that he died, he died unto sin once; but in that he lives . . . he lives . . . he lives!"

Jukes rolled his head slowly from side to side. "Dave come quick—sing plenty hymns upstairs. Hymns—no good. She die soon—singin' plenty too."

The old man seemed suddenly to understand and raised himself half out of his chair, tottering and shaking. "She died with angels 'round her," he muttered, in a hollow voice. "She kept a-sayin': 'They're tellin' me to come, Dad.' And I says: 'Go ahead, Millie, don't you be a-skeered.' She seen all kind o' things. She seen heaven openin', and she said to me again: 'They're a-tellin' me to come, Dad.' And I says: 'It's all right, Millie. Let them that is athirst come. Even so, Lord Jesus.' And she said somethin' about the girls and me, and I says: 'Fear nought, Millie. The Lord'll look after us,' I says, 'don't you be a-skeered.' And after a bit she says to me: 'I guess I'm goin', Dad,' and she sat up in the bed an' opened her eyes wide open. And I seen them angels a-takin' of her. They took her away up high, where there was harps playin'."

He began to crumple, like a man made of paper. The Canon sprang forward to save him from falling, but somehow he sank into the chair and let his head fall back, muttering again: "They mount up with wings like angels . . . like angels. . . ."

Philp, who had slowly edged nearer, said to Jukes: "Is he like this all the time?"

"Don't know," Jukes grunted sullenly. "Don't come here long time. No good. Anderson boy—him close mor'gage on me. Me lose farm."

His eyes glared. His wild glance swung toward the twisted figure in the chair.

"Hymn-sing swine!" he bellowed at the old man. "What becomes money?—hoom? Me need money. Me need money!"

Linklater's head, lolling back against the top rail of the chair, slipped a little to one side, as though he were asleep. His eyes remained closed, but his lips began to move. The Canon, leaning close, could just distinguish what he was saying: "Money . . . they're after money, all of 'em. . . . Thieves . . . thousands of 'em . . . fools! . . . do you hear? . . . Since the beginnin' men ain't heard, nor perceived by the ear . . . nor seen by the eyes . . . what he's prepared . . . for them as wait patiently . . . patiently. . . ."

Philp looked at the Canon meaningly. Linklater was too weak and crazy to give them the information they wanted. Now, while the old man was still mumbling, Philp recalled what had been told him of the case. There were two children—the old man's granddaughters—but they were nowhere in sight. The older of the two, at least, might be able to tell him something.

"Where are the girls, do you suppose?" he asked the Canon, rubbing the pale hair at the back of his head until it stood up like the crest of a cockatoo.

"Outside—'long shore—maybe," Jukes said, in a calmer tone, his anger dwindling as he became convinced of the old man's helplessness.

"What are their names?" Philp asked the breed.

"Elsie—Rosie. Rosie small."

Linklater opened his eyes. "How's that? I'm hard o' hearin'. Rosie?—where's Rosie?" he asked, in a whisper.

"Yes, where is she?" echoed Philp.

"Uncle Geoff took 'em out for a row," the old man replied, in a firm tone, raising his head and gazing slowly around. "They won't be long."

"Who does he call Uncle Geoff?" Philp said, turning to Jukes, who had begun to move about aimlessly between them and the door, as though making up his mind to go.

"Don't know," he muttered, without turning his head. Treading heavily on the squeaking floor-boards near the door, he finally blundered out.

"Tavistock," Linklater said loudly, as soon as the breed stepped out of sight. "Rosie calls him Uncle Geoff. But what's a name? Eh? We'll soon have new names—do you hear? To him that overcometh—you don't know what that means, I guess—but never mind—to him that overcometh he'll give a white stone—and in the stone a new name written . . . a new name . . . that no one knows."

He nodded his trembling head and began chuckling deep in his throat.

Philp thought he heard a boat scraping on the pebbles outside, and walked back through the house. There were children's voices and lower masculine tones floating liquidly in the air, the lake giving to the faint sounds a quality of its own.

As he reached the back door Philp saw a tall man step out of a rowboat on to the slanting old wharf alongside the boathouse, with a little girl in his arms. An older girl stood there already, coughing, with her hand pressed to her chest. Philp caught the words: "Uncle Geoff." Here, he thought, is somebody who will tell us how these people live.

The Canon came to where Philp was standing and waited beside him for Tavistock to come into the house. He began nodding when the Englishman was still a few steps away, and immediately introduced Philp. "Mr. Philp is from the town hall

—to investigate." He dropped his voice to a whisper.

The two children left Tavistock's side and ran to their grandfather, bending close to his ear and shouting excitedly about their boat-ride.

SIX

The Canon

I

"I'M GLAD WE CAME," the Canon said, over his shoulder, to Philp as they left the place and went through the overgrown garden toward the road. "The old man is much feebler."

They were walking single-file along a narrow path that had been almost obliterated by the rank growth of pig-weed. The Canon, in front, had been hurrying. It was nearing seven o'clock, and they would be waiting supper for him at home. He paused for Philp to catch up.

"Too bad to drag you out of your way just at supper-time," he said, "but you can see it was urgent."

Philp agreed. Tavistock had given them plenty of information. It was a clearly deserving case. Already it was pigeon-holed in his mind. He could see the details all carefully written out in his own neat handwriting on one of the blue forms at the office, headed—"In *re* David Livingstone Linklater."

They reached the sidewalk quickly and parted, Philp going east and the Canon turning west after a final glance back at the house, thinking how deserted and sinister it looked. It had seemed squalid enough the other evening, in the dark, when he had sat there talking to the old man and Tavistock; but in broad daylight, in contrast with the sparkling, sunlit lake, seen through the dingy windows, and with the clean young trunks of the poplars growing right up to the door, the dirt and stench of the place seemed doubly offensive.

"The misery that will not let us rest," he found himself repeating—a phrase Tavistock had quoted the other night when the three of them had sat there talking until late at night, moths fluttering around the lamp and the flame after a while dying down to a red ember of wick for want of oil, so that finally they had sat there with only the moon's glow on the lake to light the place through the open door.

At first they had gossiped of old times, he and Linklater, while the Englishman sat aside, saying nothing. Linklater had poured out a gabble of memories of the Klondike, a streaming picture that floated through his mind as he talked, gathering pace as his age dissolved in the remembered rush, and the gold rush itself burned in his veins again. But it did not last very long. The old man soon fell into mumbling, wagging his head from side to side, his mind circling again among the odds and ends of scripture he whispered to himself, hour after hour, these last few months, crouched in a chair with a huge Bible spread out on his shaking knees.

2

The Canon stepped off the sidewalk and crossed the deeply rutted road. He had reached the short-cut through McCully's bush, just back of the magistrate's house. Through a grove of cottonwoods he could see the housekeeper, Mrs. Higham, bending between the green rows in the vegetable garden. He knew every inch of the place intimately. It was a house almost as familiar as his own, and to-morrow evening he would be there again for his regular game of cribbage.

But his mind swung back to the vivid memory of the two men in the shack that night, and of the strange talk stirred up by Linklater's fanaticism. Tavistock had puzzled him, both by what he had said and by what he seemed loath to say. His tone had been lofty, paradoxical. To-night a certain mysteriousness was still noticeable in Tavistock's manner, but when he had come in with the children it was somehow attuned to their ingenuousness. Instead of arrogance—which the Canon had suspected in his attitude before—the loosely hanging arms and composed mouth had suggested a deep humility, and his voice, previously impassioned, had become low-pitched and tender.

More than ever, as he went absent-mindedly along, passing the well-kept lawns and hedges along Vernon Avenue without seeing them, this stranger he had seen occasionally in his church disturbed him by his deep-set contradictions.

That evening, a few nights ago, Tavistock had been silent at first, until Linklater's raving had given the conversation a definitely religious turn.

"You think I'm off my head since I been home this last time," the old man had rasped out, turning on the Canon with a sudden crazy light in his eyes. "Maybe I am," he had added, his nose twisted in a sneering smile. "Maybe I am—and maybe you can preach as slick as a whistle. I ain't never heard you preach. But I'm tellin' you, reverend, if you ain't been born again *yourself!*" and he repeated the words, thumping the table so that the lamp-chimney rattled in its socket—"if you ain't been born again *yourself!*—you ain't got the hang of the thing at all. Do you hear? You're in outer darkness where there's gnashin' o' teeth. What's this here about 'light in the Lord'? Eh? How can you tell what *that* means unless you been there?"

Sinking back in his chair he had jerked a trembling finger

across the table at the Canon, glancing at the same time through screwed-up eyes at Tavistock, and demanding: "Let him tell us whether he's been there."

The Canon remembered that at first he had thought Linklater was simply pulling his leg, and had let out a sort of chuckle. But he had quickly grown serious. He was sitting, hunched forward in his chair, facing the open back door of the shack, and his glance suddenly seemed to become more aware of the brilliant, broad path of moonlight across the lake. He heard, more distinctly, the water lapping against the boathouse and the bullfrogs trilling all along the marshy shore.

"You talk like a man who's been saved," he muttered, avoiding Linklater's stare.

"An' what's that?" the old man had demanded, the white of his eyes suddenly gleaming in the dim light. "You don't have revival meetin's in that there church o' your'n. You don't believe in 'em—and maybe I don't myself. It warn't no revival where I got what I got. But youse has the Bible there in your church an' you preach out of it—and I'll bet you two dollars you're stuck half the time to know what it's all about."

3

An old man quivering in his chair as though with the palsy—an old man who had lived a violent, shouldering, get-to-hell-out-o'-my-road sort of life, but converted now and changed beyond belief—sitting there with God's name on his lips, uttered reverently and even mysteriously, and waiting to be answered.

It is all vividly present in the Canon's mind as he hurries home. He remembers the tone of his own voice, replying at last in the manner one would use to a child, "I doubt if anyone knows the half—or even a quarter—of what it means, Dave. But we know pretty well what's right and what's wrong, and perhaps—perhaps it's better not to bother too much with—"

A long-drawn exclamation—a deep guttural sound—escapes Linklater's lips to interrupt him, the old man looking hard at Tavistock as though this recalls something they have talked about often before.

The Canon turns, too, and dimly makes out the Englishman's face, his head slanted as though in repose on an invisible pillow, his eyes inscrutably fixed on the tiny oblong of light reflected from the lake in the glass of the lamp-chimney.

Tavistock speaks at last in a slow, gentle voice. "A man who has been born again," he says, as though mentioning an everyday occurrence, "knows that there can be nothing evil."

"Do you mean," asks the Canon abruptly, "that the man who is living—shall we say, in *light*—doesn't need to use judgment as to what is good and evil?"

"The Comforter," Tavistock murmurs, "the Comforter—it is said—is to come to 'reprove the world of sin and of righteousness and of judgment.'"

"But surely that simply means," the Canon exclaims quickly, "to reprove *self*-righteousness—and judgment—judgment of others—'judge not lest ye be judged?'"

Tavistock answers quietly: "A man living in light is above sin and above righteousness. He becomes *innocent* of good and evil. He does only what the light makes him see as the thing to be done."

The Englishman's long fingers slide upward over his brow and brush through his hair, gripping the skull as he bends his head back to gaze upward, as though mysteries were open to him in the air.

The Canon feels the earnestness with which this youngster plunges out of the world into speculations that seem out of reach of life. But, pressing his feet down solidly, his thighs flattened against the hard edge of the chair, the Canon brings out his thought. "You mean that we should be blind to right and wrong."

"Men and women," Tavistock exclaims quickly, as though he had expected just that retort, "will not rid the world of good and evil by trying to be good and trying not to be evil. *That* is the very judgment that must be reproved. Men and women must become again—as little children—*innocent* of good and evil."

The Canon stiffens himself against the tremors that run through his body. "Aren't you twisting that to meet your own argument?" he asks. "That is in Romans. It is just there that St. Paul says, 'For all have sinned and come short of the glory of God.' St. Paul, of all men, was conscious of himself as a sinner."

Tavistock, dragging his chair an inch or two nearer the table, brings his arm down to rest on Linklater's big Bible that is lying there. "But before that he makes it clear. 'The law,' he says, 'speaks only to those under the law, that every mouth may be stopped, and *all the world may become guilty* before God.'"

For the first time Tavistock speaks with an emphasis that is impassioned, as though the vision the words call up—of millions of men and women hanging their heads in guilt before an awful Almighty—a great multitude standing in shame—were a spectacle horribly real to him. "Will you tell me," he cries, "that God—or St. Paul either—wants a *guilty world?*"

How perverse he is! the Canon thinks, growing impatient and flinging one leg heavily over the other. "My dear man," he cries, "don't you know what God has done to save the world?"

Tavistock brings his hand down with a thud on the Bible, gripping its edges and peering past the lamp into the Canon's puckered face. "The cross!" he exclaims impatiently, "always the cross! But did *he* live by the law—by judgment—by the knowledge of good and evil? Didn't *he* point to the light? Not to the mind that judges, but to the soul that is above good and evil—the *one* soul! In a life that is all one there can *be* no evil!"

The Canon sends the puzzling words out through his teeth in an undertone: "The *one* soul."

"Yes," the voice comes back, whispering across the table, with a prolonged hiss of conviction. "'*That they may be made perfect in one.*'"

"You mean—you deny the individual soul?" the Canon leans forward to ask.

"Yes."

"You are a Pantheist, perhaps."

Tavistock rises out of his chair and locks his hands behind his head, gazing steadily into the darkness under the ceiling.

"You don't like that," the Canon says, meaning it for an apology, but failing to achieve a humble tone.

"It means nothing," the other breathes into the air above him. "Call me a Pantheist, if you like."

The Canon manages a laugh—a chuckle—at the folly of all human pretensions to wisdom. "Well, God bless us," he exclaims, "how is one to deal with all these beliefs—these ideas? We all have our own ideas, I suppose, and—"

"Ideas, *ideas*!" Tavistock exclaims. "There is only the *one* truth—the way, the truth and the light! And in the light there is no evil."

The Canon feels the eyes staring through the gloom at him, and hears the voice repeating, in a prophetic accent: "There is *no* evil!"

Linklater sends a wagging finger above his head. "Be ye therefore perfect!" he mutters, nodding his chin heavily on his breast.

4

Two men—strange to him, and voicing strange thoughts—for in their mouths the ancient words seemed to be given a queer, fanatical twist—two men talking there in the dark as though the kingdom of heaven were already at hand, like a dawn breaking over a dissolving world.

He had finally got to his feet clumsily, in a sort of daze, feeling a strange vitality in Tavistock that fascinated him. The force was unmistakable—free, ascending, and revealing—somehow —the nature of the highest—the highest what?

His mind had refused to climb. Before such shining ultimates he had quivered, conscious of his flesh. His voice returned to him. "If there is no evil—if it is possible to be perfect here on earth—why do you grieve?" he had begged of Tavistock, in the tone of a suppliant, a seeker after salvation. And then, with a hint of his former argumentativeness, he had added: "Why do *you* rebel at a guilty world?"

And Tavistock had brought his head down slowly to look at him, as though amazed that he was still there. "I am one of those —that Keats speaks of," he bitterly complained, "one of those 'to whom the miseries of the world are misery, and will not let them rest.'"

His head had drooped then, and his hands had fallen to his sides. It was the same attitude, the posture the Canon had seen to-night—a posture of humility, of resignation, of a man overwhelmed by a burden of sorrow too heavy for him to bear.

The Canon found himself at his gate. His eyes were moist and his throat troubled. On the verandah steps his feet were a little unsteady. He paused with his hand on the doorknob to murmur under his breath: "God is light, and in him is no darkness at all. If we say that we have fellowship with him, and walk in darkness, we lie, and do not the truth; but if we walk in the light, as he is in the light, *we have fellowship one with another*."

He went into the house, repeating the last words—"We have fellowship one with another." His mind was occupied with wondering. Perhaps the phrase held a deeper meaning than what he had always supposed.

SEVEN

Laura

I

SUPPER WAS on the table. His wife, Jessica, sat across from him, with her expressionless, waxen face. Laura was at his side, her hair coiled low on her neck, her brow high and slanting at the temples, her eager eyes gleaming on either side of a prominent, curiously blunted nose. Her upper lip arched abruptly, while the lower curved in a full round above the cleft in her chin, which was deep, like her father's.

What a mixture! the Canon thought, looking at the strong, unforgettable face, and seeing her, not as she was now, bent over her food—twenty-four already—but as she had been all the years.

"She is like neither of us," the Canon complained to himself, his eyes swivelling under his brows between the two women. "It is her grandfather Howland she takes after," he decided for the hundredth time. He remembered the old man as he last saw him, sallow and bent among his books, yet with a kindling eye and a protuberant nose lifted eagerly if his poems were mentioned.

"It has skipped a generation," the Canon thought, recalling the Howland tradition that had made him feel inferior in Jessica's home when they were courting. The stale perfume of grandfathers, receding one behind the other into the dim past, the more revered the dimmer they grew, still clung to Jessica, but Laura had their spirit, and in her eyes he had seen gleams of their imagination.

"She will never be like her mother," he assured himself, for he had watched her and had seen she was not developing like Mildred, the married one. He had watched eagerly, his hair greying and his legs stiffening as he went in and out through a household that bore the upright, sombre imprint of his womenfolk; watching Laura grow away from Mildred and her mother, growing toward himself, and taking to Sturge Bundy, who came often to sit in a darkened corner to hear her play. The Canon had watched her, even before she began to take lessons, sitting across the meal-table, gazing at the doctor's beard, the blond point of it jiggling as he talked; or later lingering with them in the study, her head wreathed with their smoke and her eyes deepening at their talk—an alert, straight, listening girl sitting at their knees on an old foot-rest, with long, placid fingers folded in a carefully smoothed lap.

She had grown up too soon—even though they had grown together these last few years, their eyes shining at the same things, their brows arching in understanding across a roomful of parishioners, their voices brightening together if in the afternoon they were alone in the garden and wandered to and fro, bending over her flower-beds.

He was secretly glad that it had been impossible to keep her in the East to go on with her music. She was a born musician, he was sure, and when he caught her sometimes at the piano alone, her gaze fixed pensively on the still keys, he wanted urgently to sell all that he had and send her away where there would be great teachers, old men with tragic faces and long white hair, like the picture of Liszt he had seen once . . . and tiered halls in the capitals of Europe, filled with distinguished people, craning forward in their seats to see her.

Yet when he thought of the good-byes, and the months—the years—of absence, and how she would grow away from him over there, coming back a stranger and feeling ill-at-ease in the town, and irked by the stuffiness of the little house, and going away again with secret joy in her heart, he thanked God that he was a poor man, and that the Lord of all power and might—and not himself—had made it impossible, utterly impossible.

It was a small, private God that he thanked, who resided in some dim recess of his mind, whither he would sometimes steal to argue, to demand, and even—under great stress—to challenge. At times it was to offer thanks for blessings which permitted him to be the kind of man he wanted to be, poor enough to be left alone by a certain section of his congregation, and weak enough not to have to pretend sympathy with the worst of his flock. And sometimes, when the Father of all mercies so ordered his life that his most selfish desires came to fruition, even against his will, and in spite of his efforts, he crept shamefacedly inward to rejoice, displaying his tears of thankfulness only to his private, hidden deity, who could be depended on to keep his secrets.

It was impossible to send her away, and yet how much longer could they hope to keep her? She was not like Mildred, who had been accepted as a confirmed spinster in the parish years before she astonished them all by inviting that builder, Crandall, to the rectory—finally amazing the Canon beyond words, when she came out of the parlour one evening and stood in his study, her face bloodless, whispering over his shoulder that Mr. Crandall had something to say to him.

Laura was not like her, and never would be. There was throbbing blood in her, and rich, strange thoughts coursed in her mind, coming on rare occasions to utterance, perhaps at twilight in the garden, or late at night after she had been playing a long time and sank cross-kneed on a cushion at his feet, the two of them alone together in the front room, with the immense darkness of the prairie beating in against the candles.

2

But now she might be marrying soon, for she was going out with young Anderson, who had come back from Winnipeg to lead the Methodist choir and teach singing in the town. The Canon had seen her himself in the bow of Harry's new, green canoe, her shoulders arched among the cushions, her strong profile etched against the moving water.

Harry sometimes came to the house to call for her, handsome and immaculate in a light summer suit and polka-dot tie. The Canon avoided him, disliking something in his pale eyes and the set of his thin lips. Perhaps it was just that he was trying too hard to mark himself off from his shabby, boisterous, domineering father. His mother, a depressed little woman, who used to sit rocking by the hour on her verandah, darting furtive and envious looks at passers-by, was dead now, and Harry had refused to live at home after coming back from Winnipeg. He had a room in the McIllwraith Block, which was also his studio. He dressed himself and carried himself in a conspicuous way, and spoke with what seemed to the Canon to be an affected enunciation. That Laura should take to him seemed unaccountable.

She was eyeing her father now with a curious steadiness across the table, and unexpectedly mentioned Harry's name, saying she was going out on the lake with him presently. He would take her along to Linklater's with the things for the children that she and her mother had got together.

Across the pale sweet-peas which she had picked freshly, a minute or two before supper, her voice quavered with an unsureness that was strange in her. Until now she had rarely spoken of Harry in the house, and had never invited him in. Always she had come home from their outings undisturbed, speaking of the sunset, perhaps, or of somebody she had seen, somebody they all knew. But of him she had said nothing; not, the Canon felt, through secretiveness, but because he meant nothing—merely someone to take her on the lake.

But there was now in her mention of his name a tremulousness that the Canon was quick to note in her voice, striving to reconcile it with a look of studied finality in her eyes. But he could make nothing of it. He glanced at his wife, at her smooth eyes, her gaze resting absently on the bowl of sweet-peas. She was oblivious of anything unusual in Laura's tone. Her thin, unmoving head, always erectly poised, looked as though it had just been taken from a glass case in which it had been carefully preserved for years.

She gave no thought to Laura's outing with Harry, except to add something to the basket she was taking to Linklater's, when Laura was ready to go. Neither of them spoke. They nodded with slow intimacy at one another, and Laura went into the hall, stopping a moment to put her head through the curtains of her father's study—for the Canon was already at work on his sermon—to whisper good-bye.

Feeling more than ever a new, anticipatory excitement in her manner, he unexpectedly jumped up, snatching the curved pipe out of the corner of his mouth to kiss her, examining tenderly her dark hair coiled under the severe sailor hat, her high-necked blouse and the full, dark skirt curving from her slight waist to the floor.

Amused by his survey of her from head to toe, she murmured, "Am I fit to be seen?" and kissing him again on the cheek, vanished through the curtains.

3

Over young Anderson's head, as he sat paddling, Laura watched a huge, blue, pointed cloud hanging darkly against the pale, green-tinted upper sky.

"Look, Harry," she said, "there's a cloud shaped just like an anvil!"

He paused for a moment and threw a glance over his shoulder—not direct enough really to see it—and dipped the paddle again deeply into the water, driving the canoe toward Linklater's place with deft, lunging strokes.

She had left the house determined to tell him that this must be their last outing, but his sulky mood made her strangely light-hearted.

At supper she had mentioned him purposely, and with special deliberateness, to confirm the feeling in her mind by uttering it. She wanted to impress upon herself the finality that was to surround this last meeting, making it final in her thought—in her home, where she felt herself strongly dependable—so that it would be sure to come out that way on her lips in Harry's hearing and sound unmistakably finished.

She had given it all this thought because she had expected it would be difficult to tell him. There was little to object to, after all, unless she were to speak of the very things she had pretended not to notice—glances that disturbed her, a remark now and then, or something in the way he touched her arm when helping her out of the canoe. There was, besides, a curious tremor just perceptible at the corner of his mouth sometimes, which she could only construe as a mocking commentary on her—her "hypocrisy," he would call it, she supposed. It had been too often on his tongue, lately—the word "hypocrisy"—used in respect of others, of course, but with the veiled insinuation that she, like most church-going people, possessed desires and impulses carefully concealed, which everyone equally would like to indulge if only they could "get away with it" in secret.

She had suddenly seen in what direction all this was tending, and as the realization grew it became less and less tolerable to ignore his glances and deliberately misinterpret his words. She even blamed herself for pretending to be blind so long, feeling that her silence might have given him a false opinion of her.

They were among the few young people in the town who had been outside and seen something of the world. Because he was an artist and of her own generation she had talked more freely to him than to anyone else. For a while she had believed that on both sides their companionship was simply a relation between two musicians, clinging desperately to the atmosphere of high emotion associated with their art, in spite of the hackneyed, commonplace tastes of almost everyone else in the town. But she had soon discovered how shallow he was. All he had was a voice. Even his acquired manners became crudely transparent after a few meetings. And now she was rapidly re-learning a repulsion which during her schooldays had driven her away from smirking, whispering playmates.

"He hasn't changed," she said to herself, thinking of the time when they had known each other at school, "except on the outside. His mind is still . . ."

4

This errand to Linklater's complicated what she had intended. They had met at the foot of Charlotte Street, she walking down from the rectory and he paddling over from the boathouse in the East end.

"What's this?" he had exclaimed, taking the basket she held out to him. "A picnic?"

"Father wants me to take these things to Linklater's," she said, making herself comfortable in the canoe, "and then I must go straight home."

"Must?" he said.

"I meant I want to."

He looked away toward the bank they were leaving. "That's different," he said, his lip curling in a slow, arrogant smile.

"Not in the end," she said, in a severe tone.

"What do you mean—'in the end'?" He was displaying the worse side of himself. She saw the swaggering, overbearing nature of his father glowering through the mask of refinement he had lately worn.

She sighed impatiently. "I mean that when I've been to Linklater's I shall go home—at once. I don't feel like talking."

She let her hand droop over the side of the canoe, so that her finger-tips dipped and dragged in the water. "I'd rather not talk about it at all," she said quietly. "I intended to—to-night—but now I'm here I don't feel like it."

He held his paddle across his knees and stared at her through narrowed eyes, sizing up her mood. "You're offended, and I want to know why. Why can't you tell me?"

"All right, I will," she said. "But not tonight. I don't feel like it."

His head was averted, looking at a rowboat between them and the shore. There were two girls in it, one rowing awkwardly and the other chattering and laughing in a flat, raucous voice.

Laura's gaze was fastened on the rim of the sun just appearing below the huge blue cloud standing like an anvil in the western sky.

"Going to be here long?" Harry said, swinging the canoe in toward the crumbling boathouse behind Linklater's shack. His mouth was curved in a hard, superior smile, as though her moods were familiar to him and of no consequence.

"Not many minutes, I guess."

"I'll stay in the canoe, then."

She did not reply. As they neared the wharf she had noticed a rowboat tied up there with a name lettered on it which she had seen lately quite often—a name lettered large across the stern —*Sigrid*. It was one of the boats old Eggertson, the Icelander, rented out, and she had often seen in it a man who had somehow attracted her attention early in the summer. His bare head and staring, sorrowful eyes had caused her to wonder about him whenever he had passed on the lake, or when she had seen him sometimes in church.

Now that she thought of it she recalled seeing two little girls in his boat occasionally. No doubt they were Linklater's grand-daughters. Perhaps he was the man her father had spoken of a night or two before—an Englishman—she had forgotten his name—an odd name, too—who had been helping them.

The canoe ran into the high reeds that fringed the shore, and without help from Harry, who steadied the side against the wharf, she lifted her basket and stepped lightly out.

EIGHT

The Encounter

I

After Philp and the canon had gone away the two girls had cuddled down in the dishevelled bed. The old man, in a feebler voice than usual, and with a more demented look, which filled Tavistock with apprehension, began to rave about Jukes—about the old days—breed dances—poker games—trips north . . .

It was still light and the children were fidgeting and whispering and kneeling up in the bed now and then to see who was passing when they heard the splash of a paddle outside. To settle them for sleep Tavistock presently went over and told them a story. He sat on the edge of the bed, a dreamy smile deepening the two lines, like drawn-out dimples, on either side of his mouth. His slender head hung sideways and a little forward as though listening to a voice, inaudible to the children, which dictated the fairy-tale he was telling them.

A canoe scraped against the wharf. Two people spoke indistinctly. There was a sound of steps crunching lightly in the pebbles and a double tap on the frame of the open door.

The children sat bolt upright and peered across the room, trying to make out the features of the stranger who stood in the doorway—a dark silhouette against the failing light outside.

"Who's that?" croaked Linklater, looking sharply up from the Bible he had spread out on his knees.

Tavistock, seeing that it was a woman, took three strides from the bed and looked down into the lifted face. A sudden tightening across his chest prevented him from speaking instantly. At one glance he recognized her as the girl at the piano—the girl he had seen so often on the lake—who had looked at him directly, steadily, more than once, as though she knew something about him that he did not know himself. He had seen her in church, too. One Sunday night they had come out into the aisle from opposite pews, facing each other, and he had surprised on her face the lingering emotion of her prayers. The look in her eyes had haunted him because it was so close to what he wanted to feel himself. Once, he had even spoken to her, but it was in the dark, and she probably wouldn't remember. He had come across her trying to help old Pitts, who had tripped on a loose plank in the sidewalk and had stumbled into the ditch, twisting his ankle. When he saw him there he thought at once that the old man was drunk and simply said he would look after him. It was very dark and she probably hadn't recognized him. Her trembling voice, saying: "He's hurt," had not yet faded from his ears.

She spoke and he knew his memory had been faithful. She stood looking up at him, clinging to the handle of her basket, and saying, in the same soft, tremulous voice: "It's Laura Macaulay—Canon Macaulay's daughter. I've brought some things for the children."

He saw a look of sudden, half-timid recognition flash in the direct gaze of her dark brown eyes. It was true, then. They had both been conscious of each other for weeks past, meeting each other repeatedly—wondering what the other might be like. There was unmistakable curiosity in her eyes, matching the desire to know her which immediately stirred his own feelings with a quick tremor that sent warm blood rushing toward his ears.

He stepped aside. "Please come in," he said. "My name is Tavistock. I'm a sort of uncle here."

Her smile was quick, followed by a succession of little nods. There was something about her that was like her father.

He heard Linklater's feet shuffling across the floor behind him. "Who's this?" he cried, in a squeaking voice. "Is it money you're after? Eh? What's she say? I'm hard o' hearin'."

"It's Canon Macaulay's daughter—the 'reverend,' you know," Tavistock said distinctly in the old man's ear.

"Oh, the reverend's gal, is it?"

The two girls were clinging to each other, staring with round eyes at Laura. She went toward them, holding the basket out in front of her, feeling awkward and half-afraid in the gloom of an unfamiliar house with the two men standing there, saying nothing, and the children clutching each other and whispering. But the awkwardness was over the moment she spoke to them and showed them what she had brought. The old man came to lean over the foot of the bed, watching their delighted faces, while Tavistock lighted the lamp. Dusk was descending quickly.

Rosie, the younger of the two girls, looked shyly up at Laura with wondering eyes, and presently said: "Fairies are smaller, ain't they?"

Laura was puzzled. "Smaller than—?"

"Smaller than you."

"Oh, much."

Rosie knitted her little brows. "And they're prettier, too, ain't they?"

Elsie looked ashamed. "You shouldn't say that," she said, in a hoarse voice.

"Well, they have wings," Rosie cried in defence. "And stars in their hair."

Laura smiled indulgently, bending over the bed to ask: "Who told you that?"

"Aunt Julie."

"Aunt Julie!"

"That's our French aunt," Elsie said, with a serious air. "She lives across the road—in McCully's bush."

"I know," said Laura, nodding. "She is kind to you, is she?"

"Oh yes," drawled little Rosie. "She's our best aunt. She brings us pie."

Elsie stifled a cough to gasp out: "She's the *only* aunt we've got."

"Will *you* be our aunt, too?" Rosie questioned, looking up trustfully into Laura's face.

"Yes, I'd like to be."

"What's your name, then?"

"Laura."

Rosie considered it solemnly. "All right. You be our Auntie Laura. And will you come lots—like Uncle Geoff."

"Who is Uncle Geoff?"

Rosie poked a quick finger in Tavistock's direction. "That's our Uncle Geoff."

Linklater, who had been leaning over the bed-rail watching the children, straightened his back painfully. "There was a man sent from God," he mumbled, "and his name was John. The kids call him Uncle Geoff. But these here names don't mean nothin'. There'll be new names in heaven, missie."

He sat down on the edge of the bed across from her and joined childishly in the opening of the parcels, chuckling to himself and patting Rosie's head repeatedly as she crowed and blinked her eyes at everything Laura had brought. She kept the medicine until the last and explained to the old man how it should be given, handing the bottle to him timidly—still half-afraid of his haggard look and strange talk.

2

All this time Tavistock was standing by the table, which was shakily supported by four sticks of cord-wood. He was so used to the barren room that he had become half-unconscious of its squalour. But seeing her there, sitting on the battered iron bed, with the old man so close to her—his threadbare clothes hanging as though on a scarecrow—his long hair falling in greasy locks to his shoulders—the ugliness and filth of the place smote Tavistock with a pang of shame. He ought to have got them out of there, somehow, even against the old man's will.

Her voice alone, in the stale reek of the room, after Linklater's croaking, was like the morning chatter of birds after a night of bitter dreams. It was more than the stuffy house—it was the murk of his own mind—which seemed so close and stiffing in contrast with the sweet air she seemed to exhale with her words. The depths of his nature responded to her softness as he watched her hands moving among the parcels, her white brow curving under her hair with all the lure of a strange road bending behind a hill.

Her face was a perfect oval, the chin short and the forehead high. She had a curiously prominent nose, blunt at the tip, but sensitive at the nostrils. Her tiny mouth curved into little deep shadows at either side, producing the effect of an elusive smile, even when her mood was serious. Her eyes were round, dark, humid, and almost always lighted with eagerness. She carried herself uprightly, leaning forward a little, with an air of being alert for subtle ecstasies.

Tavistock had seen her a dozen times—a score of times, perhaps—and each time her round, eager eyes and parted lips had somehow disturbed him. Her face was unforgettable, and more than once he had wondered why it should be so. He had half hoped never to meet her, feeling afraid in advance that she would draw him away from what he intended to do. Yet here she was in this out-of-the-way shack, where Pitts, too, like a ghost out of the past, had come back into his life. For a moment he had a feeling of fate hanging over the house—a fate opposed to the sense of destiny which had driven him all these years toward one end.

She was beautiful. She drew his thoughts away from death and destiny. Her moist, eager eyes made him ache for life. As he looked at her the transparent, murmurous space in his mind collapsed suddenly, as though crushed like an egg-shell. The sense of mystery and miracle became a ludicrous dream. The voices that haunted him were silent. He felt something asserting itself inside him—his own voice! It rang so true, so strong, after the shadowy whispers he had lately heeded, that he was forced to accept it as his own—his own nature awaking.

"I am awake—now!" said the voice, and he began trembling with a richer sense of existence than he had ever believed possible. He had found himself. There was a man in him, after all.

She was getting up from the bed and was coming toward him. He took his hands from his pockets and gripped them together behind him.

"You don't remember it, I suppose—but I've met you before," he said, in a tone that surprised him by sounding normal, and even a little distant.

She was standing under his gaze. The lamplight glistened in her eager, lifted eyes. The rising and falling of her breast shifted the shadows of the pleats across the bodice of her dress.

"I feel sure I should have remembered it," she was saying, reddening slightly. "I've seen you, of course."

"Where have you seen me?" he asked impetuously.

"On the lake more than once," she said, "and in church a few times—and—"

He did not wait for her to finish. "Do you remember a night —perhaps a month ago—when you came across a man in the ditch on Cartier Street?"

"Yes," she exclaimed, nodding her head excitedly. "It was very dark—I—"

"Yes, the nights are absolutely black in this country, aren't they?" he said.

"You were the man who came along," she said, only half-enquiringly. "I didn't recognize you, then. I mean I didn't connect your voice with—"

"With what I look like," he helped her.

"When I came in just now I felt I'd heard your voice somewhere—and then I suddenly remembered. Did you—did you have much trouble with that man?"

He looked at her, more gravely. "No," he said. "He managed to limp along very well. I only had to get him to a place just near here."

"Julie's?" she said.

He listened to the overtones of her voice, searching for an accent of disapproval, but finding none, he said: "Yes. I know him, you know. I used to know him in Africa."

She had left her basket on the bed, and her hands, apart, in front of her, began to move to her sides, as though they had become suddenly conspicuous and she wanted to hide them.

"Did you come over together?" she said, swallowing her surprise.

"No. I found him here—working in the newspaper office. As a matter of fact, I met him right here in this house—the first time."

"What a coincidence!" Laura exclaimed.

Tavistock considered her little outcry. He thrust his hands deeply into his coat pockets, holding them rigidly, his thumbs out.

"Not much of one, I'm afraid," he demurred, with a slow squaring of his shoulders. He was thinking that he and Pitts had both drifted there. They were drifters—for different reasons—but both drifters. His impatience with himself glowed for a moment in his eyes, but she was saying something—something, he felt, to make conversation and cover her perplexity at what he had said.

"You've not been long in this country, I suppose?"

"A few months."

"Do you like it here?"

He saw her bite her lip at the triteness of it.

"I never care very much where I am," he murmured. He was trying to show her the kind of man he was, so that he would know, by her response, whether she would be like all the rest—unable to understand him. He projected his mood outward toward her as he had learned to do on the stage, affecting an audience by a mere glance or by a movement of a hand, and feeling their response in the darkness on the other side of the footlights.

He saw at once that she had sensed something strange in him. She was looking up at him with an impersonal curiosity, as she might have looked at a tree—a tree such as she had never seen on the prairies. He saw in her eyes the realization that on the prairies there is nothing tall, nothing that soars, nothing mysterious. He could feel the flatness around her and he longed to catch her up into the blue, transparent space which had receded from his mind.

"After all, what happens to the body doesn't matter," he said slowly, in a low voice. "The body is nothing."

"Doesn't matter!" she exclaimed. "I should think it mattered a great deal."

He looked over her head. "No," he said gently. "Eternity isn't something in the future. Eternity is all around us—now. If I died I should be no nearer eternity than I am in this room."

He suddenly glanced down at her, into her perplexed, eager eyes. He realized that this was a new eternity he was talking about—an eternity he might share with her.

"But—death!" she whispered, as though she felt it to be irrevocable, the end of everything.

"What makes you think of death?" he asked, his hands unfolding toward her and almost touching her. "Everything is *now*! That is what eternity is—a huge moment."

She stood close to him, nodding like her father, and smiling as though she dimly understood what he meant. She looked up trustingly into his eyes. He saw her press her hand to her breast. Her glance fell. She looked ashamed, as she might for having spied on mysteries not meant for her. Her chin quivered and the little cleft in it was drawn up nervously under her lip.

He climbed down from a height in his mind and tried to put her at ease by saying: "There is one thing in this country that appeals to me—tremendously. The sunsets—the skies."

She nodded again and looked up at him with her natural eagerness returning to her glance. "That is why you are on the lake so much," she said.

"Yes."

Her attention was suddenly caught by something moving in the garden. Through the bright halo around the lamp, which shone between them and the window, he could make out nothing. A step sounded on the verandah, and a voice called softly through the open door: "Is Mr. Tavistock here?"

"Hullo, Pitts," cried Tavistock. "Half a moment and I'll be with you."

Laura, breathing deeply, half-closed her eyes. He saw something—die out of them. It was the sense of shared eternity which he had somehow communicated to her. He wanted her to stay. He wanted to talk to her—endlessly. But he found himself moving with her toward the door facing the lake, which opened now on sheer blackness outside. He heard himself saying something about "the Canon . . . kindness . . . are you forgetting your basket? . . . Good-evening. . . ."

She was outside. The darkness swallowed her. She was gone. He heard the canoe rock under her as she stepped down into gloom.

NINE

The World's Sorrows

I

THE EVENING DRAGGED for Canon Macaulay. Thoughts of Laura's eyes as she last looked at him from under the hard straw hat—a "man's hat," he always called it—were mingled with the thoughts he tried to put down under the text he had placed at the top of the page, which had been running through his mind like an annoying melody—

> "And when he is come, he will reprove the world of sin, and of righteousness, and of judgment."

Was it because he was disturbed about Laura, or was it because the thought contained in the text was puzzling to him, that he made no headway with the sermon? Perhaps it was something in Tavistock's gently vibrating voice, uttering those words the other evening as though the text held a secret, beyond the mind of an ordinary man to conceive? Perhaps it was simply the man's voice—an actor's voice—adding to the words some deep significance by its sheer music—making mystery of mere sounds? Or was it an entrancement produced by some profundity that could be felt under his voice and behind his eyes?

Tavistock, certainly, had not made it clear. It was easy enough to see that sin should be reproved and abolished—and judgment, too. Was it not written, "Judge not, lest ye be judged."

But righteousness! If it meant self-righteousness—but it didn't! "Sin *and* righteousness"—the two placed together as opposites, and both to be reproved by the Holy Ghost, the Comforter.

The Canon bent over his notes, reading his own scribble with difficulty. He finally took a great breath when he came to the last words he had written. He thrust the chair back and began walking dejectedly up and down the study, wishing Tavistock were there, to argue it out with him. Yet he knew what he would say. He had listened long enough to grow impatient with the curious aloofness of his ideas, his thought hovering all the time in some lofty, mystical realm where good and evil, lacking men and women who were either one or the other, seemed to disappear. His voice echoed in the Canon's ears: "Men and women must become again—as little children—*innocent* of good and evil."

He recalled the emphasis, the exact tone of voice, and the intensity of Tavistock's gaze, lifted and fixed as though upon some invisible and infinitely distant point outside of the world.

He dropped into the big leather chair by the fireplace and stared at the wall opposite, but without seeing anything except his memory of Tavistock's face.

There was a sharp noise in the hall, and like a hammer-stroke against his heart his anxiety over Laura leapt into remembrance. He had forgotten. He took a step toward the door, and suddenly her face appeared between the curtains, smiling at him, smiling in a new way, as though she had come back to him from a long distance or from being away from him for a long time. And seeing his lined, worried face, she said at once: "You didn't expect me so soon."

2

She came in, and they stood a moment, his arms on her shoulders, looking at each other and exploring in each other's eyes this new thing that had happened. While in emotion he somehow shared whatever it was she had experienced, without knowing what it was, in thought he could seize upon nothing. His mind seemed powerless to create anything new that would fit whatever it was that was new in her; nor would it cast back to the old, to his youth, to his first falling in love. Only the one thought recurred—the thought that had been in his mind for days—"She will be marrying soon."

His surprise, then, at her first words, hammered his heart again so that his head shook on his shoulders as though he had been struck.

"I have quarrelled with Harry," she said, speaking with an air of finality that struggled against the other thing in her eyes.

"Eh?" the Canon exclaimed, tightening his grip on her shoulders, and knowing now that it was this he had seen and failed to interpret at the supper-table, but wondering the more at the exaltation in her eyes that was not linked with what she was saying.

"Yes," said Laura, her eyelids fluttering with irritation. "I haven't liked him. I've never liked him, but I thought . . . but it's useless . . . there is nothing genuine about him."

The Canon nodded a great many times.

"I wanted to have it over," Laura murmured, half lost in the newer thing. "I wanted to tell him—definitely to-night. He knows, really; but I suppose I shall have to tell him. I couldn't to-night, though. Something else—I don't know . . ." She was talking as though to herself. "When we came away from Linklater's, I didn't want to—to be bothered. I've promised to see him to-morrow night. I shall explain it to him as nicely as I can," she concluded, with an impatient gleam in her eyes, "and, anyway, he knows—he knows very well without me telling him."

The Canon sat down in the big chair and drew her on to the arm beside him, holding her close to him. She looked down, expecting him to speak, but he could only think, the same thoughts recurring: "She is here, she is all right, she has quarrelled with him, and perhaps we shall . . ."

She was speaking, and in a different voice—the new voice that matched what had been in her eyes, now turned away.

"At Linklater's I met that man you spoke of the other night—that Mr. Tavistock."

"Yes?" the Canon said, coming out of his thoughts.

Laura nodded several times, almost as he did himself, and turned to him quickly. "When you were talking about him I didn't know that I knew him."

"You mean you have met him somewhere—before?"

"Yes, I've seen him a number of times—on the lake—he's out there a lot in a rowboat—and in church a few times—he sits across the aisle from where mother and I sit—almost opposite."

"Yes, I've seen him there."

"And another time. . . ." She was frowningly serious. "I didn't know him then, either. I was coming home one night and found an old man in the ditch on Cartier Street—that funny-looking man who works at the *Monitor.*"

"Pitts?"

"Yes. That's his name. He'd been drinking. He drinks a lot, doesn't he? And he'd fallen and twisted his foot and couldn't get up. I must have told you about it at the time. I stopped and spoke to him, although I didn't want to—but he was groaning. I asked him if he thought I could help him, or should I try to get somebody else. And just then somebody came along—a man—who said he would look after him. I didn't notice the man who came up—I was flustered, I guess, and it was very dark, anyway—but to-night I recognized his voice. It was this man I have seen quite often—who turned out to be the—the Mr. Tavistock you spoke about."

She paused, a little breathlessly, and shifted herself sideways the better to see her father. "What is it about him?" she asked doubtfully. "You said the other night there was something about him that affected you. And that's why I have noticed him so much, I suppose. He's unusual—isn't he? I mean you can see it in his face before you speak to him. And then his voice. Didn't you think his voice sounded—it's not only English—there's something strange. . . ."

The Canon smiled at her rounded eyes. "I found out just to-day," he said, "that he's been an actor."

"Perhaps that's it," Laura admitted slowly. "Yes, you feel as though you're listening—I don't know—it is something like a play—a tragedy."

She seemed disappointed at having found this easy explanation of it. The Canon could see that she wasn't satisfied. "It isn't only that," he said, more seriously.

"No. Because what he says is strange, too."

"What did he say?"

Laura sat still, stroking her lip. "Well," she said, finally, "he didn't say very much. He's obviously English, so I asked him how long he had been out and whether he liked it here. It was just for something to say. But he answered as though it didn't matter where he was. It was like talking to a lost soul."

"Or a *found* one," the Canon murmured thoughtfully. "There isn't much difference, apparently. He claims to have found his, at any rate."

"What do you mean?"

The impatience he had felt before at the remoteness of Tavistock's ideas clouded the Canon's face as he twisted in the chair toward her. "He says that the soul exists in a state above good and evil. It isn't touched by good or evil. He says, in fact, that there are no *souls*—no plural at all—there is only one soul."

"He means God, doesn't he?"

The Canon shrugged his shoulders. "I can't make him out. His ideas sound twisted. In a sense he doesn't seem to believe in God."

Laura looked at him penetratingly. "I've heard you say that *that* isn't possible. It isn't, is it?"

Looking at her—half-comically, half-ruefully, he patted her hand and said: "A man must believe in something. That's a sure thing. And *he* does! He believes in the Comforter at any rate."

"The Comforter?" exclaimed Laura, as though she had never heard the word.

The Canon got up, locked his hands behind him, and twisted one leg around the other. "It's too deep for an orthodox old parson like me, my dear. I've been thinking that Sturge Bundy might understand him. I'd like to see them together."

"Uncle Sturge's ideas don't sound like that," said Laura, her finger at her lip again.

"No, Sturge is more human," the Canon said positively.

"Do you think so?" she almost gasped.

"Don't *you*?"

Laura shook her head and the puzzlement left her eyes. "Oh no. Uncle Sturge is scientific—colder. This man—it's hard to explain it—he is somehow—"

"Remote," the Canon said.

"Yes, remote; but the opposite of cold. I should say he was intensely sympathetic—with everyone—with everything. His sadness—"

The Canon nodded. "Yes," he said, "he's very sad. That's a sure thing."

"His sadness doesn't seem to be—for himself," said Laura musingly. "What could a man ever have done to look as he does? Or what could have happened to him? He looks as though he had the whole world on his shoulders."

3

The Canon looked at her sharply. She had removed the two blue hat-pins and was nursing the hat on her knee, the pins stuck in the band at the side. Her dark hair, falling now over her temples, narrowed her face, and he saw her—a woman in front of him—another woman in his house, but different from the others.

"Did he speak of that—of 'everybody's sorrows'?" the Canon asked, his curiosity returning.

She shook her head. "No," she said, quietly. "It was in his face."

"He didn't quote Keats at you?"

"Keats?" Her eyes puzzled over it. "I don't know."

"He didn't speak of 'those to whom the miseries of the world are misery, and will not let them rest'?"

"Did he to you?" she asked, her eyes widening eagerly.

"Yes."

She nodded. "Well, then," she said, tapping the top of the straw hat with a little thud, "that proves it. That's just how he looked to me."

The Canon touched her hair lightly with three fingers. "Yes, it proves that you're a thought-reader."

"Or," she said, smiling at him through half-closed lids, "that he is very transparent."

"Yes, he is. I think he is."

She got up and stood stroking her cheek with the cool heads of the hat-pins.

"I feel as though I have known him a long time," she said. "I think we both did. You know how you do—with some people."

She faced her father softly, her eyes half veiled, her bosom rising and falling gently in a new and slower rhythm that was strange to her and occupied her thoughts.

The Canon slanted his head at her. "And yet I thought you said he was unusual."

"Yes," she said, moving with smooth step toward the door. "Very. But—it was what I expected—somehow. I feel as though I have known somebody like him before. But I know I haven't. So it must be—I must have expected it—or made it up."

"Are you going to bed?" the Canon asked, for she had reached the door and was standing there.

"I think so. Is mother upstairs?"

He nodded. "Tell her I'm going to work for a while."

"Will you be late?"

"Probably. I haven't been getting on at all."

She smiled sympathetically with a tiny pout. "Poor dad. Good night, then."

"Good night, dear," he said, watching the curtains fall behind her and listening to her last audible step on the stairs.

4

Later, when he found it impossible to go on with the sermon, he began rummaging through his bookcases, looking for a volume of Keats. The phrase about "the miseries of the world" still revolved in his mind. Perhaps if he found the passage and read it in its context he might be able to dismiss it.

After a while he sank into his deep chair with the book, turning the leaves slowly and coming at last to the place in "Hyperion," where he knew it must be.

"High Prophetess," said I, "purge off,
Benign, if so it please thee, my mind's film."

"None can usurp this height," returned that shade,
"But those to whom the miseries of the world
Are misery, and will not let them rest."

The Canon paused, his finger-tip marking the lines, but his eyes were lured farther down the page.

"Are there not thousands in the world," said I,
Encouraged by the smooth voice of the shade,
"Who love their fellows even to the death,
Who feel the giant agony of the world,
And more, like slaves to poor humanity,
Labour for mortal good? I sure should see
Other men here, but I am here alone."

"Those whom thou spakest of are no visionaries,"
Rejoin'd that voice; "they are no dreamers weak;
They seek no wonder but the human face,
No music but a happy-noted voice:
They come not here, they have no thought to come;
And thou art here, for thou art less than they.
What benefit canst thou do, or all thy tribe,
To the great world? Thou art a dreaming thing,
A fever of thyself: think of the earth;
What bliss, even in hope, is there for thee?

What haven? Every creature hath its home,
Every sole man hath days of joy and pain,
Whether his labours be sublime or low—
The pain alone, the joy alone, distinct:
Only the dreamer venoms all his days,
Bearing more woe than all his sins deserve."

The Canon closed the book on his thumb, and sat with it in his hands, tilted forward, his black eyes staring.

"Only the dreamer venoms all his days!"

How it fitted him! And yet in Tavistock he had felt something surer than dreams—some ecstasy that transfigured misery—some *height* that he himself had never experienced.

He sat and pondered it, nursing the book tightly, knowing that his time for dreaming was past. In his own way he had felt the miseries of the world—hardships all around him—poverty—the bite of winter.

"The misery that will not let them rest!"

His thoughts went inward. "Have *I* rested?" he complained to the hidden deity lurking somewhere in his mind. "I haven't dreamed. There's been no time to dream. I've had to *do* things—I've *done* things. Thou, God, seest me!"

But suddenly he realized what he was doing—comparing himself—justifying himself—by judging others. He had fallen into the trap of judgment, which Tavistock had said must be "reproved."

Rising wearily, he went to the door, switched out the light over his desk, and slowly mounted the stairs. Under his breath he was praying: "Keep back Thy servant from presumptuous sins; let them not have dominion over me: then shall I be upright, and innocent from the great transgression. Let the words of my mouth, and the meditation of my heart, be acceptable in thy sight, O Lord, my strength and my redeemer."

TEN

The Secret

I

PITTS WENT stumbling along behind Tavistock, who was almost lost in the blackness a few paces ahead. Their legs swished through a tangle of weeds in the shadowy garden. A heavy dew, dripping from trampled stalks, sent a rank, moist smell into the air all the way out to the road.

Tavistock paused at the broken gate and threw back his head to gaze at the sky. The stars were like pinpricks through a canopy of velvet stretched between them and a domain of light.

Pitts glanced up, too, but his tongue licked eagerly against his teeth, impatient for speech.

"I didn't say anything in there," he exclaimed, stepping up on the sidewalk and cocking his head on one side under Tavistock's lifted chin, "but Canon Macaulay was in the shop to-day. They're talking of putting the old boy in the Home."

Tavistock brought his head down slowly. "Yes," he said. "He was here, too, a little while ago, with a chap named Philp, from the town hall."

"Good!" Pitts jerked out, waving his hands in the air at the humming mosquitoes. "They mean business, then."

Through the blackness of McCully's bush, across the road, a light could be seen in the back rooms of the magistrate's house. Farther along, at the bend in the road, there was a light in the window of Julie Robillard's shack. Otherwise there were no signs of the town, nor any noises, except the sustained trilling of the frogs along the marshy lake-shore. The two men, standing close together under the willows which overhung the sidewalk, could scarcely see each other. The mosquitoes were bad. Pitts slapped at his neck and finally broke into Tavistock's reverie.

"Come on in for a minute," he said, "if you've nothing better to do. You haven't been over for God knows how long. Julie was saying to me only last night: 'He never drops in, now. He's always out in that everlasting boat.' You're alone too much, don't you think you are? It isn't good for *anybody*. Don't you feel . . . ?"

"That reminds me," said Tavistock. "I've left the boat there, at the back."

"You can take it back after," Pitts said coaxingly. "Old Dan's always open to all hours. What's this I hear about you leaving the railroad?"

Tavistock suddenly started off with long strides, his heels striking a sharp, hollow sound from the loose planks in the sidewalk. Pitts, who scarcely came up to his shoulders, blundered along beside him in the dark, watching anxiously ahead for a missing plank which might trip them both.

Since he had known Tavistock it had always been like this. The younger man had always been half-oblivious of Pitts' existence, while Pitts, obsequious one minute and chiding like an old nurse the next, had taken care that his path should be smooth—getting rid of people who bothered him, explaining his foibles to those who misunderstood him, and anticipating the few wants which Tavistock, during long periods of absent-minded reverie, would completely overlook.

In Africa, as Pitts had truthfully told the Canon, they had

been boarders in the same house for a long time, and of all Tavistock's associates at the theatre, Pitts was the only one who had ever entered his room. He would trot upstairs two or three times a day, to remind him of rehearsals, to drag him out to meals, or sometimes to sit with him, a patient listener, who could respect a moody silence that was often unbroken for an hour.

In those days, although already over-fond of liquor, Pitts retained some shreds of self-respect. His mother had been a connection of the Coleridge family and had named him Samuel Taylor after his great-uncle. He had always made much of the distinction. "I've been told I resemble the poet," he would say, raising his brows and inflecting his head in a ludicrous gesture of modesty, and sometimes adding: "They say I look like him—especially about the eyes." And he would roll his eyes upward, staring off sideways into vacancy in imitation of a frenzy of inspiration.

He had always been a little absurd, even as a youth in the printshop in Clapham, where he had served his apprenticeship. But he had possessed enough ambition to practise diligently at the violin until he could qualify for a job in an orchestra. For a few years, as a musician, he had acquired a little dignity, but misfortune and bitter disappointments, and the habit of drinking to drown their effects, had caused him to drift lower and lower until now he found himself in a still stranger country, lonelier, and with little to hope for. He was almost a butt in the town, for he was often hopelessly drunk and would stand for hours with his foot on the shiny brass rail of the Bellevue bar, talking tipsily to all and sundry; or, if left alone, looking dismally at his own reflection between the necks of bottles in the mirrors that reached to the ceiling, frowning at himself or blinking his eyes in a meaningless preoccupation with the play of expression over his features.

Today was Friday—publication day at the *Monitor*—and he was sober. The talk that morning with the Canon had brought vividly to mind his former companionship with Tavistock. Since their first encounter in Poplar Plains they had seen each other rarely. Tavistock had always seemed loath to call up memories of Africa, but to-night Pitts hoped to satisfy his hunger for reminiscence.

"We haven't gassed about old times for ages," he blurted out, breaking the silence between them. "And if you're going away—"

He felt Tavistock's arm lightly dropped on his shoulder, and saw a long, earnest face turned toward him in the dark.

"You live a lot in the past, Pitts—eh?—don't you?"

"What else? What can you do in a God-forsaken hole like this?"

Tavistock drew a deep, audible breath, and asked: "How old are you now?"

"I must be fifty-two. Eighteen fifty-five—nineteen seven. Yes. And I look sixty."

Tavistock made no comment. He strode on silently.

"You must be over thirty," said Pitts in a half-enquiring tone.

"Yes. I'll be thirty-three—" A tightness in his throat seemed to stop Tavistock's utterance. "I'll be thirty-three in a few days."

"What do you talk like that for?" Pitts grunted. "Thirty-three isn't ninety."

Tavistock turned his head up to the stars.

They reached Julie's place and came to a stop. Tavistock's glance was turned aside at the lighted window in the front of the house, shaded by a tattered green blind that flapped every now and then with a slight twang against the netting of the screen. Pitts was shifting about, wondering how best he could entice him in, when suddenly, bobbing his head down to glance under the branches of the choke-cherry trees, he cried out: "Is that a fire down there?"

"No," said Tavistock. "It's the harvest moon. I saw it rise last night."

Pitts straightened himself, breathing easier. "God Almighty! It's as red as blood! Makes you think of the plagues of Egypt."

Through the foliage of McCully's bush the great egg-shaped moon, just above the horizon, glowed like a distant fire.

"Never see a moon like that at home," said Pitts, bending down to look through at it again.

Tavistock glanced instead at the stars, thickening over the treetops.

"Let's go in," Pitts said, swinging round and brushing the mosquitoes from his neck.

2

Julie peered at them from behind the lamp as the door opened. She was wearing steel-rimmed glasses that were useful only for sewing, and promptly took them off. Her dim eyes focused with difficulty across the table.

"La, eet ees you!" she exclaimed, her upheld needle glinting in the lamplight.

Pitts hung up his hat under the stairs and glanced at himself in a broken oval mirror that was nailed to a scantling near the door. Tavistock grasped the back of a high cane rocking-chair and stood awkwardly silent.

Julie was enormously fat, her chin effaced completely by bulging folds of flesh that culminated under a gaudy print dress in a mountainous bosom. Her little eyes, like the heads of hat-pins, were deeply set under brows still black, which went oddly with the untidy grey hair, almost white, bundled in a loose knot on the top of her head and skewered there with a red Spanish comb.

"Ow ees old Dave?" she asked, screwing up her eyes at Pitts until they became no more than dots in the fleshy expanse of her face.

Pitts wetted the tips of his fingers and dabbed at the mosquito bites on his neck. "You're right. He's worse, Julie," he growlingly admitted. Squatting quickly on a box by the sink, he began scratching his ankles.

"Sit down, m'sieu," said Julie to Tavistock, poking her needle-point in the direction of an old upholstered chair under the window.

"And Elsie?" she asked of Pitts again. "Ow ees her cough like now?"

"Miss Macaulay was over there with some medicine," he answered gruffly.

"Good job someone should get wise," said Julie, putting her glasses on again. "In 'ome ees place for old Dave—long time."

Tavistock, who had seated himself with his back to the window, said quietly: "He's harmless enough, surely, and he hasn't long to live."

Julie suddenly snapped her glance across the room at Pitts, who was now filling his pipe.

"What come of Jukes? He bother old man?"

"I don't know—I wasn't talking to him," muttered Pitts, wishing she would go to bed so that he could talk with Tavistock.

"He seemed quiet enough when I came in," Tavistock said. "There was a man named Philp there—"

"Freddie Philp," Julie nodded, glancing over her glasses at him with a sneer twisting her thick mouth.

"From the town hall."

"*Oui*—I know," said Julie, "fastening off" with a few jabs of the needle, and snapping the thread with a jerk.

She held the little dress she was making for Rosie at arm's length to survey the results of her evening's work.

"This Indian—Jukes—who is he?" Tavistock asked.

Julie folded up the dress and smacked it down on the table. Rocking mountainously backward and forward in the squeaking chair, she told Tavistock the story of the partnership, and how

Jukes suspected that Linklater was holding out on him and Anderson. She was in a loquacious mood, common enough with her, and much to Pitts' disgust launched into a queer, grudging eulogy of Jukes.

"He's a breed," she declared, getting up finally to put her sewing away. "White blood no good for Indians—everybody say —but Jukes, he ees very good fellow."

She peered short-sightedly across the room at Tavistock, who was sitting there listening, with narrowed eyes, nursing his knee in locked fingers.

Pitts grunted and scraped his day's growth of beard noisily across his wrist when she embarked on a long account of Juke's exploits as a guide, years ago, before the days of the railroad. He had heard the story many times before.

"He was one good guide 'round here long time—dat Jack. Marcel—my 'usband—he was one good guide also—he speak ze English very good, my 'usband," she ended, with a twisted, half-pathetic smile.

3

Behind the flimsy partition that separated the bedrooms from the rest of the shack, Julie was moving heavily about, preparing for bed, her shadow thrown hugely upward across the rafters over the heads of the two men, sitting closer now at the table, conversing in low tones.

"I've intended asking you about Clara," Tavistock said, after some talk of Africa had passed between them. "We spoke of her weeks ago, but—"

"You changed the subject," Pitts complained with a frown.

"Did I?" said Tavistock.

The protuberant eyes opposite him enlarged suddenly, popping at him in amazement. "You mean to say you don't *know?*" Pitts cried.

"I haven't heard a word since I left Johannesburg."

"What?" Pitts exploded loudly. "You've never heard of Rosa Lynd?"

"Of course I have, but what—?"

"Of course you have! Even these damned Canadians have heard of Rosa Lynd. Well, *that's* our Clara! Don't you ever look at the papers? Rosa Lynd at Windsor Castle! Rosa Lynd wedded to the Vicomte Somebody-or-other!"

"Married?"

"Yes. And to a bloody vicomte, too, if you please."

Pitts snorted and flung his hands out in a gesture of helplessness. "You see. She's not even afraid of me. She knows I haven't the guts to turn up and charge her with bigamy. I gave up writing long ago. She would never answer. She won't see me. Had me thrown out of a stage-door in London once. It's no use. She never belonged to me, anyway. I knew that all the time. You *didn't*, perhaps. You didn't know, I suppose, that the baby—you remember—?"

"Yes, it died."

"Yes. It wasn't mine. I married her that way—and not just to get her out of a scrape—although I knew it. She didn't lie to me. She told me, all right. But, do you think I cared? God Almighty! A woman like that!" Moisture trembled on his lashes, and his lips drooped like a child's in misery.

"She left you," Tavistock said, leaning across the table and speaking in a compassionate tone.

"Yes. Soon after you left Jo'burg they 'discovered' her. A great star! Another Terry! Well, that's all. I didn't count. She told me she'd send me money. She'd write. Perhaps, later, I might come to London. She sent me a little money—once!—and she wrote for less than a year. But after that—not a sound—not a word!"

"And that man—what was his name?"

"The man she said was possessed of a devil?"

Pitts' chin buckled undershooting lips in a horrible grimace. "He was the chap—the father—"

Tavistock nodded silently and drew his arm back off the table, turning sideways to glance gloomily at the floor.

"She was always talking about killing him," he said, stroking back his hair with a slow hand, as though lost in memory.

Pitts clasped his fingers in an ecstasy of recollection. "Ah, you remember that—those talks about murder—talking about killing him with her bare hands. Acting—nothing but bloody acting, of course, but—"

"No," said Tavistock, with cold certainty, "that wasn't acting."

"Well, you should know. You hated her, didn't you, eh?"

"Yes—I suppose so; but she fascinated me, too—in a way—in a curious way. The kind of mind that can kill—deliberately—has always fascinated me." He turned on Pitts a sudden, searching look.

"But she didn't kill him," said Pitts, almost frightened by the other's glance and failing utterly to understand it.

"No, but she *could* have killed him. I remember one thing she said, particularly. I remember she was lying on the couch—pale as a ghost—with her hair down. We'd been talking a long time—about murder, as usual. It was an obsession with her then. She was studying *Macbeth*, for one thing. And all of a sudden she whispered across that room of yours—you remember her whisper?—it's probably famous now. All of a sudden she whispered at me: 'Hamlet is only half a man. That's why people flock to see him. He's an abortion. *A man who can't kill is only half a man!*'"

4

Pitts didn't remember it, but it sounded like her—like those things she would come out with at times, bitter, cynical, almost diabolical, that made his blood run cold.

In Tavistock's usually gentle face the deep melancholy had given place to a reflection of that bitterness, and Pitts remembered that in those days, after performances, when they had trudged home through the bare, dusty streets—the sky around them walled in by huge mine-dumps, standing like mountains at the edges of the stark, angular town—Clara and Tavistock would fling themselves down, gulping the coffee he hurriedly made for them, and almost biting at each other across the room; while he, years older than either, did his best to humour them. They were both intense, nervous, temperamental—like flames that soar or gutter out according to the winds that blow on them. True stage people!

Pitts fell into a reverie, thinking of how at times he would pick up his fiddle and play to them, hoping to quiet them and bring them down to earth.

There was a long silence. The two men sat near one another, breathing and thinking. They were not conscious of the moths swinging in fluttering circles around the light, or that Julie's lamp had long been put out; her moving shadow gone from the rafters.

"The stage," murmured Tavistock, raising his slender head, the straight brows borne down over his eyes as by a weight of suffering. "God! how I loathed the stage!"

Pitts came out of his reverie and looked suddenly into the bowl of his pipe, at the dead ashes, and reached for a match.

"You don't know me, Pitts," said Tavistock, with an abrupt change of tone. "Do you know why I left the stage?"

Pitts let the smoke wreathe lazily from his slack, half-opened mouth. "You told me some story when you left Jo'burg," he muttered thickly. "I remember I didn't believe it."

"No." Tavistock's head went down again, cupped in his two hands. "I've forgotten myself what I said, but the truth was—I wanted to be alone. I wanted to root out of myself every last vestige of desire that a man can have. I was bound I wouldn't *will* anything. I would only wait—for—but it's no use—I can't tell you what it is. I wouldn't tell you this, but it's very close now. Perhaps I shan't see you again. I wonder, Pitts—you're the only one who knows me here—I wonder if you—no!—you'll think I'm mad, too—like all the rest."

He flung up his head and shot a glance at Pitts from the anguished depths of his eyes.

"But I'm *bound* to do it!" he cried in a loud whisper, jumping up and standing solidly before the terrified old man in the chair, as though facing a human being for the first time in the role he was determined to play.

"What's got into you?" gulped Pitts, raising himself in front of Tavistock and tightly grasping his arm. "If it's religious, as you call it—why do you look like this? And why *shouldn't* I understand it?"

Tavistock seemed unable to speak. His eyes were fixed in a stare turned inward upon a purpose so exalted as to fill him with terror.

Pitts began suddenly to tremble and to beat at Tavistock's shoulder in a frenzy, trying to recall the younger man to earth—to sanity. But slowly his fingers were stilled. His mind as though borne upward by Tavistock's ecstasy, carried him into an experience beyond anything he had ever known.

As he rose, timidly, into what seemed like a new kind of existence, he began to understand and share the terror of this man on whose strength he was borne up. The effort to cling, even for a moment, to Tavistock's shoulder, at that frightening height, unnerved him utterly. He felt his heart sink like a plummet into his breast, heaving already with quick breaths that were almost sobs. He crooked his arm over his eyes and cowered into a chair.

"Pitts, Pitts!" he heard a strange voice calling, but looking up he found it was Tavistock standing with transfigured face and speaking in a tone which was different enough to sound like another person. "For a moment," he was saying, "I thought that —you—it might be *you!*" He bent over, and with a less exalted look searched the old man's face. "Did you feel as though you were dying?"

"No," breathed Pitts, his face aghast and trembling. "I felt as though I *had* died. It was like—like the resurrection."

A triumphant smile lifted Tavistock's hair. "Yes!" he cried, in the same strange voice, "yes, 'dying into life'—it will be like that." And then, to himself, the smile fading and his own voice returning: "Yes, it's nearer—it's coming!"

5

They were outside in a night now blue around them. The moon was far up in the sky. Through the willows, as they looked toward the lake, its reflection in the water made a bright path toward them.

They had not spoken again, but now Tavistock said: "I'm leaving down there—at the pits—to-morrow. I may not see you again. Perhaps, when you hear what happens, you will understand a little—after to-night."

Pitts besought him with his eyes, staring in rounded wonder under the moon. "Tell me what it is," he pleaded. "What is it?"

Tavistock gently shook his head.

Pitts came nearer and gasped out a final question in a hoarse voice: "Is it something to do with death?"

"Death!" exclaimed Tavistock. "Why are you people always talking of death? There *is* no death!" He held out his hand, which Pitts took in his own and shook. They said goodbye—Pitts reeling back into the house, like a man in a stupor, while Tavistock went down to where his boat was beached and thrust it out into the shining path that lay across the gently swaying water.

2

Saturday

ONE

The Bunk Car

I

TAVISTOCK WOKE UP and looked across at Roff lying with his head on his arm in the opposite bunk. He was still asleep.

The sun was shining outside and a fresh breeze floated through the car. A little way off there was a rattle of pans in the cook-car where the Chinamen were preparing breakfast. The sounds came clearly through the morning stillness. Cocks were crowing in a farmyard half a mile away. There was the rumble of a train in the distance. Down in the pit there was an occasional hiss of steam. The firemen were already up and busy at the shovels.

Tavistock lay there, half dozing, enjoying the serenity which flooded his mind. The intermittent song of a meadowlark seemed to be connected with the fragments of a dream still floating hazily through his waking thoughts. He looked up through the little square window over his bunk and saw the bird perched on a telegraph pole only a few feet away. Every now and then it would lift its head and twitter a lilting, liquid call.

He closed his eyes, and Laura's face, in the lamplight, hung as freshly in his memory as though he had left her only a moment or two before. He knew her name now. He knew who she was. It was strange that he hadn't guessed.

Even though he had listened to her playing in the little house next the church it hadn't occurred to him that she was the Canon's daughter. The Canon was so squat, awkward, almost unkempt, and she was slender, graceful, eager—with a perfect head—a perfect oval—the white brow curving alluringly under her hair.

He recalled her vividly. He recalled, too, a sense of a shared eternity—a new sort of eternity—which had come to him while he stood beside her. The eternity he had talked about—this "huge moment"—was simply a philosophical idea—an abstraction. His mind had dwelt on it for years, but he had never experienced the sense of *nowness* he had spoken of so glibly, so confidently.

"I am simply a talker," he told himself. "Another Coleridge. I'm not even that. I've been simply a 'snapper up' of other people's ideas—a stewing-pot for fag-ends of philosophy that other people have discarded."

These accusations passed lightly through his mind. He felt too happy to take them seriously. He was nearer laughing at himself than he had ever been in his life. In this new mood of serenity he could see his past—even the immediate past—as a sort of nightmare. He had concocted a conception of a man who now appeared to him like a scarecrow. He had been frightening himself. But Laura had driven the scarecrow out of him. Last night he had heard his own voice asserting itself over a clamour of shadowy whispers—he had felt his blood throbbing again in unison with the pulse of a woman he could easily love. He had wanted to talk to her—endlessly.

It was no new thing for him to feel that a lifetime was far too short for all he wanted to achieve. But his belief that death must be only a passage into a larger life had been heightened while he stood there with her. He had felt a *real* eternity encompassing them—holding them together—an eternity they could share—

an eternity that would be necessary for the enduring of their love.

These thoughts poured a new meaning into a phrase of Whitman's that had long been treasured in his mind—"There is an eternity in men and women: men and women are not dreams or dots."

He had known it all along. He had felt it instinctively. Whitman had only confirmed it. And Blake, too. Both had written something—almost identical—about the body being not less than the soul. And wasn't there a passage in Goethe . . . ?

His mind and his memory were leading him off again, as usual, into literature and metaphysics—whereas his real concern was with life—the lives people actually live in flesh and blood—the sufferings they endure *here!*

"I am a breathing man again," he told himself. "She must have been sent, last night, to make me conscious of my blood, so that I feel myself again a brother of all men. I have looked inward so long, waiting for the miracle, that I've forgotten what a man is like. And yet it was because I knew so well what a man is like—because I knew the sufferings, the miseries, the curse of guilt men bear—it was because I *was* a man that I rebelled against a God who could make humanity suffer. But these voices—this damned memory of mine—these tags of poetry and God knows what—filling my mind all the time—blowing me up with bombast. . . ."

He looked across at Roff again, remembering how the Russian had sometimes stared at him, during their talks—his weak eye twitching nervously—staring at him sometimes as though he were afraid to be left alone there in the car with him.

He realized how close he had come to madness. It was all this brooding. His rebellion—his grief—had become twisted, distorted, shadowy. Last night a fresh shadow had been cast over his mind. "If I go on with this," he had warned himself, "I shall never see her again."

That alone showed how he had sunk into the little separated self which he had always denied. He had slipped back into the error of regarding himself as an individual man—a fragment *broken off* from eternity—a little piece of eternity that was worth only seventy years—and would die!

But he *knew* better than that. He *knew* there was no death. "I mustn't let myself think in terms of time," he told himself. "It's no use thinking of what may happen *after.* There is no afterness: There is only the continuing!"

It was a mystery. He could *feel* it. But he couldn't understand it with his mind. He should never have tried to. It was thinking that had delayed his act so long. And thoughts of Laura shouldn't disturb him now. He had rooted out of himself the ache for possession—long ago. It didn't matter if he never *saw* her again. What is *seeing* but the dimmest flicker of eternity? She was living—and he was living—in an eternity! They would always live! And in eternity—in unity—there can be no separateness.

2

Roff opened his eyes. He looked sleepily across at Tavistock and waved his hand stiffly as he stretched himself.

He was dark-skinned and slightly pock-marked. His high forehead and curved nose marked him immediately as belonging to the old Russian nobility. Yet he had been a revolutionist since he was old enough to think. A rifle, discharged within a few inches of his face during the attempted revolution of 1905, had caused a permanent injury to his left eye. The lid drooped almost half-way over the pupil, and trembled continually.

Roff was not his real name, but a contraction of one of those unpronounceable Russian names of four or five syllables. He had been connected with the famous "September" riots only as a publicist, but had been forced to escape from Russia after the murder of the Grand Duke Sergius. He had lived for a time in Munich with a group of exiled countrymen, but the failure of the first Douma disillusioned him. He had given up Europe as a bad job. Like thousands of others he had come to America—seeking a new start—a new life.

He and Tavistock were equally out-of-place in the camp, and almost at sight had been drawn together. At first the Russian did most of the talking, but the other's attitude, expressed more by the gentleness of his smile than by anything he said, soon softened the scornfulness of Roff's invective.

Although the older of the two, Roff became the enquirer. Under the calm of the other he felt an intuitional certainty concerning things which he himself could not accept. It was difficult, especially with his limited English, to discover just what Tavistock believed. When he pressed deeply he was struck by the apparent paradox of the other's nature—a curious reconciliation of opposites. Although feeling the deepest sympathy for suffering—one of the most frequent subjects of conversation between them—Tavistock nevertheless maintained that whatever existed was intended to be. He would declare that there was no such thing as evil, although he seemed obsessed with the idea of sin and the sense of guilt, and was always discussing criminal motives and behaviour.

As they grew more intimate the Englishman had gradually revealed an obsession which baffled Roff. The words "sin" and "evil" constantly recurred in his talk. In the last few days, particularly, he had shown signs of intense inner excitement, and his tone had gradually grown ominous. He began to talk as though some terrible event, which caused him to shudder when he allowed his mind to dwell on it, would somehow—and very soon—end his life.

3

Roff sank back on his pillow of gunny-sacking and half closed his eyes. He was trying to find words and presently spoke with a strong foreign accent. While Tavistock dressed, the two men carried on their talk from the previous evening as though it had been interrupted by only a few minutes.

Roff knew that this was Tavistock's last day in the camp, but the Englishman had not made it clear where he was going or what he intended to do. His own mind was not made up about it.

They talked of his departure, and Roff made a final attempt to discover what it was that Tavistock feared in the future.

"It happen soon—this—what you say to me?" he enquired, peering inquisitively into Tavistock's face. His injured eye, working spasmodically, added to his look of eager excitement.

"Yes, I expect so," said Tavistock in a numbed tone. Talking with Roff destroyed the serenity he had felt on awaking. It recalled their discussions about suffering and guilt and evil.

"But you go—to-day. You escape this?" the Russian asked.

"No," said Tavistock. "Maybe—in a day or two—I shall move on. That's all. Maybe I'll hit for the mountains. I don't know. There's a matter that may keep me a day or two—I didn't tell you. I've come in for a bit of a legacy."

He bent over and began lacing up his high boots.

The Russian blinked. "What is that—you call 'legacy'?"

"Money."

"Ah, yes!" cried Roff. "Fortune! Somebody die and leave you this."

Tavistock managed a sort of smile. "My parents died when I was a youngster, but the thing's been in chancery—in the courts, you know. It's nothing. It isn't much."

"But you quit—because—"

"No."

Roff screwed up his face. "It's this—you say so much about—some evil business?"

Tavistock looked up at the Russian. "Yes," he said. "Only it isn't evil."

"You talk queer," said Roff almost irritably. "Nobody understand you."

"I don't want you to understand me," said Tavistock.

"Why you talk like that?" urged Roff in a friendlier tone.

"I've scarcely talked to anybody. I really haven't talked about it at all—until last night." Tavistock closed his eyes, and his chest rose in a long-drawn breath. "There's an old chap here—a musician I used to know in Africa. I got talking with him. You and he are the only people I really talk to here. I haven't seen him for weeks. But last night . . ." He stood up, locked his hands behind his head, and stared at the low ceiling a few inches above his raised face. "When I talk about it," he whispered, "it sounds—it sounds mad—fantastic—like an old myth."

4

The muscles of Roff's face were tautly drawn as he concentrated on Tavistock's words and tried to make them mean something in his mind, a mind in which English was extricated as thought only after it had been separated from a succession of unfamiliar sounds.

When Tavistock ceased speaking Roff lifted his hands in a helpless gesture and said, as though speaking to a man from another planet: "You die?—some way—strange? Is that it?"

"Yes," said Tavistock wearily. "That's what everybody will say—death! Always death!"

Roff dragged his legs slowly out of the bunk and sat up, his injured eye blinking. "You—you kill yourself?" he asked steadily, in a harsh voice.

Tavistock swung his eyes round at him as though this were something he hadn't thought of. He shook his head. A second later, with the definiteness of a man who wishes not to be misunderstood, he added: "No."

Roff looked hard at the watch-chain dangling from the pocket of Tavistock's khaki shirt.

"When this happens—people say—a crime—this. Eh?"

Tavistock looked quickly at him, his eyes enlarging. "What makes you think it will be a crime?"

"That is all you talk—long time now—crime, always."

"I've told you I don't believe in crime. No matter what a man does—but we've talked of all that, Louis."

He suddenly sat down and dragged the valise from under his bunk, turning it sideways and pulling it out between his heels.

"Yes, but you talk always crime."

"No, I've just been trying to find out how you feel about things—how you regard murder, for instance. It seems to me the whole world is wrong about what it calls evil. That's what I would like to change, Louis. Change *that* and it would be a different place—a different life."

"This is not crime—this what happens? Eh?" Roff demanded impatiently. "Not like all this you talk—not the same?"

"It's connected—yes," said Tavistock, throwing open the lid of the valise and eyeing his few belongings indifferently. He pulled out a tie, and when he had buttoned his shirt collar, knotted it about his neck. While his fingers continued to shape the knot, he said: "People will call it a crime, I suppose."

He looked at Roff almost defiantly. "You'll wonder what sort of man you've been living with. If I could tell you—but there's the rub—if it could be told—if people would understand without—

without the act—then I shouldn't have to—I shouldn't be . . ."

He began absent-mindedly to look about for whatever he had to pack.

5

After the midday meal they came back to the car together. Tavistock had spent the morning in the pits with the new timekeeper, who had arrived from Winnipeg the night before. He had turned over to him his books and records. He was free. He was ready to go.

Roff had come back to the car to say good-bye—away from the gang. They walked along the tracks and climbed the ladder without speaking. Tavistock made a pretence of looking for odds and ends that he might have forgotten to pack. He stood between the two bunks, looking around out of the corners of his eyes.

Across the prairie, like a hoarse bird cawing, the long hoot of a freight train sounded. Roff, standing in the doorway, leaning against the stove, watched the train swing into sight around a bluff of poplars.

When he looked back Tavistock was tightening the straps of his valise.

"Where you go now?" Roff asked. "Where you stay?"

"At the Manitoba, I think."

"How long you stay there?"

"Just overnight, perhaps. A day or two at the most."

Roff puzzled a moment, his weak eye straining to maintain a steady, penetrating glance. "That is all you tell me."

Tavistock seemed not to hear him. He was looking about the car for the last time, his eyes strangely hard. Lifting the grip quickly he took three strides and thrust out his hand and said, in an even voice: "This is *adieu*, Louis."

"No, Tavistock," said Roff, his hand feeling cold in the other's grasp. "*Au revoir!*"

In a moment he was looking down at the head of the only man he had talked to in that place—the bare head dropping out of sight as Tavistock descended the ladder.

Roff moved forward, on to the iron sill of the car door, and watched him step from the last rung on to the cinders—expecting an upward look, a raised hand. But with a sudden squaring of his shoulders Tavistock strode off between the tracks toward the town.

Roff stood watching him until he went out of sight behind the water-tank, thinking of the months together there in the car, lying across from each other, a foot apart, arguing in the dark.

Leaning in the doorway his gaze wandered across the rusted rails—over the long, waiting lines of box-cars and the tar-paper roof of the oil-house—straying into the distances of the vast sky, in which thousands of flat white clouds receded with the orderliness of a marching army to the clear blue at the horizon. The normal mirage of a sunny prairie day lifted bluffs and farmhouses as though above a flood . . . the seeming water shining. . . .

TWO

Gawthorp

I

TAVISTOCK WENT into the Manitoba Hotel and walked directly up to the desk. He had stayed there on his arrival in the town a few months before, and knew the ins and outs of the place. Behind the desk, which served also as cigar-counter, there was a tiny alcove, known as "the office." In this few feet of space two men were sitting, their heads close together, and a third—the day clerk—was leaning over, discussing something with them in a low voice.

Out of the corner of his eye the clerk saw Tavistock reach the desk. With a capering step and brief slide he confronted him, twirling the register with one hand, whisking the pen out of its groove with the other, and sliding shut the back of the cigar-case with his foot. These agile motions were accompanied by a simultaneous nod, grin, and muttered, "How'r'ya!"

Tavistock remembered him at once, by his quick, juggler-like movements, his slick hair, and the massive horseshoe pin in his tie. He recognized one of the men behind the counter, too. One of them had his back turned, but the stout man facing him was Mark Ivey, the proprietor, a barrel of a man, with a face as ruddy as a tomato, and melting eyes, like an animal's. He was one of the best sources of news in the town for Gawthorp, who now sat opposite him, his big broad head thrust forward and his ear cocked in a listening attitude.

"Isn't that him, right here—the guy you was talkin' about just now—from the railroad?" Ivey whispered behind his hand.

The editor had to twist himself in his chair to see who had come in. "That's the fellow—the very man," he muttered in Mark Ivey's ear out of the corner of his mouth.

The day clerk swung the register around on its pivot with a flourish and spelled out the signature: "Tavistock. Oh, sure. You was here in the spring."

Gawthorp gave Ivey a meaning glance and got up. The clerk was discussing with Tavistock the kind of room he wanted, lounging forward over the open book, his elbows widely spread.

The editor of the *Monitor* limped forward and came out from behind the counter. "Good day," he said affably. "How're things at the pits?"

A trace of surprise disappeared quickly from Tavistock's face. "Oh yes, you're the editor, aren't you?" he said. "How are you these days?"

"Fine and dandy," Gawthorp said briskly. "It's funny I should run into you right now. I was just asking about you."

"Yes?"

"Yes. I heard yesterday you'd come in for some money."

Tavistock slowly shrugged his shoulders and looked at the editor without speaking.

Gawthorp dug his stick into a crack in the worn oilcloth, and wriggled his twisted foot into a more comfortable position. "Are you going to be busy for a minute or two? You're going to your room, I guess."

"If you're looking for something for your paper," said Tavistock, with a guarded smile, "I can tell you now I'd prefer you said nothing about it."

"That's all the more reason why I'd like to see you—if you really want it kept out," said Gawthorp significantly.

"Come up to the room, then," Tavistock said abruptly.

The clerk went ahead of them up the wide, old-fashioned staircase, carrying Tavistock's valise, to a room at the back of the first floor. Gawthorp awkwardly stumped along behind the Englishman, who marched ahead, preoccupied, without a word.

The clerk flung up the window, which overlooked the stables. In St. Stephen's churchyard, on the other side of the lane, trees were swishing against the high board fence as they nodded violently in the wind. Above their tossing foliage rose the squat spire of the church.

2

"The trouble is, Mr. Tavistock," Gawthorp said, as soon as the clerk was gone, and they had settled down in the room—Gawthorp alertly upright in the only chair, and Tavistock half reclining on the bed—"news gets about mighty quick in a town of this size. The Chief was enquiring around for you the other day. He's a bit of a mutt, the Chief. So there's rumours around town already. I ran into talk right downstairs there—'Who's this man Tavistock the Chief is looking for, and what's he done?' Do you see what I mean? Wouldn't it be wiser to say something—just something to stop that sort of gossip?"

Tavistock waved his hand as though gossip meant nothing to him. Instead of answering he went to the window and stood looking out.

Gawthorp felt at once that there was something queer about

him, after all. Out there at the pits, at the time the Irishman died, he had seemed just thoughtfully melancholy in the presence of death. But Gawthorp could see now that what he had mistaken for a temporary sadness was deeply ingrained. The man looked as though he had been through some sort of hell, and was marked by it—for life.

He began to wonder if the legacy meant that someone very near to him had died. His grief over such an event would account for his indifference to the money. But before he could pursue the thought Tavistock turned and dispelled it.

"It's funny," he said, with a half smile which failed to disperse the shadow hovering across his eyes; "it's funny how things turn out. I've been waiting for this money for years. And now it's come—I don't want it. I've a purpose in life that makes it—well, I don't need it—I don't want it. It's a nuisance. It—"

He stopped and looked at Gawthorp with an air of gentle curiosity. "I wonder what you'd do," he said, smiling still more, as though to conceal an earnestness which might spoil the editor's response to his question. "If you were left some money—well, put it this way. If you had a purpose—a determined purpose—and this money tempted you to discard it—would you give the money away? How would you get rid of it?"

Gawthorp screwed his heavy head on one side in a sort of shrug. "It would depend, quite a bit, wouldn't it, on what the purpose was?" he said soberly.

A quick flash of exultation appeared in Tavistock's eyes. "Suppose it was the highest possible purpose," he said bluntly, without any hint of concealing anything.

"Yes, but there you are again," Gawthorp said diffidently. "You see—your idea of 'highest' mightn't be the same as mine."

He paused, and then blurted out: "Why can't money be used for the highest purposes?"

"Ah!" exclaimed Tavistock. He slanted his head and looked at the editor with new interest. "What do you think is the highest aim in life?" he asked, half smiling again.

An echoing smile, drooping at the corners of Gawthorp's mouth, expressed his helplessness at facing such a thought.

"If you possessed unlimited power," Tavistock added quickly, "and you were able to *carry out* the highest purpose you could conceive—here, on this earth—what would it be?"

Gawthorp settled back a little more comfortably in his chair and laid his stick against his knees. "I used to be a great fellow to read, when I was younger," he said slowly, "but there's hardly a soul in this town to talk to. All we talk about here is crops and the weather." His broad, square forehead was deeply lined. "But I guess the grandest purpose I ever heard of is the notion of 'the greatest good of the greatest number.'"

Tavistock nodded slowly twice, as though he had expected just that answer. "What do you—?" he began, but checked himself. "I was going to ask you what you mean by 'good'—but I'll put it this way. How would you go about it?"

Gawthorp looked at him doubtfully. "You mean, as I am now, or if—if I had unlimited power?"

The direction of Tavistock's thought—reflected in his deep eyes—underwent a sombre change. "Suppose," he said, "that you had only two or three days—or let us say, twenty-four hours—to live. And suppose that instead of being ill, you had all your powers—and felt that during those twenty-four hours you ought to make a prodigious effort toward achieving this idea you speak of—the greatest good of the greatest number. What would you *do*?"

Gawthorp passed his hand tremblingly over the lower part of his face and ended by rubbing his chin. "I'm away out of my depth, I guess," he said, staring at the floor. "I haven't given any thought to these kind of things. You should talk to Canon Macaulay or Sturge Bundy. Doc Bundy is—"

Tavistock interrupted him by jumping up from the bed. Gawthorp watched his glance roam excitedly around the little room, from the jug on the washstand to the fluttering curtains at the window.

"It would never occur to you, I imagine," Tavistock said, ignoring the editor's suggestion that he should talk to these others, "that something usually called evil—a crime—a murder, let us say—could conceivably bring about the greatest happiness of the greatest number?"

Gawthorp met his eyes. "No," he said decidedly. "I can't figure how that could come about. Unless you're thinking of—" He stopped, and then added quickly: "Perhaps you're an anarchist?"

"No," said Tavistock, with a weary smile, "I'm not an anarchist." He sat down on the edge of the bed, balancing himself there temporarily and uncomfortably, and yet with the air of having given up his curious catechism.

3

Tavistock sat perfectly still, balanced, nursing his knee. The conversation appeared to be ended, but Gawthorp felt no impulse to get up and go. He was diffident about breaking the silence. Besides, there was something about Tavistock's attitude which held him there. There was a queer kind of magnetism about him, even in repose. His head was slanted away from the editor, leaning on one side, as though he were listening. Perhaps he was simply trying to remember something, but Gawthorp felt that he must sit quiet and listen, too. He sat there, gripping his stick to prevent himself from trembling. A vague excitement had taken possession of him. He couldn't account for it, but it was very strong and disturbing. It sent a curious tingling across the top of his head. He began to feel that they were both waiting for something—something supernatural. He had fooled with a ouija-board once, and had experienced a queer feeling of suspense—a sort of ominousness in the air—before the pencil began to write. This was the same sort of feeling—only stronger. He didn't like it. He couldn't stand it any longer. He purposely let his stick slip so that it clattered lightly against the thick sole of his boot.

"They might mourn the loss of one. . . ." Tavistock murmured in a half-whisper, as though coming out of a dream. Then he turned his head quickly and said aloud and abruptly: "Pascal—have you ever heard of the Frenchman—Pascal?"

The lines across Gawthorp's broad forehead deepened and drew together, but before he could even shake his head Tavistock swung himself around and spoke in a great hurry.

"Pascal was a doleful philosopher—but there's one thought of his—I was just recalling it—about the man who has lost an eye. There is something about man's present state, Pascal said, that makes us all miserable. We are always wishing for some happier condition. We long for an ideal state—a Utopia—a paradise. You've known plenty of people who feel that way, haven't you?"

Gawthorp nodded.

"Pascal," Tavistock went on, less hurriedly, "has an interesting explanation of it. At least, it has always seemed so to me. He says that we must once have known a happier state—and lost it—or we shouldn't long for it. A man who has two eyes, he says, doesn't long for a third. But a man who has possessed two, mourns the loss of one, if an accident happens to him. It sounds plausible, don't you think? It fits in, doesn't it, with the myth—or whatever you like to call it—of man's lost innocence?"

Gawthorp leaned forward and looked sideways at the floor. He felt that Tavistock did not expect him even to nod.

"Personally," said Tavistock, "I think it's much more than a myth. I think it's a symbol of something that has really happened to us. It's queer—but we've got it into our heads that Adam *gained* something by eating the forbidden fruit. Actually—I'm quite sure—he *lost* something. Humanity has lost something. We're supposed to have gained *knowledge*—but what we've lost was infinitely more precious. After all, what *is* knowledge? We know how to separate things—events—acts—calling some good —some evil. But think what innocence must have meant. Nowadays we think of it simply as ignorance of evil—absence of evil. It's negative. But innocence—at the beginning—must have been a positive thing—an acceptance of whatever happened. An acceptance of everything! Everything was right—perfect—harmonious! And it can be again. It *is* again, the moment we stop thinking—questioning—accusing God of bringing evil on us."

4

Gawthorp raised his head heavily and looked out of the window at the tossing tree-tops. There was something behind all this, in Tavistock's manner—an eagerness, an urgency, that excited him. It was no ordinary talk about religion that a couple of fellows might drift into—late at night, when things sometimes seem kind of mysterious, and a man gets going—talking about queer feelings he's had or about what's going to happen after you're dead. And it wasn't preaching, either. Not like the way a fellow sometimes gets hold of you—on a train, or some place like that —and starts telling you what he felt like when he was saved. There was nothing sanctimonious about this Englishman. There was almost a sort of fierceness. . . .

Tavistock was moving. He got up from the bed and stood with his back against the dressing-table, his hands pressing down heavily and gripping its edge. Gawthorp looked up at him and something in his glance made him understand why the Englishman was talking like this. He had only met him two or three times, but there was a look in his eyes as though the two of them had known each other all their lives. It was even more than what you might call a brotherly look. You'd think the fellow had sort of picked him out—out of the whole world—to tell him something he'd kept a secret from everybody else—something he had to get off his chest or die, or go mad, or something.

The tenseness, the excitement Gawthorp had felt, was suddenly gone. In its place there was a queer softness. He had never felt such sympathy for anybody in his life. If Tavistock should ask him to help him some way—anything at all—any old thing he asked him—he knew he would do it. He said to himself: "He's a wonderful fellow. I've never met such a fellow."

"There isn't a doubt in my mind," said Tavistock, beginning to talk again as though the interval had been no longer than a breath, "that some day we'll be shown a way back to innocence. Some man will do it, I suppose. A man like Christ—only Christ didn't do it—not for everybody, at any rate. This man will face evil and *see through it!* He will *do* what is called evil and yet be innocent. Do you see what I mean? He will overcome evil by doing evil innocently."

Tavistock smiled enigmatically over Gawthorp's head. "It isn't easy to talk about, let alone to *see!*" he declared, in a more doubtful tone.

"I don't understand it," said Gawthorp, shifting his stick and leaning forward as though he were anxious to have it explained.

"No," said Tavistock. "But—look—you know what it's like to have a very strong presentiment. Not just a hunch, as you say in this country, but a feeling that's like certainty—certainty that something is going to happen?"

Gawthorp nodded slowly. "Yes," he said, "I had a feeling like that after my wife died. I had a feeling that somehow or other she would speak to me—just something—some message. Even after the funeral I still felt she'd get it across to me some way. I used to sit by myself at night—sit up for hours—and wait. But nothing ever happened."

Tavistock took three strides to the window, almost striking his head against the raised sash, and came back again.

"But *this* will happen," he declared, lifting a rigid finger, and dropping it immediately. "I've been waiting for years. I know exactly how it will take place. This man I speak of will commit a murder—the crime we all think the most evil. He will murder somebody—innocently—and then we shall all see that there *is* no evil."

"I don't understand it," Gawthorp said again.

"No. I don't understand it myself—*in my mind.* But I can feel it. I'm so certain of it that I've sometimes wondered if—perhaps—I'm the man he will murder."

Tavistock said this in a curiously deliberate tone which made Gawthorp look up in surprise. The brotherly look had gone from his face. The fierceness was growing.

"You and I can't understand it," Tavistock said, "but we can *believe* in it. The people who lived at the time of Christ couldn't have understood what he was sent for—perhaps Christ himself didn't know—but people *did* believe in him. If you'd been alive then, do you suppose you would have believed?"

The taut feeling of excitement rushed back across Gawthorp's head. "I don't know," he said huskily. "I've never thought much about—"

"But suppose you felt as I did," Tavistock interrupted, his former urgency of tone returning. "Suppose you firmly believed that a superhuman person was alive who *could* commit murder innocently—and bring about the greatest good of the greatest number—would you run away from him?—would you try to escape?"

Gawthorp saw an inner flick of horror flash for a moment in Tavistock's eyes. His strange words recalled what Canon Macaulay and Pitts had been talking about yesterday—about him being "dedicated" to something—living a lonely life, devoted to some queer idea. He had been thinking too much about it. If he didn't watch out he'd go crazy.

5

"You won't answer. You don't know," Tavistock said.

"I don't believe this—this—"

"No, but I do—and I'm just asking you. If you felt as certain of it as I do—so certain that I can *see* it happening—would you run away from it?"

"I tell you what I think," Gawthorp said, letting his stick fall against his thigh and dropping both hands on his knees. "If you worry around with this notion much longer you'll be getting it into your head that *you* ought to murder somebody. It's a dangerous business—monkeying with religion. I knew a fellow once—"

"Never mind your fellow," Tavistock exclaimed abruptly. "Suppose I *am* the man who is to do it. Suppose *that* is the reason I'm so certain it will be done. What then?"

"What do you mean—'what then?'"

He felt himself in danger, and in the face of it his courage, welling up inside of him unexpectedly, doubled his confidence in himself, almost to the point of bravado, so that he was prompted to say: "What's to prevent you killing me?" But he swallowed down the words and licked the roof of his mouth.

Tavistock's lips were parted in a curious smile. "You think the idea is mad—but don't you suppose a lot of people thought Christ was mad?"

"Maybe they did."

"Perhaps you think I'm mad," Tavistock said, in a dry voice. "But if I were a lunatic—if I were just a man with a mania—why didn't I kill the clerk down there at the desk?—why don't I threaten to kill you this minute?—why do I go about without weapons? Eh?"

The editor shrugged his head down and sniffed a grim, chuckling breath through his taut nostrils. "Just what I was thinking myself," he said.

"No, I'm not a maniac," Tavistock said, speaking with real solemnity for the first time, and raising himself to his full height. "But I know this thing is going to be done. I seem to be the only one who knows it. I'm certain of it—and I can see how it will change everything. Misery and evil will disappear. The miseries of the world—"

His voice became a mere breath. He walked again to the window and leaned his head against the frame.

Gawthorp got up. The clatter of his stick against the chair disturbed Tavistock's reverie. He turned slowly and said: "You can't believe?"

"No," said Gawthorp shakily. "Notions like that aren't safe to be going around with. I'd do something about it, if it was me. I'd see somebody."

Tavistock stretched his arms out widely to right and left, his fingers rigidly bent, as though trying to drag help from the air.

Gawthorp put his hand on the knob of the door.

"I'm sorry," Tavistock said, dropping his arms to his sides with a thud. "I've disturbed you. I thought—but it's no use. I'm sorry."

"It's you," Gawthorp said considerately, holding open the door. "You're in a bad state. You ought to—"

"No," exclaimed Tavistock, "you don't understand me—nobody does. But I must expect that, I suppose."

He clasped his hands behind him and forced a smile into his hollow cheeks. "Good-bye," he said.

"So-long," said Gawthorp, limping out and closing the door quietly behind him.

THREE

Questions

I

Gawthorp went slowly along the dusty avenue to his office. Already his encounter with Tavistock had grown unreal. The man haunted him as sometimes a character in a book, after the book is closed, lingers in the memory. But the lanky, strutting figure of the magistrate, passing with long, bird-like steps, distracted him from a puzzled concern over what had happened in the hotel. The high wind, which had been blowing all day, carried great clouds of dust along in spite of the spray from the rattling old water-cart, trundling noisily half a block ahead. The magistrate stalked past, his hand across his eyes. Beyond the water-cart, in the middle of the avenue, drawn by six heavy horses, was a frame house, squeaking along at a snail's pace on wooden rollers that were thrust in front of it and caught up from behind by a gang of four or five men.

"Billy McEwan must be moving the old Slade house out to that lot of his in the West end," Gawthorp said to himself, his slow mind feeling at ease again among familiar sights, and gradually becoming aware that it was Saturday afternoon by the unusual bustle along the sidewalks. As far as he could see there were buggies and democrats drawn up at the stores, the heavy country horses standing quietly at the hitching-posts, while farmers went striding dourly in and out under the awnings, their arms burdened, letting screen-doors slam behind them.

Gawthorp limped along, nodding and hailing at almost every step, flinging up his stick now and then as he passed the Fire Chief tilted back in his chair outside the Fire Hall, or the furtive-eyed Postmaster whispering into Jim Hallett's ear on the Post Office steps, or Rod Inkster, standing at the side door of the Bellevue bar, his hands under his apron, glaring sideways at nothing across his twisted nose.

The bus had just brought a load of harvesters up from the depot, and they were standing all over the sidewalk with their packs, gazing dully around. The editor made his way awkwardly between them, turned the corner and reached the stoop of his printshop.

2

Through the screen-door he could see Clem Anderson inside, talking to Pitts. Philp was there, too. He and Pitts were sitting on a long table littered with proofs—Pitts in his shirt-sleeves, while Philp looked dressed up as usual in his grey trousers, black coat and hard black hat. They were both gaping at Anderson, who was uttering loud and extravagant prophecies about the future of Edmonton.

"What's this—about 'thirteen million acres'?" demanded Gawthorp, with a smirk, as he came through the door.

Firmly standing his ground, Anderson swung his heavy shoulders round at the editor and sucked in his cigar. In one hand he held a roll of blueprints which he had been banging on the table for emphasis. His vest-pockets were bulging with pencils, cigars, the protruding edges of a card-case, and a huge watch-fob.

"I was just tellin' the boys, Dick," he went on, his strident, auctioneer's voice reaching to the street, "there's thirteen million acres of farm land up there between the North Saskatch' and Battle River—just waitin' for the white man. And Edmonton's the nat'ral centre. What a town, boys! They're diggin' coal right out o' the river bank, an' just a mile from the fort there's bog iron to smelt it with. An' that ain't all. There's gold washin' down the river all the time—within a stone's throw of the town, b'God!"

Gawthorp flung his stick down among a sheaf of papers heaped up to the pigeon-holes of an open roll-top desk, and sank into a swivel chair that lurched treacherously back under his weight.

"You're *good*, Clem," he growled, stretching out his legs with a sigh of relief.

"Why, Dick," Anderson bellowed, waving his cigar aloft so that it nearly touched the ceiling, "I could sell lots in the middle of the bloody lake if I had to. I've sold property in this town, boys, that's been lying idle twenty years. I sold the government the site of the new Land Titles Office for fifteen thousand dollars. Nobody around here could get a better offer than six for it. You ain't never really seen me workin', Dick. How long you been here now?"

"Ten—eleven years, I guess," said Gawthorp. "Ninety-six, it was."

"Yup," snapped Anderson, "eleven years. Well, this town ain't boomed in that time. It's gone all to hell, this town has. It's a hoodooed town, I'm tellin' you. I'm through with it."

"How is it hoodooed?" asked Philp, opening his mouth timidly for the first time.

"How! How!" snorted Anderson, grandly thrusting his fingers among the litter in his vest pockets. "How should I know?

—but I'm tellin' you it's hoodooed—it's a Jonah town. Look at 'eighty-six—the biggest year of the boom. There was thirty real estate offices in this town in them days, when there was less than three thousand people here. Yes, and what happened? Just as things was goin' nice the Assiniboine overflows and floods the crops around here for miles. Put the town on the blink. People was afraid to come here. And then in 'eighty-eight there was the cyclone. That's how I got this." He jerked his thumb in the direction of a long scar across his cheek.

"And in 'ninety-one we had a fire-bug here. Fellow named Weir got sore on the town on account of the taxes and hired a poor old nit-wit of a breed to set fire to places. Why, it went on for two years before they found out who was doin' it."

He stopped as though he were finished his catalogue of calamities, but seeing Pitts' mouth opening, he blared on: "In them years you could buy lots for a dollar at the tax sale. Rod Inkster bought a whole block across the tracks for a five-spot. She'll go that way again—sure as God made little apples! You watch. You see what happens when they close down them gravel pits out there. This town'll just be a bloody one-horse place, like it's always been."

He threw his burnt-out cigar in the waste-paper basket beside the desk and pulled out his watch.

"Yes," said Gawthorp quietly, out of the corner of his mouth, "but things have been going a damn sight better around here since 'ninety-two, you've got to admit. These last fifteen years have made a big difference. The town's growing—and she's the finest wheat country in the world, right here on these plains."

"That's the old stuff—that's the stuff to feed 'em," sneered Anderson, putting his watch away. "Go ahead, Dick," he added, hoisting his shoulders belligerently, "stick it out as long as you like—but I'm through. I'm off as soon as this auction sale is over at Jukes's."

"You figure it'll go to an auction, eh?" said Gawthorp, tilting forward in his chair.

"Sure. Jack can't raise any money. Where the hell would he get it?"

Pitts got off the table and hitched at his braces. "The poor blighter's pretty down in the mouth about it," he said.

Anderson wiped his hand across his chin. "Well," he blared, "that's *his* funeral, ain't it? I'm gettin' out—lock, stock and barrel—with everything I can lay my hands on. This Edmonton thing is a whale of a big fat juicy chance for yours truly."

"What's Harry going to do?" asked Gawthorp.

"God knows," said Anderson, his mouth dragging at the corners in a sour smile. "Now he's taken up this singin' business he's too damn high and mighty to live with. He'll be hittin' back to Winnipeg one of these days. You'll see. This town's too small for him."

He looked at his watch again. "I've got to be movin' along. Don't forget that notice, Joey. On the back page, in among the locals, S'long, Dick. S'long, Freddie."

3

Philp had come with some legal notices and an advertisement for a pound-keeper. As soon as the door closed behind Anderson he unfolded the half-dozen sheets of paper, covered with his neat, slanting handwriting, and ran over them with Gawthorp to see that everything was understandable.

When he went out the editor picked up a spike-file from the top of the desk and stood absent-mindedly with it in his hand, looking through the front window at Philp going down the three steps outside.

Gawthorp jabbed the papers down on the spike and stood

fingering them, gazing abstractedly through the dirty window.

Across the street a youngster sneaked past the open door of the blacksmith's shop and began rummaging among the litter of old iron heaped around the rain-water barrel, looking for horseshoes. The glossy rump of a big dray-horse glowed ruddily just inside.

Gawthorp stood there dreaming. Something had come into his mind—but he had lost it again. The ding-dong of two sledges swung on glowing iron in the darkness of the blacksmith's shop, and the shower of sparks—but that was nothing to do with it. He had been dreaming of a face. And now it came back to him—the face of that man who had run out of a barber shop one day when he was a boy in Brantford.

A man had run out of Hayling's barber shop, yelling at the top of his voice, with one side of his face shaved, and the other covered with lather. He had suddenly gone mad in the chair—a fit, or something. They had caught him and tied him up—a big crowd around him—and had taken him away in the back of a delivery wagon, but not before Gawthorp—a youngster ducking under people's elbows—had seen his staring eyes. He had dreamed the eyes were following him for weeks afterward.

It had come into his mind because he was thinking of what had happened in the hotel; yet Tavistock hadn't looked like that, not even that once when a gleam of horror had flickered for half a second in his eyes. Now that he was away from him something surrounded the man—something that aroused his curiosity—his sympathy—a desire to do something for him.

Damn the hammers! The persistent clang—clang—clang—from the blacksmith's shop was deafening, irritating. Ignoring his stick Gawthorp grabbed at the door and flung his twisted leg into a long stride, clutching at the walls, the cases and cupboards, as he waddled lamely into the back and confronted Pitts with his lower lip squared to speak.

4

Pitts was working over one of the "formes" of yesterday's paper, scrubbing the type with alcohol to clean it of the clotted ink.

"Say, Pitts!" the editor shouted over the noise of the ringing hammers, "this friend of yours—this man Tavistock—when did you see him last?"

"Last night," said Pitts, rolling his watery eyes at Gawthorp in a quick, perplexed grimace. "Why—what's up?"

"What's up!" the other echoed, mimicking his accent from habit, "that's what I'd like to know. *You* know him. What's he got on his mind?"

Pitts waved the flies from his bald head with an inky hand. "What's he done?" he demanded, puffing himself up. "Has he done something?"

"I've just been talking to him," said Gawthorp, his brows lowered. "The man's mad—he's not safe."

"Why, what was he talking about?" gulped Pitts.

"About murder."

"God Almighty!" Pitts groaned, throwing down the brush and shooting his glance first one way and then another over the discoloured ceiling as though looking for some explanation there. He brought his head down, and stood bowed for a moment, his fingers fiddling with his brace-buttons, as he recalled what had happened the previous night.

"What did he say, for Christ's sake?" he suddenly asked.

"He says a murder's going to be committed—an 'innocent' murder!" Gawthorp shouted over the din of the hammers. "It's a mania he's got. For a holy minute I thought he was going to strangle me."

"No!" cried Pitts. "No! I don't believe it! I'll swear, by God, he couldn't do it. But—I'll tell you—I think he expects to die any minute. That's what it is."

"Did he talk about it last night?"

"Yes," nodded Pitts, his eyes bulging under thick, black brows. "Something happened to him. I felt he was *going*—if you know what I mean. Damn it, it sounds silly when you say it, but—you know this business about 'walking with God.' *Like that!*—As though he was going to float up through the ceiling —and I thought I was going, too. I hadn't been drinking, either. One beer when I went to supper was all I had—and this was near midnight."

"Well, but what did he *say*?" Gawthorp barked at him impatiently.

"He asked me—he asked me if I felt like I was going to die."

"Yes. Well?"

"And then he said something about 'it's nearer' or 'it's coming,' or something like that."

"But he asked you if *you'd* felt it?"

"Yes. 'Did you think you were dying?' he said, or something like that."

"He didn't threaten you."

"Good God, no."

"And he didn't try to hypnotize you."

"No, no. He was just standing there."

"And that's all he said about it."

"God's truth," declared Pitts solemnly.

"Well, he's talking about murder now. I told him I thought he was crazy. I told him he ought to see somebody."

Pitts's eyes popped at him. "*You* did," he shouted. "You said that to—to—"

"Why not, when the man's stark mad? He's dangerous. I'm going to see the Chief or Doc Bundy. He can't be—"

"No, no," pleaded Pitts, his eyes watering and his head rolling from side to side. "Don't talk like that. I know it sounds queer. He's got some funny kind of religion—that's all's the matter with him. What are you giving us?—saying he's mad. He's got more brains than all this un-Christly town put together."

"Maybe he has, but if they're addled—"

Pitts edged himself with sideway steps around the stone and patted Gawthorp's sleeve. "I think he knows that he's going to die—*you* know, in a few months. Perhaps the time's up, I don't know. He knows he's going to die and he's made up his mind that death don't amount to much. He's gone past it—if you know what I mean."

Gawthorp looked sharply at him. "This is *your* notion, now —this what you're saying. *He* didn't say that, did he?"

"Not last night, but he's talked to me a lot in a funny way— and that's what I make of it," Pitts said, puffing himself out as he imagined the great Coleridge might have looked, and glancing with a certain defiance at his employer.

"Well, why the hell, then, does he talk so much about murder?"

"If you ask me," muttered Pitts, "I'd say that he's got death and murder and God all kind of mixed up—well, maybe not mixed up—but he's queer about religion. He asked me once if I thought Jesus Christ really suffered all the sorrows anybody ever had."

Pitts paused and fixed his glance on the brush lying there on the type. "*That* sort of thing," he said slowly, trying to remember the whole conversation, and what had led up to the question. He shook his head. "If you ask me," he said, in a low, scared tone, "I think he believes God is responsible for everything—you know what I mean—for sin, and—all kinds of evil—and death. One time he said something about an 'act of God.' *You* know, like on a bill of lading. I believe he thinks God is a sort of murderer."

Gawthorp drew back from the stone and perched his elbows on a half-open tray in one of the cases behind him. "Well, what's *that* but madness?" he demanded doggedly.

"I told you he was queer," Pitts declared, his eyes rolling loosely. "But he ain't *dangerous.* And don't you go using what I've told you," he added quickly. "This is all just between you and me. I wouldn't open my trap to your Chiefs or your bloody doctors."

"You wouldn't, eh?" Gawthorp snapped at him. "Not even for the man's own good."

"What do you mean 'for his own good'?"

"Well, if he's mad—"

"How do you know who's mad and who isn't?" cried Pitts, flinging out a blackened finger at him.

Gawthorp passed his hand over his brow, feeling a strange guiltiness inside.

"He isn't a spiritualist—is he?" Gawthorp asked thoughtfully.

"What d'you mean—one of these blighters that ask five bob for looking in a glass bowl?"

"Yes."

Pitts fairly grinned in Gawthorp's face. "What do you take the man for, for God's sake?" He picked up the brush and brought it down with a resounding whack on the type. "You'll be going off your own head in a minute." He spat on the floor. "Yesterday you couldn't see anything wrong with him, and to-day you've got him on the brain."

"Well," muttered Gawthorp, dragging his leg from under him and making a movement to start back to the front office, "well, I'll tell you, Pitts—" But he limped away without saying more, his brows knotting thickly and drawing his eyes together in a squint of horror.

FOUR

Jukes

I

TOWARD DUSK Jack Jukes walked into the police station. The dust that had been blowing all afternoon had settled in the deep lines that seamed his face, and in the hollows of his eyes. He had wiped off an occasional trickle of perspiration with his sleeve, and his smudged face looked more Indian than usual.

Inside the storm-vestibule was a room for examining prisoners. When Jukes went in the Chief and one of the constables were questioning three Galicians who had just been arrested for petty burglaries in the north end of the town. They handled the men roughly, going through their pockets and placing everything they found in three heaps on a large table.

Jukes closed the inner door of the vestibule and stood watching.

"Lo, Chief," he said, when Kitson presently looked in his direction.

"What do *you* want?" the Chief said, turning his back on him and continuing the search.

"Me wait. Me come see you."

"What do you *want*?" bellowed the Chief, his fleshy jaws bulging as though his mouth were full.

"Me come see you—speak business. Me wait," insisted Jukes.

He sat down in a chair by the door, under the clock. Taking off his cap he wiped the sweat from his forehead with a greasy, red sleeve, and sat nursing the cap while the Chief questioned the Galicians and wrote down their names and addresses and details about their birth, their arrival in the country and their occupations. Only one of them could speak any English, and he had to act as interpreter for the others. It took a long time.

Finally, the Chief, who had seated himself at the table to write down these particulars, got up and squared his shoulders in a martial way. "All right," he said to the constable. "Lock 'em up."

Constable Burnand, looking very much like an overgrown farm boy, in spite of his uniform, unlocked the door to the cells and pushed the three Galicians through. He closed the door behind him and Jukes heard the bolts thud into their sockets on the other side.

Chief Kitson bent over the table, his pointed moustaches moving like the feelers of an insect over the prisoners' belongings, which he bundled separately in the men's handkerchiefs. These he took into the vault. Coming out, he closed and locked the door, moving with slow, military gravity, his jaws tightly locked together, his small grey eyes fixed in a slanted gaze.

Jukes stood up, and Kitson spoke from across the room. "What do you want?"

The breed advanced a few steps, his head doggedly down between his shoulders. "Me speak business—go office," he said, nodding down the corridor toward the Chief's office. He had been arrested a good many times and was familiar with everything around the station.

"What's it about?" said Kitson, jerking his tunic down over his hips.

"Bout old Dave."

"What about old Dave?"

"Dave—him money belong me and Anderson."

"What about it?"

"Me get money—pay Anderson Monday. Anderson no close mor'gage—me stay farm."

The chief looked down his nose at Jukes as though he were about to startle him with a peremptory order to stand at attention or make a right turn. He was a South African veteran who had spent most of his time as a drill-sergeant and bore himself toward those he considered his inferiors in the manner he had used with an "awkward squad."

"What's your idea—coming here?" he blared at Jukes, running the words together in a gruff blur of unintelligible sound.

Jukes slapped at his thigh with his cap. "You come search warrant. You come search Dave's place. Lawyer say get Chief—him search."

"What lawyer?"

"Old man Carey."

The Chief thrust his thick chin forward threateningly. "Old man Carey sent you to me?" he asked incredulously.

"Yup."

The Chief looked down the corridor toward his office. "Come in here," he said, and led the way, twisting the waxed ends of his moustaches with a neat fillip of his finger and thumb, first one side and then the other. He sat down ponderously at his desk and Jukes stood just inside the doorway, fidgeting with his cap. The Chief moved some papers on the desk to one side, picked up his pipe and lit it.

"Now, then. What's this all about? Out with it."

The breed's eyes brightened and the lines through his cheeks grew lively as he leaned forward to pour out his story. "Me go friends—me go lawyer. Me ask loan all over. Nobody come loan. Old man Carey say get Chief come search warrant—come Dave's place—find money."

"What money?"

Jukes glared with impatient disgust and then looked around on the floor.

"Don't spit in here," the Chief shouted at him.

Jukes flung his cap in the chair facing the desk and took a step nearer. "Me and Anderson give old Dave money—go north—prospect. Before you come. Chief Hendry here them times. Old Dave strike rich—go Winnipeg—no divvy up. Me get money quick—pay Anderson—must have."

The Chief sat bulgingly back in his chair. "Any proof you lent this money to Linklater?"

"Me no understand."

"Did old Dave sign anything?"

"No. No sign. Him take money—go north."

The Chief cocked his head on one side and looked hard at the ceiling. "We can't do nothing for you," he said.

Jukes squirmed on his heels. "Lawyer say go Chief—get search warrant."

"I can't swear out a warrant," Kitson hurled at him in one long blare. "You'll have to see the magistrate. Come in after the court, Monday morning."

"No good Monday. Clem say close mor'gage Monday."

The Chief stood up and stretched himself. "You come Monday," he gurgled, his mouth wide open in a prodigious yawn.

Jukes' close-cropped head settled still further down between his shoulders. "Me see worship right now—me come house—get search paper. You come get it—search Dave's place."

The Chief laughed. "A fat chance—*you* have—of seeing the magistrate to-night."

"Me come see right now."

"He won't see you, I tell you."

"He see me—sure. Me push door. Must have."

The Chief stood up to his full height, and arched his upper lip so that his moustaches performed a quick gyration. "Don't be a fool, Jukes. We can put you in jail for pushing doors. Forget it, now, till Monday. Come round Monday, after the court."

The breed held his clenched fist near his temple and shook it. "Me no forget. Must have."

The Chief stepped from behind the desk and stood in front of Jukes, bending his head slightly so that the breed should get the direct glare of his glance. "Don't be a fool," he repeated, slurring the words into a sharp bark. "If you're not careful I'll put you in the cells right now for threatening violence."

"Me no understand."

"No. Well, get out o'here, before you're locked up."

"You come worship's house."

"Shut up, you, and get out o'here." Kitson took him by the arm. "Get your cap there."

Jukes picked up his cap.

"Now, come along."

The Chief led him by the arm into the examining room and opened the inner door of the vestibule. "You come Monday."

"Me come worship," said Jukes, glaring over his shoulder.

The Chief violently whirled him around. "You're looking for trouble," he growled.

The breed looked with steady savagery into Kitson's little grey eyes. "Trouble hell! Much plenty trouble now."

"You go home."

Jukes put on his cap and the Chief let go his arm. "You go home," he said again.

"You go hell," said Jukes, and opening the outer door he let it slam behind him.

2

Magistrate Moffat lived on Vernon Avenue, which ran parallel with the lake road. The old house backed on some vacant property which belonged to the Hudson's Bay Company, known to everybody in the town as McCully's bush.

The magistrate was elderly, a widower, and had lived there a long time with a housekeeper almost as old as himself. In spite of twenty years on the prairies he had retained his English accent, his Tory allegiances, Anglican beliefs, white waistcoats and spats. On Saturday nights he was visited regularly by Canon Macaulay, who played cribbage with him, and they were well into their game when Jack Jukes approached the house. A tall glass of whisky-and-soda stood at the magistrate's right hand. The Canon had just drained a glass of port wine. He permitted himself two glasses of the magistrate's port on these weekly occasions.

Jukes' knock at the front door was answered by Mrs. Higham. It was just getting dark and in the twilight the breed's grimy face and bloodshot eyes—inflamed by the dust that had blown into them during his tramp from place to place since early afternoon—gave him a sinister look.

Mrs. Higham opened the door only a few inches. Seeing a rough, unfamiliar face, she almost closed it again. Through the narrow slit she poked out a long, thin nose.

"What do you want?" she demanded.

"Me come see worship," said Jukes.

"You can't see the magistrate this evening. He's engaged."

"Me come see. You tell Jack Jukes come—speak business."

Mrs. Higham withdrew her nose. "The magistrate won't see you. You should go to the court on Monday morning."

"No wait Monday. Me see worship quick soon."

He made a movement to push open the door, but Mrs. Higham slammed it and shot the heavy bolt. Jukes immediately began to hammer at the door with both fists.

While the housekeeper stood waiting to see if he would go away, the magistrate came out into the hall, looking short-sightedly through his spectacles, and bending at every step with a birdlike strut. Canon Macaulay, looking very squat and undignified beside him, stopped in the doorway. There was a gentle, ruminant expression in his eyes as though nothing could disturb him.

"What is it?" said the magistrate, standing excessively straight in the middle of the hall.

"An awful-lookin' Indian, your worship. Said 'e wanted to see you."

The knocking on the door continued.

"What did you tell him?"

"I said for 'im to go to the court on Monday, your worship."

The magistrate nodded his approval, smiled at the Canon, and asked: "Did he say who he was?"

"Yes, sir. Jack Duke—or somethin' like that."

"Jack Jukes, perhaps. Was it Jack Jukes?"

"Yes, your worship—that's it."

"Is he drunk?"

"I don't think so, your worship, but 'e looks very dirty."

Moffat turned and looked over his shoulder at the Canon with a smile that was half-amused and half-impatient. "He'll soon go away," he said thickly. "Let's go on with our game."

"Jukes is an old friend of mine," the Canon remarked, in a reminiscent tone. "We've bucked wood together more than once. You remember when that poor fellow Archer died—dear, dear—and his wife in bed with twins—"

He looked quickly at Mrs. Higham, coughed, and began

fidgeting with the few curling hairs in the cleft of his chin.

"All right, Mrs. Higham," said the magistrate. "He's gone, I think."

The housekeeper rustled out of sight, behind the stairs, sniffing, and the two men went back to their cards.

FIVE

The Lake

I

THERE WAS no wind now, but the sky was overcast, threatening rain. It was still warm, and Jukes continued to perspire as he went dejectedly out of the magistrate's gate and struck along the path through McCully's bush to the lake road. He walked slowly with his head bent, stumbling every now and then over the willow roots embedded in the path, like a man in a stupor.

When he came out of the trees on to the lake road he stopped and raised his head. It was lighter there. The lake reflected what little glow there was left in the sky, toward the west. The water, still rough from the wind that had been blowing all day, washed noisily against the reeds on the other side of the road.

Jukes seemed to sense a stir in the air that had nothing to do with the lake's agitation. Standing still, he raised his head and listened. Faint noises could be heard a long way off, confused with the sucking sounds the water made against the bank. The breed looked along the road toward the town and saw people coming. Some were running. Ahead of them was a man on horseback coming at a gallop.

Jukes looked westward and there were more people, going

away from him. There were lights by the shore about a half a mile away, and he saw a boat pushed out from one of the boat-houses with a lantern in it. There were lights out on the lake, too, moving very slowly. Opposite the lights a crowd was gathering on the bank. Jukes could see tiny dark forms passing to and fro in thc faint glow of the lanterns.

The thud of hooves in the sandy road grew close behind him and he stepped nearer the ditch to let the horseman past. The man shouted at him as he went by in a cloud of dust, but the breed did not hear what he said. While he stood there, gazing after the rider, some boys came up, puffing.

"Who's drowned?" one of them called across the road.

Jukes grunted and shook his head. They ran on, and Jukes followed them, walking fast. Other runners passed him.

2

The crowd was thickest around Bruce's wharf. A long continuous murmur, like the buzzing of flies, came up the bank, louder than the sounds of the water as it slapped against the piles of the dock.

Jukes pressed into the edge of the crowd on the bank. There were a lot of youngsters there, standing under people's noses, listening to everything that was said. Two or three old breed women, with shawls over their heads, were mumbling together in broken Cree and English. Everybody was asking questions. The crowd was milling around, asking questions and moving on nearer the water's edge when they could not find out what had happened.

Somebody had just driven Dick Gawthorp over from the other side of town. He limped into the thickest part of the crowd, making way for himself slowly with his stick and peering into every near-by face. Almost at once he caught sight of Philp, who had been dancing around asking questions for twenty minutes.

"Who's drowned, Fred?" asked Gawthorp in a low whisper.

"Hello, Dick," answered Philp's high-pitched voice, as he made out the editor's face in the growing darkness. "Don't *you* know?"

"I've just got here."

"Nobody seems to know who it is," Philp squeaked over the buzz of the crowd. "Old Mrs. Spencer heard shouts down opposite her place and saw a boat out there. She ran down here to tell Dan, but Dan was half-way out there by that time. Then she ran up to Enos Sadler's place and Sadler sent his boy down to the police station on his wheel."

"Is the Chief here?" asked Gawthorp, standing on tiptoe to look over nearby heads.

"They say he came down with two of the boys from the Fire Hall. They're out there now with irons dragging."

"Hasn't anybody come in?"

"Not that I know of, Dick," Philp answered, in a bewildered voice. "Nobody seems to know anything. I heard somebody say there were two boats out there—two boats close together. Somebody else said it was a boat and a canoe, and maybe they'd run into each other. But it couldn't have been very dark when it happened."

Gawthorp looked over Philp's shoulder at the people feverishly moving about. "If this is a drowning," he said, in a shaky voice, "it'll be the first in three years."

"Yes," said Philp dolefully, "young Allison was the last."

"Yup—pretty bad, that was," Gawthorp said, in an absent-minded way.

At his elbow a voice suddenly spoke with a foreign accent: "Good night, Mr. Editor. Is it somebody drown?"

Gawthorp turned and recognized at once the twitching eye of the railroad interpreter. "You're at the pits, aren't you?" he said, by way of greeting.

"Yes. My name is Roff."

"Sure. I remember. I don't know what's happened. They're dragging out there. Mr. Philp knows more about it than I do. Fred, this is Mr. Roff, the interpreter out at the pits."

"Pleased to meet you," said Philp.

"How you do?" said Roff. Then he addressed them both at once. "It is not—is it?—what you call?—suicide?"

Gawthorp looked sharply at him. "I don't know. More likely an accident, I should think."

Roff leaned closer to him, so as not to shout. "There is a man —very strange—timekeeper at pits. I wonder just—"

"Tavistock!" exclaimed the editor.

"Yes. Man named Tavistock. He go in boat very much. Maybe him."

"But what makes you think it's suicide?"

Roff backed away a step and raised his head in the air. A moment later his lips were again on a level with the editor's ear. "I talk from him this morning only," he whispered loudly. "Very sad man. In Europe I meet these type—they think much. This man think too much also—sad man—maybe suicide."

"I was talking to him myself, just this afternoon," Gawthorp twisted his head around to say. "He talked very queer—about some kind of presentiment."

"Ah, yes," cried Roff excitedly. "That is it. And he is on lake much."

"Who's this?" said Philp, in a piping voice, looking up the bank.

Somebody had just driven up in a buggy and several of the crowd were turning in that direction, craning their necks to see who it was. There were two men in the buggy. The driver pulled up his horse violently in the midst of the crowd, and while its front hooves were still in the air the other man leapt out. He was short and was immediately lost to view.

"It's Canon Macaulay," said a voice.

3

"Is that you, Gawthorp?" the Canon asked a moment later, having pressed through close to where the three men were standing together.

"Yes, Canon. Have you heard who it is?"

"God bless us—no! I was hoping you could tell me. Laura is out there somewhere."

"Laura!" groaned the editor.

The Canon couldn't keep his hands still. One was plucking constantly at his lips and the other at his coat buttons. "I was at the magistrate's and they sent a message to me. Mrs. Macaulay is beside herself. It's all over town, apparently. Doesn't anyone know what has happened?"

"We can't find out a thing."

The Canon stood a moment, knotting and unknotting his fingers, as he sometimes did in his sermons.

"Isn't there a boat around here?" he cried suddenly. He raised his voice to a shout: "Hey! Bruce! Is there a boat here?"

The murmur of the crowd stopped and heads were turned. There was no answer. In the silence the Canon raised his voice again: "Has anyone seen my daughter, Laura—Laura Macaulay?"

A murmur of, "No, Canon, "No, no," ran through the crowd.

The frenzied man grasped Philp's shoulder. "Where's Dan?" he said. "Is he out there?"

"Yes, Canon," said Philp.

But the Canon had already turned away. "Where's Jud Heath?" he was shouting, and then, turning back: "Come with me, Philp." He flashed a frantic glance at every face around him. "A couple of you men—come on. Let's get one of Heath's boats."

He began ascending the bank, the crowd hurriedly making way for him.

"They're coming in," somebody shouted.

"The boats are turning this way," cried another voice.

For a moment the Canon hesitated. He turned, as though he were going to the wharfside to look, but instead, he flung up his arm, and shouted: "I can't wait. Come on, Philp. We'll meet them."

The crowd watched them run along to Heath's boathouse and saw a rowboat pushed out. Three men dropped into it. The Canon had his coat off already, and he and another began to row like mad.

Gawthorp pressed through the crowd and leaned on his stick at the edge of the wharf, peering over the dark water. At his side a drunken, babbling voice was muttering unintelligibly. Turning, he saw Pitts leaning heavily on Jukes' shoulder, talking into his ear. He heard something about "the bloody moon . . . just like the plagues of Egypt . . ." and moved away, hoping to avoid him.

The little fleet of boats was now clearly making for shore. Some were simply dark shapes on the water. Others had lanterns in them.

"That's Dan, I'll betcha," someone said, close at hand.

"And it looks like the Chief—the other one."

"It's Dan and the Chief—look at 'em pull."

There was a lantern in the bottom of the foremost boat which illumined the rowers.

Gawthorp heard behind him a familiar booming voice. "Been here long, Dick?"

"No, Clem, I haven't," said Gawthorp, glancing round into Anderson's face, which he found drawn with anxiety.

"Haven't seen Harry, have you?"

"No, not to-night."

"He's out on that blasted lake—I know he is." Anderson lowered his harsh voice to a whisper. "If Laura Macaulay's out there, *he's* out there, that's a cinch."

He squeezed the editor aside and stood on the wharf's edge, straining his eyes to watch the progress of the incoming boats.

"Here's Doc Bundy," a commanding voice cried over the

general murmur, and in a moment the doctor came perspiring through to where Anderson and Gawthorp stood craning forward over the water.

"Hello, doctor," said Gawthorp gravely, in a half-whisper.

"Who is it, Dick?" panted Bundy through his beard.

"It's not a girl, anyway," a hoarse voice said, near at hand.

"I can see a man's legs hanging over the seat," cried another, from the extreme end of the wharf.

Anderson suddenly dragged off his hat and crushed it in his hands. "It's Harry—look! I'll bet money! Look, Doc! look at that ice-cream suit! As sure as God made little apples! It's Harry, I tell you."

"Hold on, hold on, Clem," cautioned the doctor. "You can't tell from this distance."

"Chief! Chief!" Anderson yelled across the intervening water. The two words, bellowed at the top of his voice, rang out over the lake. But there was no answer. Kitson and Dan Eggertson were bending at the oars.

"Chief!" roared Anderson again, flinging his right arm commandingly upward. It was a gesture he used at auctions to compel attention.

Dr. Bundy put both hands on the distracted man's shoulders, and thrust his pointed beard in his face. "Pull yourself together, Clem. Whoever it is can't have been down long. Chances are they can be brought round . . ."

The Chief shipped his oars for a moment and blared with military peremptoriness toward the shore: "Clear that wharf there! Clear that wharf!"

Gawthorp turned and pressed back the crowd. Some had already moved up the bank. The editor, limping about, flourishing his stick, coaxed the others back. The doctor was already on one knee, opening his bag. A boy stood beside him holding a lantern. Anderson hung out over the water, in danger of toppling in at any moment. It was shallow there, and suddenly Anderson flung himself in. The water came up to his waist. Talking unintelligibly to himself, he started wading out, his broad shoulders swaying in a grotesque exaggeration of his usual swagger as he trudged with difficulty through the water.

"Hold on, Clem," the Chief blared at him. "There's a good chance yet."

Clem stopped dead in the water and raised his clenched hands over his head. "I knew!—I knew God damn well!" he bawled, and threw the hat that was crushed in his hands as far as he could throw it, out over the water.

4

The boat shot alongside the wharf. They lifted the dripping body out awkwardly and staggered a few steps, Anderson shouldering every one aside and repeating his boy's name a dozen times. "It's Harry . . . it's Harry . . . it's Harry!"

"Take his arms, Clem," cried Bundy. "There. Turn him face down."

"Keep back there!" roared the Chief, the words rolling together in an unintelligible blur, as the crowd surged forward.

"Is Laura all right?" whispered Gawthorp in Kitson's ear.

"Yup," the Chief snapped at him as he went down on his knees alongside the body.

"Hold him up in the middle," ordered the doctor. He looked quickly over his shoulder. "Is there any brandy in the crowd? Get some brandy?"

Gawthorp went hopping over to the bank and sent somebody up to Sadler's place for spirits.

The men worked feverishly over the body, Anderson's tears

dropping on the blue, unconscious face. The doctor puffed and grunted as he bent and straightened the stiffened legs.

The other boats neared the wharf, and in the nearest the white shirt-sleeves of Canon Macaulay showed conspicuously in the lantern light. He was sitting in the stern with his arms around a limp figure in a light-coloured frock. Two men were rowing. One was quickly recognized as Enos Sadler, but the other was a stranger to most of the crowd.

A voice over Gawthorp's shoulder startled him. "It is *him*—Tavistock."

Roff stood at his elbow, his eye twitching nervously.

"Feel his pulse, Doc," cried Anderson. He stopped his rhythmic pumping of the boy's arms and dashed tears from his eyes with the back of his hand. "Is he coming round?—eh?—is he?"

"Keep him moving, Clem," grunted the doctor. "It may take an hour. Let the Chief there for a spell."

"No, no, no! Go ahead."

He grasped the boy's wrists again and began doubling the limp elbows over his chest. The wrists were very cold. Mechanically he dragged them backward and forward. The doctor, doubling the legs, brought Harry's knees to meet his elbows in the pit of his stomach, then back again, out to their full length. The Chief was kneeling close, rubbing the boy's chest.

Anderson no longer looked up every little while into the doctor's face. His stare was fixed on the damp brow. He pumped mechanically. Nobody spoke.

Suddenly Anderson dropped the cold wrists and burst into a wild shout that boomed over the hubbub of the crowd and echoed against the side of Sadler's barn high up on the bank. "It's Harry! It's Harry!"

"Take his arms, Chief," ordered the doctor between two gulps of breath.

Anderson raised his arms and shook them frenziedly in the air. "Leave him alone!" he cried. "Leave him alone!"

"Get out of the way, Clem," the Chief blared at him.

"Don't I know when he's dead?" sobbed Anderson.

A girl's voice, close to them on the wharf, made him look up quickly.

"Let me see him," Laura was saying.

Laura and her father came up and looked down at the body. Dan Eggertson and Tavistock were close behind them. Roff and Gawthorp were standing to one side. Pitts, who had been talking tipsily to Philp, edged his way through the crowd, slapping at the mosquitoes on his neck and cursing in a drunken undertone. He managed to break through, and reeled across the open space to where Tavistock was standing, but the Englishman did not turn his head. He was watching Laura. Her lavender-coloured dress was bedraggled and soaked and her wet hair hung down her back like a little girl's. She stood there, grasping her father's arm, staring and shivering.

Anderson awkwardly got up and faced her and looked at her intently. It had grown quite dark, and he stood close, looking at her in the dim lantern-light, as though this little girl of the Canon's he had known from childhood had suddenly grown up. He tottered toward her and held out his hands helplessly.

"What happened?" he groaned.

She shuddered, stepped back and clutched at her father.

"Don't ask her now, Clem," said the Canon hoarsely. "I must get her home. There's hope for your boy, isn't there?"

The distraught man did not answer, but Laura was suddenly talking.

"There isn't much to tell, Mr. Anderson," she said, her soft voice, after all the shouting, carrying a long way in the silence that had fallen over the crowd. "He stood up in the canoe. He—he was cramped—and stood up. And getting back he slipped and the canoe went over. I got hold of the side of it and hung on, but when he came up he was turned away from it. He couldn't seem to get turned round. He kept sinking."

She shuddered and looked wildly about until she saw Tavistock.

"And then—this gentleman came and got me into his boat and began diving for Harry. And then Dan came. That's all—really that's all, Mr. Anderson. And, oh, I hope they save him."

Tavistock met her glance as she looked at him over her shoulder. He stood there, dripping, behind her, motionless and grave.

"Come to the rectory when you can, Clem," urged the Canon in a husky voice that was hardly audible. "I've got to get Laura warm—and this man, too," he added, looking behind at Tavistock. "Take heart, Clem. Look, they still have hope."

At that moment the doctor was pouring brandy between the swollen lips.

"My buggy's up on the bank there," Jud Heath said quietly to the Canon. "I guess the three of youse can pile in."

Laura suddenly dropped on one knee beside the body. Dr. Bundy and the Chief knelt back. She leaned over, and looking at the still face, shuddered again. She tried to rise, began to tremble, and fell on her side in a faint.

There was a hushed stir. The Canon and Tavistock lifted her and carried her up the bank.

Anderson stood open-mouthed, staring after them until the buggy had driven off. Then he turned and gazed down blankly at the men still bending and unbending the arms and legs of his dead boy.

SIX

The Drive Home

I

SHE FOUND HERSELF wrapped in blankets, her head against her father's shoulder. It was dark and the buggy was rattling under them. The bare head beside her father's flapping round hat was no more than something solid and grey against the sky.

Stars were out overhead. The clouds, which had piled up in the west toward sundown, were sinking below the darkened horizon. The freshening night air blew gently across her cheek, between her and the bare head moving against an immense serenity of blue.

It was over. Against her flesh she felt the chilling wet folds of her clothes. She was alive, and they were going home. It was over, and there was this serenity in the sky . . .

Jud was shouting over the noisy rattling of the wheels, his mouth against her father's ear. Trees were gliding blackly past. She felt her eyes closing again, and the rattle sank to a gentle refrain, soothing her . . .

Again she opened her eyes. It was dark, and the bare head was still there, gliding through the blue. She looked ahead into the darkness. There were arc-lights at the corner of each block, but the trees, grown up around them, prevented the light from carrying very far.

They reached Vernon Avenue and turned east, past the magistrate's house. Under the light at the corner Laura glanced up at Tavistock. There was an expression in his eyes as though he had been looking at her, in the dark, a long time. While the light lasted their gaze held, and when it grew dark again, between the lights, they made no motion or sign.

Jud and the Canon went on talking.

After a while they approached another corner. The light, screened by the thick foliage of a maple until they were almost opposite it, shone suddenly on Tavistock's face. Laura's glance had been fastened on the dark, slender shape of his head. She now looked deeply into his eyes. He did not smile, but as he answered her eager, seeking look his eyes enlarged with an intensity she had never seen in his face before.

She began to shiver. The Canon, feeling the tremor of her body under the blankets, leaned over and looked at her; but by this time they were past the light. Darkness again engulfed her head.

"She's shivering," the Canon said, turning to Tavistock. "Aren't *you* cold?"

"No, no," the other answered quickly. "Just a bit clammy."

"You must come in and get warm," the Canon shouted at him over the noise of the wheels. "I'll find you some clothes."

Tavistock was about to say something, but the Canon went on: "You'd better not go out to the pits to-night—we can put you up somewhere. You must have some hot brandy. I think there's brandy in the house."

"I've left the railroad," Tavistock shouted back at him. "I'm staying at the Manitoba. It's just near you, and I can run in there and get warm in no time, thanks."

Laura stirred. "But please come back to our place when you've changed," she said anxiously, raising her head under her father's chin. "I want to thank you. I want to talk to you."

"Are you all right?" the Canon said to her, shifting her weight closer to him.

"Yes, quite. I fainted—didn't I ?"

"Are you cold?" her father asked, ignoring her question.

"Not very." She turned in the darkness to Tavistock. "You *will* come back, won't you?"

"Yes—if you wish," he replied, his voice trembling slightly for the first time as though he might be shivering.

"But, bless your soul, Laura," the Canon objected, "you should go to bed and get thoroughly warm. And Mr. Tavistock won't want to come out again, surely."

"Won't you?" asked Laura.

"I don't mind in the least. It's not a cold night—luckily. But there's nothing to thank me for."

"My dear fellow," the Canon said.

Laura moved under the blankets. "You'll come, won't you?" she said, in a determined tone.

"Yes. I'll come. I'd like to."

"Good!" said the Canon heartily. "Mrs. Macaulay will want to thank you, too."

"Really, you know, it was nothing," Tavistock demurred, brushing back his damp hair. "I just happened to be near when the canoe turned over." He looked down through the darkness at Laura. "You could have held on for some time, I imagine. It might have been anybody. Old Dan would have . . ."

"But it wasn't anybody," said Laura decisively. "You must let me thank you properly."

"And I'll have some hot brandy for you," said her father. "Come right back when you've changed. We'll have a fire going and I'll have some brandy for you."

"Here we are," Jud bellowed, digging his elbows into the

Canon's ribs as he drew the lines taut. The horse pranced a little and came to a stop on the boulevard beside the rectory.

"Will you get out first, and I'll give you the bundle," said the Canon to Tavistock, with a quick, excited chuckle.

"Oh, I can walk," exclaimed Laura.

"Not in all these blankets."

Tavistock had jumped out and was standing on the grass. He held out his arms, and the Canon let Laura slowly down until Tavistock bore all her weight.

While her father was getting out of the buggy Laura whispered to Tavistock: "I *must* talk to you."

"Yes," Tavistock said. He looked understandingly at her. She could just see his eyes, and suddenly she smiled at him for the first time. His eyes softened. There was an ache in them which made her tremble.

"Let me help you," said Canon Macaulay, stepping from the wheel-hub to the ground and offering to lend a hand.

"She's not heavy," said Tavistock. He looked down at her. "Shall I carry you in?"

"Come on in, Jud," called the Canon, leaving them and running ahead up the path. He flung open the front door, thrust his head inside and called: "Jessica! Jessica! She's all right! She's here!" His voice was lost in the hall as he ran in.

Tavistock walked slowly up the path, carrying Laura carefully.

"This is another strange meeting," Laura said to him, lifting her face from his shoulder.

"No," he said. "This is not so strange." His voice trembled again, but she could tell now that it wasn't with cold.

She shook her head free from the blankets to peer at him. They were on the verandah. They could hear the Canon running out through the hall toward them. Tavistock took another stride, and the light from the hall shone on Laura's face.

The Canon was in the doorway, jumping with excitement.

"That's right—stand her down. Thank God!"

Tavistock gently lowered her to the floor. The Canon bent and flung the blankets away from her feet. She stood up. "There I am," she breathed out in a deep sigh.

"Hurry now and get dry," the Canon said to Tavistock.

He went out and ran down the steps of the verandah—passing Jud Heath going in—and hurried around the corner to the hotel.

2

It was Saturday night, and the hotel was busy. A great roar from the bar reached the sidewalk and echoed all through the house. Tavistock squeezed through the tipsy crowd on the verandah, crossed the rotunda, ran up the stairs and entered his room. He threw off his dripping clothes and attacked his chilled flesh with a towel.

He was soon dry and warm, and began to dress. The suit in his grip was badly crumpled. He had packed very carelessly. Dragging out the trousers of a grey suit, he began to put them on, when there was a knock at the door.

"Who is that?" Tavistock called.

"Roff," came the muffled answer from outside.

Tavistock pulled the trousers around his waist. "Come in, Louis," he called back.

The Russian stepped in, removing his shapeless hat. He frowned gravely. "I drive with foreman," he said. "That Swede."

"Johnson?"

"Yes. Before that—I am at lake."

"Oh, were you?" cried Tavistock, puzzled by his manner and flinging a quick glance at him. "Were you there when we came in?"

"Yes, I see you."

Tavistock was at the dressing-table, putting on a soft collar and tie. He could see Roff in the glass, looking at him seriously.

Roff said: "Is *this* what you mean?"

Tavistock looked over his shoulder. "What, Louis?"

"This evil something. Is this it?"

Tavistock wheeled round and looked full at him. "No," he said, thoroughly astonished. "No. This has nothing to do with it."

Roff did not drop his glance. "This was just—accident."

Tavistock considered a moment, and took a step toward the Russian. "The chap got cramped in the canoe, and stood up. He slipped, and the canoe turned over. I couldn't get there before he went down. I kept diving, but I couldn't find him. He got himself all tangled up in the weeds."

"The lady? She hang on side?"

"Yes."

Roff looked at him more meaningly than ever. "It was—accident?"

Tavistock smiled at him indulgently. "Yes, it was an accident."

"I am friend of yours," said Roff, in a whisper. "Maybe I help you. It was not—murder?"

Tavistock suddenly sat down on the bed. He propped his chin in both his hands and looked hard at Roff.

"You're a strange chap, Louis."

Roff stared. "*Me? Me* strange! It is *you*!"

"Well, yes, I am strange, I suppose," Tavistock muttered gloomily, half to himself. "But that is because I think of only one thing. You think all sorts of things."

Roff sat down beside him. "What you mean—I think all sorts of things?"

"Why do you ask me if this was a murder?"

"Well—all the time—you say murder—murder—all the time."

Tavistock had been looking at the floor. He twisted himself round on the bed and faced Roff, and looked at him with a puzzled expression.

"The curious thing," he said, as though talking to himself, "is that this—this *could* have been a murder."

"What you mean?"

Tavistock jumped up. He put both his hands on Roff's shoulders. "No. It was an accident. Not quite the way I told you, but close to it. And, anyway, it doesn't matter now. It doesn't matter to anybody . . ."

"He is dead," Roff said very quietly.

"They gave up before you left, did they?"

"Yes."

"The doctor said he was dead."

"Yes."

Tavistock walked about the room. Suddenly he stood still, felt at his tie and looked at Roff. "I must go, Louis. I promised to go back to the rectory."

"That lady. She is all right?"

"Yes. It was simply a faint. She is all right now."

He dragged a coat out of the valise and put it on.

"Then this is not *it*," Louis said deliberately.

"No, old chap," said Tavistock, brushing back his soaked hair at the dressing-table. "This isn't what I was talking about. Will you believe that?"

He was ready, standing waiting to go.

Roff got up from the bed.

"You believe me, don't you?" Tavistock said.

"Yes," said the Russian simply.

They moved to the door. When Tavistock took hold of the knob, Roff placed a hand on his arm. Tavistock looked sharply sideways at him.

"Tell me," Roff said, "what is this *it*?"

"No, I'm sorry, Louis," said Tavistock, opening the door. "I can't tell you that."

3

Canon Macaulay opened the door himself when Tavistock rang the bell at the rectory. "Good," he said, nodding his head a great many times. "Good. Come in."

He shook Tavistock's hand repeatedly. "I can't tell you how grateful I am—and Mrs. Macaulay. God bless you. We are all in here."

He was moving toward his study on the right of the hall.

"We've heard from the doctor," he said in a lower tone, coming to a standstill. "Dr. Bundy. He is an old friend of ours—the head of the Home for Incurables. You saw him down there on the wharf, I guess. He sent word. Young Anderson is dead."

He paused and looked down, still holding Tavistock's arm.

"I thought I would tell you," he said, looking up into the other's face again. "Perhaps when we go in—you understand—there will be no need to mention it. Mrs. Macaulay—especially—is very upset."

He seemed about to move on, but paused again. His black eyes curiously scrutinized Tavistock's face. "Laura asked me to get the others out of the room when you came. She wants to talk to you—"

Tavistock returned the Canon's anxious glance without a change of expression.

"Is there something about this," the Canon asked hesitantly, "that isn't—that the rest of us don't know about?"

He took his hand from Tavistock's arm and began plucking at his tiny beard in a nervous way.

"I haven't any idea," Tavistock said slowly, "why she should want to talk to me."

"You haven't?"

The Canon was lifting his heels and letting them drop again. He was very excited. "Perhaps after you've talked to Laura . . ." he began, but suddenly stopped.

"Possibly," said Tavistock, inclining his head.

The Canon took his arm again to lead him into the library. "Good," he said, nodding uncertainly. "Well—shall we go in?"

4

Firelight was gleaming on the backs of books, shelved against all four walls of the library, and on the old-fashioned, shabby furniture—the desk, a littered table, and three or four high-backed chairs.

Laura, in a kimono and wrapped in a travelling-rug, sat close to the tiny fireplace. Beside her was Jud Heath, his long, solemn face looking more dejected than usual as he glanced up out of the corners of his little eyes at the newcomer. On the other side of the fire, with her back to the door, Mrs. Macaulay was sitting up very straight in her chair.

"Jessica," said the Canon, bending close to her ear and speaking loudly, "here is Mr. Tavistock."

Mrs. Macaulay raised herself slowly. The voluminous dress fell and settled in dark folds about her. The tight black sleeve made the hand thrust forward seem even whiter than her pale, rigidly composed face. Her smile came deeply from within to warm this severe appearance.

"I hope my husband and Laura have thanked you—adequately—Mr. Tavistock," she said, in her usual husky undertone. "I haven't his command of language," she continued, looking at the Canon quickly, "but perhaps you can guess how a mother feels when—" She couldn't go on. Her lips seemed to click mechanically together, and she looked apprehensively out of the corner of her eye at Laura. "I wish I could thank you—I—I—" She looked dismayed, glancing first at Laura, then at the Canon, as though this were unheard of.

The Canon stepped behind Tavistock to her side.

"This is silly, Malcolm," she whispered brokenly, "but—you see—I sat here—I—I thought she was *gone*."

She dabbed at her eyes with her white hands and went quickly out of the room.

Laura and the Canon glanced after her until the heavy curtain over the door into the hall had stopped swaying. Then they looked at each other in astonishment.

"My wife so rarely gives way," the Canon said, in explanation to Tavistock, who stood rather awkwardly beside him.

"I guess you met Mr. Heath," Laura said, recovering herself and looking across the room at the stooped old man who was still sitting on the edge of a chair, eyeing them with a solemn sideway glance.

"Good evening," said Tavistock, stepping forward and grasping the shyly offered hand.

With his wet hair newly brushed Tavistock looked thinner than before. Laura was looking at him in a good light for the first time. Holding the rug about her, she got up and moved a step toward him. "I haven't really thanked you yet," she said, in a soft voice, as though they were alone together in the room. "It's like a story-book to be thanking somebody for saving your life. And yet I've forgotten how they say it. I only know you were very brave—and—and I shall never forget."

The Canon moved awkwardly across the room, sliding his blunt fingers nervously over the little silver cross on his watch-chain. He stopped in front of old Jud, and surprised him by abruptly swerving his eyes toward the door with a short jerk of his head. The old man put his hand to his back and raised himself slowly. He looked over the Canon's shoulder at Tavistock and Laura, whose faces were turned away, and suddenly winked, without a trace of merriment in his eye. He lifted his feet two or three times, as though to make sure they were there, and wobbled across the study toward the doorway, the Canon closely following.

"Good night, Laura," mumbled old Jud.

She turned fully around and just touched his arm as he passed her. "Good night, Mr. Heath," she said. "Thanks so much for bringing us home."

"Thank God you was here to bring home," he jerked out, in a cracked voice.

The Canon followed him into the hall, pulling the curtain close as he went through the doorway.

SEVEN

Togetherness

I

As she stared at the fire Laura felt the height of him beside her. His silence seemed to add a tremor to the stillness of the room.

Looking up suddenly she saw that his head was poised in a listening attitude. "What is that?" he asked in a half-whisper.

Music from somewhere was floating through the window open on the garden.

"It's the organist practising," she said, her glance drifting back to the fire.

"Oh, of course," he nodded.

"Please sit down," Laura begged, raising her hand as though to drag farther forward the chair the Canon had placed for him.

He grasped the arms of it and sat down, crouching forward, his face level with hers, but avoiding her eyes.

"You know what happened, don't you?" Laura said, with a note of bitterness in her voice.

He shaded his eyes with his fingers, his thumbs sunk in his cheeks. "Yes," he said with an effort.

"But you couldn't have expected it," she declared, as though nothing in his mind was hid from her.

"No," he said. "I didn't expect it."

"Yet you kept near us all the evening." Her voice did not accuse. She was simply letting him know that she had somehow anticipated everything he had done.

He raised his head and looked at the little black marble clock on the mantelpiece. "I was rowing up and down," he said softly.

"But when we stopped paddling, you drifted, too," she persisted, glancing across at him eagerly.

"What made you notice that?" he asked. "I was a good distance away." He made a triangle of his hands again for his head to rest in.

Laura touched his sleeve. "What did you see?" she whispered.

He did not move or speak. The music stealing through the window swelled into a crescendo as she said: "You saw him get up?"

Tavistock still did not move or make a sound.

"I *must* talk to you about it," she insisted, hunching herself forward to be nearer to him.

"No," he said, in a deep tone that rang under his arched fingers.

"I must!" She gently drew his nearest hand away from his brow and made him look at her. "I can't talk to my mother—or to daddy."

His eyelids were heavy. "No," he said. "Talk to no one."

Her cupped hands were ready to grasp his arm. "We don't know each other," she breathed through the little space between them, "and yet—we *must* talk."

"No," he said, shaking his head and thrusting a foot toward the fire, "we must *forget*!"

An unexpected light burned for a moment in her eyes. "*You* can forget, perhaps, but I . . ."

He looked at her quickly. "It is *you* who must forget," he said emphatically. "You are young. You must forget it all—anything about it." With a gesture that struck her as forced and theatrical, he added: "Most of all—you must forget me."

"But why *you*?" she demanded quickly.

He flung a second sudden look at her. "Most of all—*me*," he whispered.

He was about to get up, but her two hands swiftly grasped his arm. "We don't know each other, but . . ."

Her voice broke and she threw her head back to inhale a deep, trembling breath. Immediately his manner changed. He looked at her as he had on the verandah when he was carrying her in. "Ask me anything," he said.

"Tell me, then," she said severely, "why I must forget *you*."

"No. That is the one thing you mustn't ask me."

"Ah, you see," she sighed.

He stretched out his hand as though to touch her. "Well, yes," he said, "I *will* tell you. *That*, really, is why you can ask me everything else. To-morrow I shall—I shall be gone."

"You are going away?"

He hesitated, and then answered abruptly: "Yes."

"You mean," she faltered, "you'll not come back."

He nodded his head slowly, three or four times, so that she knew he was determined not to speak. Taking her hands from his arm she turned away and looked into the fire. There was no longer any blaze. As she looked, the red coals shifted and fell together in a new pattern that seemed to hold her gaze.

Presently she leaned nearer and looked searchingly into his face. "You saw the canoe upset."

"Yes," he said, in a sort of groan.

She looked over his shoulder at the curtain closing the doorway, and lowered her voice to a whisper that could just be heard. "*You saw me upset it.*"

"No!" he said.

"But you knew I *did*."

He shook his head widely from side to side, and she remained silent, stroking her hands together in her lap as though they were cold.

"He had a chance to hang on," Tavistock said.

"Yes, a chance," she said bitterly.

He turned, looked at her and took her two hands. "You're *making* something in your mind," he said softly, in the tone one uses to a child.

Her glance roved about the walls.

"May I ask *you* something?" Tavistock said.

She curled her two hands more tightly in his and nodded.

"Did you care for him?"

She looked at Tavistock with a slow gaze that wandered from his brow to his chin. "Do you want to know?"

"I would like to know."

She watched his mouth as he spoke, and continued gazing at his closed lips. Then she suddenly dropped her head and shuddered.

He released her hands slowly and placed his own, which had held them, against his cheeks.

2

After a long silence he said: "It is getting late."

She looked up and shook the smouldering look from her eyes. "Yes," she whispered, leaning toward him again. "I must tell my father—but no one else need know. That is what I wanted to say to you. Let it be—an accident."

"The canoe upset—just as you told it on the wharf."

"No. I can't tell daddy," she said quickly. "And yet he will wonder. I told him I *had* to talk to you. And if you go away tomorrow—I shall be left alone with this . . ."

He took his hands from his cheeks and clasped them tightly together. "It is best," he said, forcing decision into his tone. "I should only remind you of it."

"No," she said, at once, starting out of her dreaminess. "You wouldn't remind me of this—but here I've been worrying you with—with this—and you—I know you are *really* suffering."

He looked gently at her, his lips opening slowly to ask: "How do you know that?"

"I can feel it," she whispered, crossing her hands on her breast and pressing against them toward him. "How many times have I met you? Is it only three times? But I've seen you on the lake. You've had some terrible trouble, haven't you?"

He got up and stood looking down into the fire. It had long ago sunk into a heap of embers, and these had now ceased to glow. He looked at the faint red veins of heat mottling the burnt-out ashes, and moved his lips over each other, holding back the words that were crowding his tongue.

"Shall I see you again?" Laura asked, without looking up.

"I hope not," he breathed above her in the gentlest of whispers.

"You *hope* not?" she repeated, with a rueful smile.

"Yes. There is something I have to do—and when I look at you—when I think of you—I want to give it up. And yet—I cannot."

Her two hands fell away from her breast like petals opening and wilting in one long slow sweep of inevitable motion. "And we shall have no chance to know each other," she said, her voice drifting through her lips in a prolonged sigh.

"No," said Tavistock, his face setting grimly. "For some reason we have met—last night—and to-night—at a crisis, apparently, in both our lives." He paused and seemed to be listening for a faint echo of his own voice against the walls of the room. "It makes what I have to bear," he added, as though to himself, "even more bitter."

Laura looked up at him in bewilderment, knowing that he was talking, as she often did, in a sort of dream. "I thought your trouble was in the past," she exclaimed.

"No," he said, in deeper tones than he had uttered yet, "it is to come."

"It will be there," she murmured breathlessly, "where you are going?"

"It will be in—in the nature of the going."

She jumped to her feet, holding the rug about her, and flung out one arm toward him.

"What is it?" he whispered, looking into her terrified face with amazement.

"You said something last night," she said, "something about if you died . . ."

"Yes."

"But it isn't that, is it? You're not . . ."

"Not in the way you think."

"You are ill, is that it? You have given up hope. Oh, tell me." She clung to him with a feverish tremor agitating her face.

"No. I can't tell you."

She tried to soften the rigidity of his body with her arm's pressure on his shoulder, lifting her face nearer his and plunging a frantic glance into his eyes. "In a moment daddy will be coming in. Promise me that before you go—you will see me—you will tell me—you will let me help."

"You only shake me," he groaned.

"Promise," she cried, her fingers gripping him fiercely. "If anyone can shake you it means there is hope, doesn't it? It can be changed—prevented. Oh, what is it? Oh, tell me what it is."

"It isn't what you think."

"How *can* I think? You have saved *me*, but you won't let me help *you*."

She was looking into his eyes, thinking furiously. Suddenly

she became calm and stood away from him. "We have confessed a lot in these few minutes," she whispered, leaning her weight on his arm with one hand, so that he could not move.

"Yes."

"More than we have actually said."

"Yes."

"And in the buggy, coming here, without speaking, something happened, too."

"Yes."

"And even last night."

He nodded silently.

"And it isn't . . . I mean, it's not just an ordinary . . ."

"Why do you say this?" he asked breathlessly.

"I shouldn't say it," she cried softly. "I *wouldn't* say it, if we were not—if there were not this need to know each other—so that I can speak to you—as though I had some right. I can't see you go—now—wondering what will happen to you. Can't you see? If nothing else—I owe you so much."

"Nothing," he said sadly.

"I owe you so much, and you won't let me do *anything*. If you would even talk to daddy . . ."

"I *have* talked to him."

She looked at him, almost angrily. "But you won't talk to *me*. Do you think I am just—just a little girl?"

"How you have changed," he said thoughtfully, "since last night."

"Last night," she murmured, "perhaps I wasn't—I wasn't—but I know what it's like to be a woman now."

He stood watching her, holding his hands behind him rigidly.

"Always," she went on, "I felt my heart was . . . but I can see now that hearts are to break—that is the excuse for them—that is what life is *for*."

"No," whispered Tavistock, his brows arching in pain.

"I have *his* life on my conscience," she went on sorrowfully, "and in the same night I turn to you—for someone to bear this with me—the only one who knows—and I—I find *your* heart breaking, too, with some trouble you won't let me see."

Tavistock grasped her hands, held them tightly, and pressed them against his breast. She looked up at him, trembling, her eyes seeking.

"Is it always like this?" she asked, as though he knew all mysteries. "Is this what life is like? I have never felt *alone* before."

"And I," he said, his sadness suddenly vanishing in a smile that was like the coming out of the sun, "I have never felt *togetherness* before."

She broke her hands out of his grasp and clutched his arms as though she would sink without him. In his eyes she sought for what had been in his voice. It was there. He could no longer hide it under his grief.

"I love you," he said.

Her eyes flashed with a passion of curiosity, and her lips parted as though she must ask him "why" and "how." But he bent his head swiftly, and her open lips were stilled by his sudden kiss. She flung her arms about him and stood on tiptoe to peer with unbelieving wonder into his eyes.

"I love you—I want you," he breathed, touching her damp hair tenderly.

"I can help you—now," she said, looking at his eyes, his cheeks, his mouth, as though a man's face were something totally strange.

"Thank God!" she whispered. "We can think of to-morrow now!"

Her words sent a sudden quiver through him. "To-morrow!" he cried, under his breath, in a tone that made her fling her head back to look at him.

"Remember," she said. "We are together."

"Yes," he said, like a man in a trance.

"Come to the church—to-morrow—after Sunday school," she whispered. "There will be no one there. Come about five o'clock. It will be quiet."

A sudden sound in the hall made them both turn their heads. It was the whirr of the grandfather's clock just before striking. It slowly struck the hour of eleven.

They heard the Canon's footsteps in the hall.

"Promise!" Laura whispered.

"Yes," said Tavistock.

The Canon called quietly from the hall, after the last stroke of the clock: "Laura!"

"Come in, Daddy."

She wrapped the rug more tightly around her. Tavistock stood facing the doorway, his head leaning into the air as though listening to sounds a long way off.

EIGHT

The Comforter

I

THE CANON stepped into the room, locking and unlocking his fingers nervously in front of him. He came to a standstill on the edge of the carpet. The smile he attempted broke over his face awkwardly, without in the least concealing his embarrassment, as he glanced enquiringly from one to the other.

"Where is mother?" asked Laura, to put him at ease.

"She's gone to bed," said the Canon. "You'll excuse her, Mr. Tavistock, I hope," he added, turning to their visitor with what he conceived to be the air of a host. "She is quite unlike herself."

"We are all unlike ourselves," said Laura, looking at him thoughtfully, and seeing the backwoodsman in him more definitely than ever before, in contrast with the waiting Englishman beside her.

"Your daughter was worrying about—about the accident," Tavistock said, in a manner the Canon found youthful for the first time. "That is what she wanted to talk to me about. She was disturbed—and exaggerated—this—this—but it's nothing."

How quickly he changes, Laura thought, recalling how his reticence and gloom had melted into sudden sympathy for her—his sympathy becoming infused all at once with a passionate hunger for what he had called "togetherness"—his tenderness giving place to some secret fear—and now, an unexpected, halting awkwardness, like a boy caught in mischief.

Yet in spite of these swift turns of mood, which made him almost a different person at different moments, to be reckoned with in a new way whenever he veered, she had a vivid sense of him as one man, a man who could be made whole again—his trouble healed, whatever it was—if he would only share it with somebody else.

She looked from her father up at him, feeling how little hold she had on him—how difficult it would be to make him talk of his trouble so that she could help. . . .

Her father's voice broke into these thoughts. "I'd like to ask one thing," he was saying, unlocking his fingers and putting his hands behind him.

Laura looked at Tavistock.

"If you don't mind me saying so, sir," he said, "I wouldn't—not to-night."

The Canon brought his hands from behind him. He crossed the room and touched Laura's arm. She looked at him and saw that he was no longer her father in the same way. He was a man who had brought her up and from whom she now had a secret, shared with someone else. She saw that he looked at her differently, too.

It was in a new tone that he said: "You are satisfied about it, Laura?"

She could no longer call him "Daddy." In her eyes was a mature, unsmiling tenderness that was new to him, as she said simply: "Yes."

"Are you going to bed now?" he asked. "You must be worn out."

"Yes, I'll go now," she said, and with that abrupt directness which had amused him since she was a little girl, he saw her hold out her hand to Tavistock with a sure, frank, unhesitating gesture. "Good-night," she said softly, and when he echoed it, looking at her forehead instead of into her eyes, she drew away from him with a deep breath. Turning to her father she sought in his face a new relationship that would replace the old one that was gone. Quickly she invented a new name for him.

"Good-night, dear," she said.

2

The Canon pushed a chair nearer the burnt-out fire and waved Tavistock toward it. On the mantelpiece was his pipe, and he reached for it eagerly, taking two quick steps and clattering against the fender in his haste, knowing that even the feel of the round bowl in his hand would put him at ease. Grasping it, he turned, and, finding Tavistock still standing, he nodded and gestured again at the chair, muttering, "It isn't late," as he leaned over and busied himself by elaborately knocking the ashes out of the pipe against the bars of the grate.

Tavistock sat sideways on the arm of the big chair, as though not wishing to settle himself.

"I'd like a pipe before I go to bed," the Canon said, slanting his head on one side to inspect with scrupulous care the inside of the bowl, satisfying himself that it was clean, and blowing through it toward the fireplace.

"This has been very hard on all of us," he said, looking directly at Tavistock at last. "You know, I remember when Mrs. Chesley lost her daughter—it was her only girl—drowned out there five years ago—or maybe six, perhaps. Yes, it must be six."

He took his pouch from his pocket and shook down the tobacco before opening the flap. "I had to take the funeral service, and I remember trying to enter into that woman's feelings. A widow, she was. Florence was just about Laura's age, too. But, you know, with all the will in the world, it's hard—next to impossible, isn't it?—to put yourself in somebody else's place."

The Canon looked up from his pipe, which he was energetically stuffing with tobacco, but Tavistock seemed lost in thought, his gaze fastened on the whitened ashes littering the hearth.

"Just the anxiety," the Canon went on, "was bad enough. When I started out in that boat to-night I thought she was gone. Even that much of the experience—you know, it confirms me in a favourite notion—an idea of Virgil's—you'll recall it, perhaps: *Quidquid erit, superanda omnis fortuna ferendo est.*"

"No, I don't recall it," said Tavistock, wrinkling his brows, "but—"

"Roughly, I suppose, you could translate it—'Nothing is overcome until all has been suffered,'" the Canon continued, noting Tavistock's nod of acknowledgment.

"Curious—that you should mention that," the Englishman said suddenly, slipping down into the chair and leaning forward in an attitude of intentness. "I didn't expect this," he added, with a puzzled air. "I didn't expect to be in your house. I've been avoiding people. It never occurred to me that I might get to know a clergyman out here."

The Canon paused with a lit match in his hand. "You don't mean, I hope, that you have a dislike for the clergy."

"No, no—by no means," said the other hurriedly. "I'm far from orthodox, I suppose, but that doesn't mean I dislike clergymen. I hope I didn't give you that impression—the other night—at Linklater's." He looked up and smiled thoughtfully. "I was brought up in the church."

The Canon threw away the match. "You've broken away,

have you?" he asked, without anxiety. "I thought I had seen you in church once or twice."

"Yes," said Tavistock, "I have been there."

3

The Canon sank comfortably into his favourite chair, puffing evenly at his pipe. Tavistock glanced toward the door and lowered his voice. "You can see," he said, "that your daughter has grown—has grown up, so to speak—in a few hours—because she has suffered something."

As he said this Tavistock swung his body slowly round to face the Canon, and went on in a slow, measured tone: "Do you remember—that night—the other night—we were talking about evil done innocently?"

The Canon nodded, stroking his lower lip with the curved mouthpiece of his pipe. A double grunt of assent sounded in his throat. "I don't understand it," he said slowly. "That's one of the things I wanted to talk to you about. Your ideas disturbed me—quite a bit—do you know that? I tried to write a sermon around what we were talking about that night, but—but it wouldn't come. This idea of yours about the Comforter—it doesn't come out right, somehow—I mean, I can't reconcile it—"

Tavistock hunched himself farther forward, impatiently, burning to speak. "Well," he exclaimed, his fingers gripping the arms of the chair, "this—to-night—was almost an example of it. No, not really, but—it might have been." He stopped, and suddenly slanted his head as though listening to himself. "No," he went on in an agitated way, "it wasn't really—it wasn't evil—and it wasn't—" He paused, but immediately broke out again: "You're quite right, though. She has borne something—she has overcome something by bearing it."

"What do you mean?" the Canon demanded, using his elbow to lever himself quickly upright.

Tavistock clenched his fists and struck them twice on the padded arms of the chair. "You know," he said, leaning away from the door and speaking just above a whisper, "it wasn't only death that she faced."

The little black eyes, meeting his, suddenly widened, and the squat features were drawn sharply together in a bewildered expression, but before the Canon could speak, Tavistock said: "I told her she'd better not tell you—but she'll never be able to keep it. It will be easier for her if you—if you *guess*, now."

The Canon snatched the pipe out of his mouth. "You don't mean—"

"I don't know myself exactly," Tavistock whispered, leaning close. "I don't know—just what he intended. But I saw him get up in the canoe. She was afraid. She called to me . . ." He stopped and drew his knees up under his chin, clasping them tightly.

"You were near, then," the Canon gasped, thrusting his quivering face forward as he started to rise.

"Yes."

He scrambled up and grasped the mantelpiece, his round head still jutting forward in his clerical collar as though it were awkwardly stuck on an ill-fitting body. "When he got up," he muttered, his eyes boring into the top of Tavistock's head, which was bent over his knees, "when he got up—he—he upset the canoe."

"No," said Tavistock evenly and quietly. "Laura flung herself into the water."

"God bless my soul!" Canon Macaulay said, with solemn deliberation. He paced up and down, nervously, between Tavistock and the fire. "This is terrible!"

"But it need go no further, sir," said Tavistock, following him with anxious eyes.

The Canon stopped short in the middle of the floor and stood looking at him, shaking his head absent-mindedly. "No, no, no. Oh no." His eyes gradually focused on the man sitting there in front of him. "Just—just the three of us."

"Yes."

"Tell me," the Canon said more calmly, coming back to his chair and sitting down again. "Are you interested in—in Laura?" The Canon shot it out quickly, as though he might be prevented from asking it if he gave it consideration.

"I've no right to be," said Tavistock gravely. "All this is very unexpected. That's what I meant just now. I didn't expect to be here—in your house—in your daughter's confidence. That, above all, was the furthest from my thoughts."

"That, above all . . ." the Canon repeated. "What *is* your tragedy?" he asked, with sudden directness. "It's clear you have one. Are you married?"

"No."

The Canon placed his pipe between his teeth to disguise the relief which spread over his features. "Don't answer me if you don't want to—but—but have you something on your conscience?"

"No," said Tavistock almost wearily. "No. But in a few hours . . ." He checked himself with an effort that distorted his face. "No, that's not the way to tell you." He leaned back in the chair, his fingers sliding upward over his brow and brushing through his hair. "The other night you asked me: 'Why do you grieve? Why do *you* rebel at a guilty world?' Do you remember?"

"Yes. Very well."

Tavistock dragged his fingers from under his thick hair. "*You* do not grieve," he said, in a bitter and yet reverent tone, "because you believe—in—in the Lamb of God that taketh away the sins of the world."

Canon Macaulay bowed his head as he did in church when reciting the name of Jesus.

"You believe that someone who never sinned can take away *our* sins," Tavistock added.

The Canon laid his pipe away carefully, but before he could answer, Tavistock quoted in a low, sonorous voice: "'Surely he hath borne our griefs and carried our sorrows.'"

"Yes," came in a deep whisper from the Canon.

"Can that be true of one who did not sin?" Tavistock demanded. "To bear our sorrows—to overcome them by bearing them, as you were saying just now—surely one must *experience* them—where they occur—here—in the flesh. To be overcome they must be *suffered.*"

The Canon's squat face, troubled with thought, looked almost repelling. "You think he did not bear all our sorrows," he questioned sternly.

"He did not sin."

The Canon looked at him as though he might have been a stubborn, badly behaved boy. "He was tempted, and withstood the temptation," he declared, beating emphasis into the air between them with a pointing finger.

"Ah yes, but doesn't most of *our* suffering spring from just that—from *yielding* to temptation? Isn't remorse for sin the worse suffering we have to bear? But he—!" Tavistock shrugged his shoulders and blew a deep breath through his nostrils. "He died the death of a malefactor—yes—but he was innocent! He was innocent! What did he know of the pangs of the guilty?"

4

The Canon, with a twisting smile, tried to throw off the intensity of feeling which Tavistock communicated to him. He looked deliberately at the man before him, at the outside of him, at the shape of his brow, the sweep of his long cheek and the tense line of his mouth. "You have some idea back of this," he said, with intent to put Tavistock on the defensive.

"Yes," came the ready answer. "It is this that is troubling me."

The Canon sat back. "You sound," he said, "as though you do not believe that our Lord was 'a full, perfect and sufficient sacrifice for man, once offered.'"

Tavistock looked darkly into the corner of the ceiling. "You have put your finger on it exactly. I do not. If God is greater and more merciful than I—and if *I* suffer—if *I* rebel at a guilty world—then God must suffer—God must realize—"

He stopped, but immediately went on again. "It was in Christ—wasn't it?—that God is supposed to have come down to suffer all things in our flesh? Who was it said: 'He became as we are that we might become as he is?' Yet he knew nothing of what we call guilt. I agree that if he were truly God he could not—it would not be in his nature—for there *is* no sin. But there is the *sense* of guiltiness in the world—which must be reproved—and it is for that end that the Comforter will come."

Something like a smile passed over the Canon's face as he listened with a curious, grudging admiration to Tavistock's passionate explanation, almost envying his fervour, although he felt it to be mistaken—even wilfully mistaken. It was this sense of wilfulness in the man that continually set the Canon against him. He found it difficult to believe that the man was not posing—attitudinizing—manufacturing a grievance against which his turbulent spirit could beat.

The Canon brought his feet together and looked down at the shabby, scuffed toes of his shoes.

"Of course," Tavistock said, after a brief silence, "I have been using your terminology. I've been speaking as though—in Christ—God approached man. I think, of course, that it's the other way round. In Christ man approached God—and God is made—made in *us*—by these approaches to the guiltlessness of a perfect being."

Still the Canon did not look up. This was simply twisting things upside down. He had no patience with it.

"I feel," said Tavistock, and the Canon suspected in his tone the deliberate forcing of a tremulous, hypnotic vibration, as of a man determined to conquer by the sheer exertion of his will, "I feel that another approach—will occur soon. It is almost here."

Suddenly he jumped up and looked fiercely down at the Canon. "It *is* here!" he cried. He struck his breast. "It is *here!* That is what troubles me."

Raising himself and standing half-crouched, pale and disturbed, the Canon said: "You mean that this—*this*—is *all* your trouble?"

Tavistock flung back the lock of hair that had fallen over his brow. "Yes," he whispered. "I am obsessed by this new sacrifice that is going to be made."

The Canon looked at him steadily through narrowed eyes. "But what—*what* sacrifice?" he gasped, his tongue rolling uncontrolled against his teeth.

Tavistock thrust his hands into his coat pockets and stood a moment, his thumbs pointing downward. The heat of rebellion was quenched in his eyes, and a strange, unearthly compassion renewed the tragic lines long worn in his face. "Another Christ-like man," he said humbly, "must sacrifice himself for humanity."

The Canon watched this change come over Tavistock, a change so complete that it was almost as though another soul had entered his body. The clash of their personalities had died out of the room. A deep tranquillity settled over them both, the Canon leaning against the mantelpiece, one leg twisted around the other, while Tavistock stood squarely upright, engrossed in thought.

"This belief of yours—about the Comforter," the Canon finally said in a patient, conciliatory tone, "it's your own, is it?

—I mean, you've thought it out—like this. There's no new sect that—?"

"I simply believe that he *must* come—to save the world from its sense of guilt."

"And how do you think it will be done?"

Tavistock said: "He will do what is called evil—innocently—to show his innocence of good *and* evil."

The Canon tried to smile sympathetically. His straggling moustache went up and his eyebrows came down, but the grimace that resulted was scarcely a smile. "I'm afraid I can't follow you," he said. "I can't see how evil can be done innocently."

Tavistock slowly brought his hands out of his pockets. "The lightning is innocent when it strikes," he declared, his voice sounding against all the walls of the room as his tone deepened. "Man must be like that—the pure instrument of the world's unity!"

Lifting his head, he gazed at the ceiling, alertly, intently, as though listening or waiting for something that would come down through him from above.

The Canon stiffly untwisted his legs and straightened himself. "Sturge Bundy would understand all this better than I do," he said. "He has a philosophy that amazes me, too. What are you doing to-morrow night? He often drops in after church. I believe you'll find him something of a kindred spirit. Could you come in about half-past eight to-morrow night—eh?—will you?"

Tavistock stirred and drew down his head, flashing a look over the Canon which sent a chill through his blood.

"To-morrow night," murmured Tavistock, half under his breath. "Sunday night! Yes—perhaps I shall be able to tell you something then—that I can't now."

He drew back his shoulders and moved away to the door with the air of a man leaving words alive in the room to haunt it.

3

Sunday

ONE

Laura Awakens

I

LAURA AWAKENED just as the sun was rising. She stretched herself sleepily and watched the slow infusion of colour creeping over the pale sky. A broad ray suddenly climbed to the zenith from the hidden horizon. Another crept up beside it, and across the ceiling and walls of the room floated the first rosy hint of coming glory.

These gleams of daybreak were accompanied in her drowsy mind by a distant, continuous sound, which softly encompassed her, and in which she seemed to float, unconscious of its meaning. As her eyelids fluttered open she felt that in the dream, now fading quickly, her surrender to that sound had been like the delight of lying in the sun—a surrender so complete that the tiny effort needed to lift her eyelids seemed like a formidable task.

Her body lay in the bed as she had lain in the dream, her limbs restfully composed, her head deep in the pillow, intently listening to the spell-like sound which now grew more meaningful and intimate—more curiously disturbing as it came to resemble a sound she knew—the sound of Tavistock's voice—his whisper—breathed last night against her cheek while she clung to him, astonished at the newness, the unexpectedness of love.

In her dream it had been a tender monotone in which she had caught no words, nor wanted any. It was simply around her, like the light on the walls, as though he were shining upon her. But words came, now, threading dreamily through her thoughts—words he had uttered last night—his question about Harry: "Did you care for him?"

Her eyes were wide open now, staring at the ceiling, after a quick glance about the room—taking in the knobbed wooden posts at the foot of her bed, the wash-stand, the jug and basin and soap-dish ringed with blue, the dressing-table with its china trays, the picture of "Jesus among the Doctors in the Temple," and her clothes hanging tidily over the back of a chair. Her quick glance, after running over everything, fastened again on the blankness of the ceiling, where her eyes could rest while her memories circled on.

"Did you care for him?" It had caught her unawares. She remembered that she had been thinking of Harry, living over again what had occurred in the canoe, and feeling she might have stopped him with a look, a word, a cry for help. She might have stopped him without throwing herself over the side. There was nothing masterful about him. Whenever they had been together she had felt herself the stronger of the two.

No—she could have stopped him—by the mere exertion of her will, by forcing into her voice the confidence she always had in being able to take care of herself. She could have stopped him by simply uttering his name in a tone that would have chilled him. But she had wanted to be speedily out of his way, out of his reach.

She might have stopped him, but the thought of sitting there afterward, silent, or wrangling, while he took her back to shore, had seemed more than she could endure. The thought of him walking home beside her in the dark, sulking, or taunting her, had been unbearable.

2

The night before she had discovered something. She had learned what it might be like to fall in love. It was new to her, and it made Harry's outburst even more detestable. The discovery had come with the force of a revelation, because no one had ever given her a hint of it. The boys and men she had met had sometimes talked of love in a sly, frivolous way, as though it were a prank; or sentimentally, with an effusive, flattering extravagance that was wholly unreal; or else as Harry had done, making it merely a matter of heated blood.

But in Linklater's shack, looking up at Tavistock, she had sensed what love might be like. If it happened to her it would give her life a purpose stronger than any that had ever swayed her. There would never be enough moments—enough life—in which to give all one would want to give.

She had become aware of all that, and had even felt that Tavistock had made the discovery with her. They were sharing the same thoughts, she felt, for how could she have surrendered herself so completely to that revelation unless on his side there had been some response.

To go out of that house and get back into the canoe with Harry had been distasteful enough, even though she was hardly conscious of him. But it was an even worse ordeal to go on the lake with him again the following night, after she had dreamed all day of what had happened at Linklater's. He had made it doubly hard for her by sulking from the outset. They had quarrelled in a way she had hoped to avoid, and finally, in a sort of desperation, he had talked wildly of how grudging and cold she was. In a sudden panic she had cried out that she wouldn't listen to him, that he must turn back and take her home.

"You *will* listen to me," he had answered threateningly. "You're out here and you're going to stay out here till you've heard what

I've got to say. You're going to hear a lot, young lady. I'm going to knock some of this damned prudishness out of you, if I never do another thing."

The words rang again in her ears with a distinctness that made her shudder. Somehow she stopped the sound of his voice in her mind. But the picture of him suddenly getting up, grasping at her ankles as he leaned over her, was not so easily banished.

She might have stopped him—even then. But she wanted him to know that she would take any consequences rather than submit to his talk. And it was all complicated by the knowledge that Tavistock was only a stone's throw away, drifting behind them in the dark. He was following them—drawn by something in her as she was drawn by something in him. She wanted to take the quickest means of getting to him or of bringing him to her side. And the quickest way would be to throw herself in the water. He would come, then, and take them both into his boat and row them back. He would be there to prevent Harry from talking.

3

All this had passed through her mind very quickly—and she did it quickly, in an instant, kicking her ankles free of Harry's grasp, and rolling over sideways out of the canoe. She raised her voice in a loud cry to Tavistock before her head went under, grasping the side of the tipping canoe with both hands as she went.

As soon as the water rushed together over her head, roaring in her ears, she realized that Harry was half-standing and would be thrown farther away from the canoe. She remembered, suddenly, that he couldn't swim. A gasping moment of horror shook her as she came up, her body scraping against the canoe as it leapt like a cork, upside down, out of the water.

Clinging to it, she frantically turned her head and saw Tavistock in the half-light rowing toward them, each violent stroke of his oars sending the prow of the boat clear of the water.

Taking a fresh hold on the slippery bottom of the canoe she flung an anxious glance over the water, but there was no sign of Harry. Farther away—much farther than she had expected—there was a movement under the surface, and suddenly his hand came up—one hand—the fingers clutching at the air for half a second, and sinking again, limply, forlornly, as though the wrist were broken. He was beating about blindly under the water.

Would he come up, breathe, and then go down again? Didn't they go down three times? She knew almost nothing about it. There was the hand again, weakly groping—but not his head. Would he, perhaps, never come up at all?

She let go her hold and plunged in Harry's direction. Her soaked skirts clung to her legs. She found she couldn't kick out. Her arms threshed the water helplessly. Tavistock, now only a few yards away, shouted at her to turn back and hang on. She went under, but struggled up again, panting, flinging herself around toward the canoe.

Tavistock's boat shot through the water beside her, and he, ready, his oars shipped, his feet braced in the thwart, leaned over and grasped her shoulders. The impact swung the boat around and almost threw him out, but he flung his weight backward just in time, slipped his hold under her arms, and raised her waist-high out of the water.

Was it the relief of his arms about her, lifting her into safety—or was it mostly the joy of his nearness? She had only a moment or two to clutch at him, her head crushed against his shoulder as she tried to drag one leg over the stern of the boat. Her skirt, like a soaked rag about her knees, prevented her, but Tavistock, raising himself with a quick, powerful twist, flung her clear of the thwart. Her feet struck the bottom of the boat and she rolled over in his arms, a rush of words pouring from her—thanking him and asking about Harry in the same breath.

She could feel his gentleness even in the hurried way he sat her down, hoarsely directing her to row after him to the spot where she had last seen Harry struggling. Before she knew it he was over the side, swimming under water, and as she grasped the oars and dipped them weakly forward, she watched his dark head plunging down.

She sat there, while he dived again and again. Shaking with cold and fear she watched his head come up and go down again, his back arching out of the water as he gathered impetus for the downward plunge.

She called to him to be careful. She was afraid Harry might grab him and drag the two of them down. She called to him each time he came up, growing more frantic each time, and finally screaming at him to come back. He didn't hear her at first, and when he did he couldn't make out what she said.

"It's no use!" she cried. "Let's go for help."

He trod water and called back to her. "Shout!" he gasped, and went under again.

She began to shout—"Help! Help!"—her eyes wildly scanning the shore, where lights were beginning to twinkle through the willows that lined the bank.

Pulling the boat close to where Tavistock had last gone down, she waited for him to come up and begged him to rest a minute, holding an oar out for him to grasp. He came to the side and hung on to an oarlock for a moment or two, looking up into her frenzied eyes.

"I can't find him," he panted. "I can't see a sign of him."

They looked at each other fixedly, their faces twitching, their open mouths gulping quick breaths.

"Someone's coming," she cried.

She had seen a boat with a lantern in it push out from the shore.

While she was looking away he let go the side and went under again. It gave her a start to find him gone, and her heart began pounding furiously. There was no light left in the sky, and the water looked cruelly black. She was afraid—afraid, now, that something would happen to Tavistock. Her fear was more chilling than the wet clothes clinging to her flesh. She drifted into a sort of stupor. Her head slipped slowly forward and wet strands of hair fell over her eyes. When Eggertson and the other man arrived she was sitting there, staring down at the water washing back and forth over her ankles in the bottom of the boat.

4

The whole picture and all her thoughts about it at the time circled through her mind again—each incident moving more slowly than when it had occurred, as she went back over it, examining it, probing her selfishness, and blaming herself again and again. But gradually the yearning, the response to Tavistock, drove out the darker pictures and severer thoughts. Her memories of him in the water and in the boat again, rowing back, became mingled with what had happened later while they were driving home and when he came into the study and they were left alone together. His sorrow and his tenderness took possession of her.

As the sunlight slowly warmed the room she slid her limbs into an easier posture, turned her body toward the window and rested her cheek on her elbow, her eyelids drooping as she picked out of all that had happened the sweetest moments.

That there could be an emotion more absorbing, more poignant, than the tempests of feeling which music had aroused in her seemed unbelievable. Music had previously carried her to what she had thought were the peaks of experience. At times the invincible, upward march of tragic chords, storming her heart, had left her breathless. The final resolution had somehow emptied her. But this new emotion filled her. The assault of love clamoured in her pulses. Lying awake, last night, she had listened to its beat, until her eyes, roving in the dark, grew heavy, and the new, slow rhythm of her breath lulled her to sleep.

Now, in broad daylight, it surprised her more than ever to feel again this tremulous tingling, like tiny bells ringing rapturously through her body.

She began to imagine his eyes—his voice—when they should be again alone—and a sudden curiosity as to what she must look like to him made her sit up quickly in the bed, craning her neck to see herself in the mirror of the dressing-table. She flung off the bed-clothes impatiently, grasped the foot-post and hoisted herself into view. But she was too far away. Dropping her feet to the floor, she hurried to the mirror and held her face close up to it. Her nose—the Howland nose—was too prominent. Her eyes, like her father's, slanted a little upward toward the temples. Her upper lip was too thin and the lower lip too thick, and there was the funny cleft in her chin. But her eyes, meeting their reflection in the mirror as she scrutinized each feature, surprised her by their brightness. She was plain; but it didn't matter. He loved her. He had said: "I love you."

Watching the slow wrinkling of her chin and the flutter of her lashes as her face broke into a smile, she flung herself shamefacedly away from the glass, and stood looking down at her toes, thrust out from under her nightgown as she leaned back against the dresser.

TWO

Struggle

I

TAVISTOCK ROSE LATE, after lying awake most of the night. Through the open window, as he dressed himself, the church bells could be heard ringing for the morning service. Nearest and loudest was the little bell of St. Stephen's, which he could see, over the stable roof, tossing briskly to and fro under a tiny cupola. Each stroke of the swinging clapper shook the room and left a murmurous hum clinging to the walls.

He went down to breakfast, startling the day-clerk at the desk, who suddenly saw his haggard face over the banister as he descended the stairs. The hotel was quiet on a Sunday morning, and the thud of his step across the tiled rotunda rattled emptily against the windows.

He ate sparingly and in silence, and returned immediately to his room. Flinging his valise on the tumbled bed he turned out its contents in a heap. From the litter of soiled, crumpled clothes he separated the few papers and letters that had accumulated during the last little while. There was a black leather writing-case containing a few documents and clippings which he had preserved much longer. He took these out and folded all the papers together so that they would go into his breast-pocket. He intended to go out somewhere and burn them.

It occurred to him that he would make a sort of ritual of it. He would go far out of the town and find a spot where he would be out of sight of everyone, on the bare prairie, where there were no farm-houses within miles. Under the lonely sky he would make a little fire and watch the ashes of these few mementoes blowing far away over the withered grass. He felt in his jacket to make sure he had matches in his pocket.

"I've been dreaming all night," he said to himself, as he stood there planning this last day—the day he had been dreading.

All night long his mother's face—and Laura's—had been queerly mixed in his dreams—Laura's face as she had looked when the Canon stepped awkwardly into the boat and almost fell into the seat beside her, staring blindly at her through sudden tears and stroking her wet, tangled hair—Laura's face, shuddering at death—and his mother's face, as she lay dying, with the others, the older ones, around her, and the bishop, his uncle, breathing noisily in the still room. He had dreamed again how Gladys had come to wake him, calling to him in the middle of the night: "Geoffrey!—Geoffrey!—You're to come and say good-bye to mamma."

His father gone—it seemed so short a while!—and now to go in and stand solemnly in that room again, with all their eyes on him, so that even his chin mustn't quiver—feeling her wasted fingers clinging in his hair as she kissed him—and to say good-bye to her in a steady voice as though she were going to sleep. He had kept his head up—they expected it of him!—and had gone out with Gladys's arm around his shoulder, his eyes staring, his heart like ice.

The Maunders were used to freezing their feelings, even in secret; looking at life fixedly, belligerently, as though they said: "We'll stare you out!" He had their cold blood in him, he knew;

but it was to the Tavistocks that he really belonged. As a child they had said he had his father's eyes—those eyes he could just remember!—kindling easily, either in tenderness or anger, so that people loved and feared him at once, and leaned on his strength, even when it bruised them.

He had needed both—the cold fixity of the Maunders, and the passionate tenacity of the Tavistocks—to become as he was, a man driven by an all-absorbing aim.

The sense of destiny, strong in him since boyhood, had been tremendously heightened in the past few days. All these bewildering hints—these moments of exaltation—they had been *sent*, he supposed, to prepare him. And Laura!—she, too, had been sent. He had seen her suffering—blaming herself—believing herself half guilty of that fellow's death. That very sense of guilt which he had sworn to root out of human consciousness!—he had seen her bowed with it, sitting there dazed, sobbing, wringing her hands.

He had wrestled all night. He wanted to live. In all his past arguments with himself his own life had not been the issue. Horror of the act he must commit and pity for his victim had been warring for years against the miracle which hovered over his head, ready to strike. But, last night, at the same moment that his own life roused itself, hungering for love, he saw that Death had joined with Destiny against him.

If it had not been for Death he would never have known this "togetherness" which he and Laura had experienced. Death had kindled it with grim mockery within a few hours of parting them for ever. Death, slowly creeping into the veins of old Linklater, had brought them both in pity to the crumbling shack. Death, again, the following night, lurking under the water, had flung them together. Death, tainting her with guilt, was urging him now to perform his miracle of innocence. Death—always stalking him. Death turning his pity for humanity into a task that must employ Death. Death—always at his elbow. And to-day, before he slept again—if he should ever sleep again—he would confront Death and "stare him out."

Now, with this hunger, this new warmth in his blood, he could see that his long-held idea belonged to the cold Maunders, after all. His aim was to stare out Death and Evil and prove that there could be *nothing* evil. And yet it was Death itself—Evil itself—that seemed to be driving him. What he had thought was Destiny was the twisting flaw of Death running through his life. He could see it now, widening into a chasm that would engulf him.

2

He suddenly flung himself down on his knees and buried his face in the crumpled quilt at the foot of the bed. He wanted to live. Laura's face, the weight of her in his arms, her tense fingers clinging to his shoulder, her voice, her smile, her love!—all night he had tried to doubt it, but it had flooded him afresh with the first ray of dawn—he couldn't forget her!—he couldn't give her up!

But one of the thousand voices in his mind that he was accustomed to, came to his comfort. The voice became his, saying to himself: "There is neither Time nor Death! Everything is immortal! She and I are immortal. Whatever happens to *me* cannot part us. I have felt 'togetherness' at last—and that is the secret—the answer! That is what life is for—that we have fellowship one with another—that *we may be made perfect in one!*"

But the voice—whether it was his own, or an angel's—did not satisfy him. He began to pray: "O God, I have waited patiently for the miracle all these years, believing I was on the side of

Life—on the side of Mercy—and Love—but it is Death, now, that is standing over me—and I want to live. I can't give her up."

He tore his hands from his eyes and glared across the room. A sterner voice was speaking, as though from behind his shoulder: "Yes!—because you love her—you would give it up! You!—who called yourself the Comforter—a greater Christ—you'd give it all up—on this last day—because a woman has smiled at you—because you want . . ."

"God in heaven!" groaned his own voice inside him as he jumped up and stood transfixed by the conflicting emotions warring in his mind. He remained motionless a long time, his head sunk on his breast. His fingers, tightly locked behind his back, began slowly to writhe. He put Laura out of his thoughts, and the old struggle, pursued in loneliness all these years, the old struggle of his horror and his pity against the mercilessness of his "idea," clashed again with greater vehemence.

As so often before, he saw again, even more clearly, that love alone—pity alone—could never have implanted this awful aim in his mind. The aim had needed a man just like himself. All this was also his destiny—to have been born as he was, to have suffered as he had, to have rebelled and denied, pitting his ego against the profundity of life—"staring it out," as he had often said—and determining that he, alone, by the pitiful, flickering passion of his revolt—could somehow shame a heartless God into a miracle of mercy!

All around him sounded nightmare voices as his mind opened downward, deeper and deeper, into a chaos of thought. He reeled for a moment on the edge of a precipice and experienced the frightful nausea of falling—falling for ever.

3

He grasped blindly at the bedpost and sank down in a sitting posture on the edge of the bed. He conquered the horror of falling in his mind, and slowly there came back to him the hours when his destiny had seemed really Christ-like—hours when a burden of sorrow—the whole world's sorrow—had crushed him under its staggering weight.

He was a man sent from God—and he knew it—had always known it. It was only when he forced himself to think of murder, in cold blood, that his whole nature revolted. All he had to do was to stop thinking and surrender himself to the miracle. Once he stopped thinking—once he was utterly selfless—the miracle of innocence would make him its instrument; and though, in his mind, it had the appearance of murder—now—it would be transfigured, he knew it would, in the moment of achievement. In a mysterious way, that he could not understand or predict, but in something like the way that Christ's crucifixion had become the symbol of atonement, this act of his would become the symbol of guiltlessness.

This was his destiny, and like Christ he had been forced to suffer in his flesh and in his mind the pain and bewilderment of a man who slowly discovers a god coming to excruciating birth within himself. It was his destiny to suffer these pangs—these throes of the superhuman driving out the human. It had been *meant* that he should live in isolation—loving no one, possessing nothing, clinging to nothing—so that he would be empty of all resolve, innocent of desire, and free to obey—*to obey whom?*

But the questioning voice needed no answer. His heart was filled with the fervour that had always answered his doubts.

What does it matter whether God sends down his Son from a heaven beyond the world, or whether he ascends through the world in Son after Son for ever? It is God—the unity of all—that drives or draws us—descends into us—or ascends out of us! On Jacob's ladder the angels ascended and descended. Whether ascending or descending—or both together—all in one—it is all God's will. There can be no other will.

Tavistock opened his eyes and saw sunlight in a golden patch on the floor in front of him—a brightness beyond understanding. He bowed his head and murmured: "Thy will be done."

THREE

Surrender

I

LATE IN THE AFTERNOON Tavistock turned along Charlotte Street from the lake road, walking slowly, his head bent. He passed the rectory without looking up, and stood a moment, hesitating, in front of the church.

It was an hour when there were few people on the streets. The usual week-day noises were hushed, so that the town seemed asleep—motionless and quiet in a serenity of pouring sunshine. The walls of buildings stood so perpendicularly still, the shadows lay so solidly on the ground, and each blade of grass pointed so erectly upright, that the whole neighbourhood felt becalmed, as though under the breathless suspension of a spell.

Tavistock went up to the little porch, his tread on the wooden steps echoing back at him from every nearby fence. The blistered door flung a wave of heat over him as he lifted the latch, but inside it was cool, and he paused again.

All day long he had kept himself from thinking. He had gone about like a person in a dream who questions nothing that he sees. In the morning he had succeeded in silencing his mind. His will was numbed. In a mood of resignation he had started out, going down to the boathouse, and across the lake in his boat. On the other side of the lake, in a great stretch of unturned, barren prairie there was a rock he had seen many times, all by itself—a huge slab, like a lonely altar, rising out of the earth. There were no other rocks anywhere in the neighbourhood, and more than once he had puzzled as to how it had come there. He had gone back to it, drawn by its loneliness, and sitting down on a ledge, with his back to the sun, he surveyed the immensity of isolation around him. Toward the west the bare prairie stretched to the horizon. On the north and east a fringe of yellowing bush glimmered against the sky. Southward a single field of wheat shone in the distance, and one house, in all that panorama, stood half-concealed in a poplar bluff, miles away. Colossal white clouds were banked all around him like mountains, their summits dazzlingly bright; and above him, the vast sky trembled with heat.

He sat there, scarcely moving, for an hour, keeping his senses continuously alert, watching every nearby movement in the grass, or following the slow drift of a majestic cloud swinging behind the rest and dissolving in the farthest light. His concentration on these barely perceptible changes in the scene kept his mind closed and still.

He became as immovable as the stone on which he sat, and all sense of separateness from anything on earth was swallowed up in the feeling that the day flowed through him as it did through the clouds and the grass.

After a long while he roused himself and took the sheaf of old papers from his pocket and burned them on top of the rock. The flame soon sank to a smoulder. The ashes smoked a while and crumbled into dust. There was not enough wind to blow them out of the hollow in the rock.

Tavistock resisted the temptation to scatter the lifeless, grey powder with a puff of his breath. He submitted to the will which held it, faintly stirring, in the shallow bowl of the rock. He had relinquished all desire to do or to be other than the day and the coming miracle should dictate.

He turned back to the lake, to where he had pulled up his boat among the blueberry bushes. There was a muddy creek there which ran up behind the Indian village. Through the poplars he could see three fat squaws bending in the underbrush, gathering berries. The air was so still that he could hear the berries dropping into their pails.

Crossing the lake again, he had gone into Linklater's, and was shocked to find the old man in bed, peering crazily at him as he came in, without a sign of recognition. The pallor of his brow was ghastly, as though his bony head were illuminated by an unearthly light from within. He moved his lips two or three times, but was unable to speak.

Tavistock sat down beside him and touched him. He, too, tried to speak, but there seemed to be no will left in him. He sat there, stroking the threadbare sleeve of the sweater Linklater had put on over his shirt.

The old man presently fell into a doze. Tavistock could see his eyes rolling under the closed lids. He was dreaming and his lips moved every now and then in a faint whisper. Bending over him, Tavistock caught the sense of a refrain. The old man was humming a familiar melody. His eyes slowly opened and his voice grew stronger, so that a few words became audible:

"... lift up the fallen,
Tell them of Jesus, the mighty to save.
Rescue the perishing, care for the dying,
Jesus is merciful, Jesus will save."

Tavistock sat there until the glazed eyes again rolled upward under the lids, and the old man fell asleep.

The children were nowhere to be seen. Julie must be taking care of them, Tavistock thought, and rising quietly, he went out on tiptoe. His calm was shattered by concern for the old man and the children.

As he strode rapidly along the lake road to Julie's place his face became clouded with anxiety and his heart began aching again—the deep, splitting ache he had suffered so long. But when he came to her door he could hardly speak to Julie.

The children ran to the screen before her and pressed their noses soberly against it, regarding him with curiosity, as though their grandfather's collapse had caused them to see strangeness in everyone. Julie waddled laboriously across the floor behind them, puffing out a volley of words as she came, explaining everything and saying she would go back and sit with old Dave as soon as she had made a meal for the children.

Tavistock could express nothing of what he felt. The numbness that had come over him stopped his tongue, so that he answered her with "yes" and "no" or with deep noises in his throat, hoarse with sympathy. Finally he took from his pocket all the money he had and gave it to her, saying he might not see her again, but to do what she could. He held open the screen door and patted the children's heads, silently, with an attempt at a smile. Then, with an understanding nod at Julie, he went down the path, returned to his boat and took it back to Eggertson's.

He asked old Dan how much he owed him, meaning to settle the acount, but when he felt his empty pocket he stood a moment, nodding absent-mindedly, and explained to the old boatman that he would look after it some other time. He seemed annoyed at not being able to settle with him, and strode abruptly away.

Half-way up the bank he turned, looked back at old Dan, and suddenly raised his hand. The Icelander, surprised by the gesture, took his pipe out of his mouth and waved it. Long after

Tavistock had disappeared down the road under the arch the willows made, old Dan stood gazing after him, shaking his shaggy head slowly from side to side.

2

Inside the porch it was cool and he stood a moment, hesitating, with his hand on the red-baize door. No sound came from the church. He pushed gently, while his head was still bent in a listening attitude. Raising his eyes slowly he saw Laura, only a few feet away, in one of the back pews, kneeling, her folded hands against her eyes.

He went in and trod carefully along the side-aisle. The matting deadened the sound of his steps. Beams of dusty light were falling aslant the pews from the south windows. Beyond them the tiny chancel looked dim and separate.

Tavistock stepped into the pew where Laura was kneeling. She looked up with that hushed, absent glance of one who has been praying. He knelt down beside her, resting his knees on a thick hassock, and let his head sink into his hands.

She was wearing a straw hat trimmed at the side with a large flower. The full sleeves of a blue silk dress billowed outward from her small, slanting shoulders. She was almost a stranger, but through one long night—last night—he had loved her. He could love her now. He could turn, now, and face her, and sweep the numbness from his brain, and take her white hands . . . and tell her. . . .

But the miracle, hovering so close that his head had seemed all day to be moving separately, above his body, in a sphere of mystery—giving him a sensation of lightness, of floating!—the miracle, hovering so close, drew him up from the pew, away from her, to a great height. And a voice that was not so much as a breath said to him: "What have you to do with her?"

In the same instant he felt her moving beside him. She was getting up from her knees and settling back in the pew. She was looking at him. He could feel her glance—and his heart responding to it. In the perfect silence of the church he could hear her breathing.

He turned and looked at her, intently, eagerly, and found an unspeakable tenderness in her eyes, which he knew would be there, but which rocked him as though a storm had suddenly surged into an enormous swell under him, flinging him toward her. A quick breath helped him to hold himself still. She wrenched her glance away and bent her head slowly, as though in obeisance to some overpowering presence. A gold cross, pressed in the cover of a Prayer Book on the book-rest in front of her, held her gaze. She felt for his hand on the cushion beside her and curled her fingers softly over his tightened knuckles.

"Tell me—now," she said simply, as though nothing else had been in her mind since she had left him the night before.

When he did not speak she looked up under the drooping brim of the hat, lifting her head to the level of his high shoulder. The green-grey pupils of his eyes held two tiny pictures of her, extraordinarily sharp and vivid. But she saw the reflection only for a second. His deep, hungering desire for her overwhelmed her senses, bursting the too-narrow gateways of sight and touch, and reaching her somehow in its wholeness, so that she felt encompassed—trembling from head to foot—in a strength she had never suspected.

His voice, strangely remote from the force that burned in his eyes, sounded above her as though muffled by the throbbing of her blood.

"You are the last person in the world I want to tell," he was saying. "When I am with you I want to forget it—I want to live."

"Oh, you *will* live!" she declared imperiously.

He leaned so close to her that she could feel his breath against her cheek. "I *want* to live," he said. "I want—to love you."

She turned and faced him, her lips parted, her moist eyes seeking his. She felt both her hands swiftly caught up. "Could you love me, Laura?" he begged awkwardly, as though strange to the ways of love.

An ache that engulfed him and herself in a closed moment, took her breath. She felt herself toppling into a flood that would be merciless, and tore one hand from his grasp to steady herself, her fingers clutching his shoulder.

"Could you?" he said again.

"I do," came quiveringly from a parched throat that seemed no longer hers.

He was plainly astounded. Dropping her hands, he grasped both her shoulders and held her away from him, searching her eyes with an intensity which a minute before would have set her shuddering. But now she could bear it, and even challenged him, by the steadiness of her upward, burning glance, to look deeper and as long as he would, until there could be no doubt in his mind that she meant it with all her heart.

"How can you know so soon?" he asked her incredulously.

Her face crumpled suddenly, like her father's, into a curiously quaint and uncontrolled smile. It was a grimace so tender that his anxiety vanished. He leaned forward, driven to kiss her. She closed her eyes and her whole body seemed to melt as their lips joined and clung quiveringly together.

"I have loved you a long time," he said presently.

"How long?" she asked.

She knew, as he sat there, looking at her hungrily, that he was remembering all the occasions—many, perhaps, that she knew nothing about when, from a distance, he had watched her, here in the church, or out on the lake—with Harry. With Harry! The thought of his body there on the wharf as she had last seen it, with half the town crowding the bank, watching her—the thought of herself fainting—the thought of *him*—this man who loved her—being always, until last night, a distant onlooker, unknown to her, while Harry had been about with her so much . . . all these thoughts flew through her head in the instant between her question and his answer:

"A long time—months—at least," he said. "It was here in the church. You stepped out of the pew into the aisle. Your mother was with you, but I didn't see her till afterwards. We came out into the aisle at the same time—facing each other—and you looked directly at me. You had just got up from praying and your face—" He paused and looked slowly at her from brow to chin. "But how can you love *me*?" he asked, the lines in his face deepening with gravity again.

"Why not?" she demanded, genuinely astonished.

"When did you see me first?" he said.

"Weeks ago," she answered, her eyes fixed on vacancy. "It was on the lake. We passed you in the canoe. It was nearly dark, but your face was toward the light—you were sitting quite still in the boat—thinking—or praying, perhaps—oblivious of everything, anyway. Even that first time I knew you had some trouble worrying you. You looked so sad—so isolated! We passed quite close to you and I remember—I remember feeling that I wanted to touch you or speak to you—to bring you out of your misery. And after that I recognized you over and over again—as the same man—always so sad. And I used to wonder what your trouble could be."

He closed his eyes.

"You won't grieve any more," she whispered, impulsively pressing his hand.

He looked at her again, with a gleam of hope in his glance. "When did you know you loved me?" he asked her urgently.

"Last night," she declared. "Last night—when you lifted me into the boat. I was exhausted—almost frantic. You held me—

do you remember?—do you remember when I looked at you?"

"I shall never forget."

"At first I was only thanking you—but—before I could close my eyes—so that you wouldn't see—I—I was loving you."

"Laura!" he murmured, looking down at her hands.

"And then you put me down in the boat," she went on, more excitedly, "and started diving—for *him*. I was afraid all the time you would find him—and he might grab you—and drag you down."

She shuddered and her head sank on her breast, but only for a moment. Raising her chin she looked through the oblique beams of light between her and the chancel, her eyes dwelling on the words—"Holy, Holy, Holy"—written above the altar. "Fancy," she said, in a dreamy voice, "fancy facing death so suddenly—and then—even more suddenly—*beginning to live!*"

"That is just what I felt," he said tenderly, "when you looked at me that first time. But while I was diving—while I was actually under the water—groping about in those weeds—I wondered what sort of fool I was. I thought—after all, your look *was* only thanking me."

"But you looked at me again, on the way home," she said, "under one of the lights."

"Yes."

"And wasn't it the same?"

He nodded his head slowly without taking his eyes from her face.

"So you knew, then," she declared, tilting her head back to look directly at him.

"No. I didn't know." He picked up her hand and looked at her long, pointed fingers lying across his brown palm. "I still thought that perhaps your eyes—" He stopped and shook his head, almost in agony, as though her eyes had wounded him.

A slow smile curved her lips, and her white fingers crushed

his hand. "But now," she whispered breathlessly, "you believe—*now*—don't you?"

"Yes," he said, with a sudden chill in his voice. "But—I shouldn't have let myself . . . or you . . ."

She stopped him with a sudden cry. "You haven't said a word about—what is troubling you. That is what we came for. Tell me—tell me, now!"

3

She sat away from him and looked at him, realizing how strange he really was to her—how much of his life had been lived apart from her, in countries unfamiliar to her, and among people she would never meet. She saw his face, suddenly saddened, and almost aghast with the recurrence in his mind of the anxiety she had seen so often there before.

"What did you mean, last night, about 'preparing to die'?"

He did not answer immediately. He thrust his legs out beyond the hassock under the next pew, and bent his head deliberately.

"I was talking in riddles," he said slowly, without looking at her. And then, with an attempt at a lighter tone: "It's a bad habit of mine."

"You mean," she said, touching his sleeve eagerly, "that it was—a sort of figure of speech?"

He hesitated again, looked fixedly at his stretched legs, and muttered: "What did I say last night?" But he swung quickly toward her before she could answer. "I was excited," he said. "The excitement—the accident—and the hope that you would love me. It was like—oh!—it was like a way back to life." He took her hands anxiously. "What do you remember that I said?"

She was puzzled and bitterly disappointed by his manner. Her voice trembled. "You said something about a crisis—in both our lives. And something you had to bear—in the future. I couldn't understand you. I thought—at one time—I began to wonder if you were trying—after all—not to love me. I wondered if there was some—some reason—"

She stopped, seeing his face go suddenly pale, and grasped his arm, clinging to him as though afraid he might leave her without another word. He turned a tortured glance on her and closed his eyes. In a whisper he said: "I must tell you—at least *this*." He opened his eyes again and looked at her forlornly. "There is no *reason*," he said, "no *ordinary* reason why I shouldn't love you."

These words puzzled her still more. He could see her anxiety and bewilderment deepening into fear, and yet he seemed unable to say anything that would comfort her. She had stirred him so deeply that his numbed will had failed him. He had let her see how much he desired her.

"I am human—all too human!" he said to himself.

He began to accuse himself of weakening—touching her—kissing her—so that it would be impossible—hateful—to leave her and let her hear—to-morrow—that he was . . . ! But he couldn't frame the word—even in his mind.

"Did I do it purposely?" he asked himself.

And a voice clamoured: "Yes—yes—yes!"

"Yes!" his own soul echoed. "I wanted another excuse—the hundredth excuse—for giving it all up. A good one, too. How can I leave her, now? I should have come—humbly—ashamed of my weakness last night. I should have told her at once that I have no right to love her. I haven't any right. Whether I succeed or fail, it's all the same. If I give it up—I shall never be content. The failure to be what I hoped will haunt me all my life."

He felt a presence, as of angels, all about him, and he began complaining to them, asking them why they had offered him this destiny. The presences seemed to leave him, but he went on complaining, even more bitterly, to himself.

"If Christ had borne, once for all, all sufferings—I shouldn't have this to bear."

Laura stirred beside him, as though she were shivering.

"Yes," he cried, almost aloud, "yes—and now I must give her up. Something more that Christ never suffered. He never had to give up a woman."

He suddenly looked down at her, fiercely. He had declared himself to her, and now he would have to leave her—leave her wounded, after pitilessly awaking her love.

"And when she learns," he thought, rolling his eyes away from her white, shocked face, "when she learns what I intend to do—what I have *done*—it will scar her life! It's as good as killing her. It's another murder. I am guilty already. Who am I to prove to the world there can be no guilt? I am guilty already. I have tortured her. Why, I am not even a decent man—let alone a god! I have nothing godlike in me. They have chosen the wrong man. I have sinned and am not worthy of the miracle. Pass on, angels. Find a purer heart somewhere else."

4

When he had made this declaration his heart seemed lightened, and he took Laura's hand very tenderly in his own. He still did not look at her, but she could see that he was no longer staring.

"I have no right to love you—to ask your love," he said. "Almost all my life I have been dedicated to a single idea—an ambition. It is too great for me to achieve. I know that now. I have failed already."

He looked at her and smiled in a way she had never seen before.

"I am a failure," he added, the muscles of his face sinking through sheer weariness into his habitual haunted expression.

"You must have nothing to do with me. You must forget me. Go home, now, and pray—to the God you believe in—for a lost soul."

Laura peered up at him through a mist of tears.

"Whatever you have done," she said brokenly, "or failed to do—whatever *happens*—surely it can all be right—as long as you love me—if you *do* love me. As long as I cling to you—what can happen?—except—death!"

As she uttered the word a sudden horror grew in her eyes.

He regarded her sternly and said: "I must give it up—this death—or it will kill us both."

"Oh, why don't you tell me?" she begged.

"Perhaps, when I am gone," he said, "I will write and tell you about it. You will perhaps be the only one who will understand me. In twenty centuries only one man has conceived this idea—and if I fail—but I have—I have failed already. It won't come again perhaps for years—for centuries. Do you see? I have had this chance—and I haven't been true to the highest I know. I couldn't stay here and look you in the face. How can I look in anyone's face?"

"Oh, look in mine," she pleaded. "I know something about it."

"What?" he cried.

"My father told me to-day about his talks with you," she said, brushing the moisture from her eyes. "And from what you have told me—from the way you look—I can guess—it's something—some sacrifice for humanity. Isn't it? But I can't believe in it—even though I don't know what it is. It's wrong—I'm sure it is—or it wouldn't worry you so. If you really loved me you wouldn't let it—you would give it up."

He took her hand from his shoulder and suddenly stood up.

"If you never see me again," he said, "remember that I am not a man."

She stood up beside him and looked into his face, half-patiently, half-defiantly.

"Even Christ was a man," she said.

"Yes," he cried, grasping the rail of the pew until his knuckles went white. "Yes—but he never loved a woman."

He turned away from her and took a step toward the aisle.

Laura stood her ground and whispered through the space between them: "No. Poor Christ! But *you* do!"

He swung round as though he had been struck, and stared at her in amazement. He could find nothing to say, but he stood there staring.

"Promise me you'll come—once more—if only once," she said, "to our house to-night—after the service. Come and talk to my father—if you won't talk to me. Promise me—for the sake of what has happened—and because—because—God help us both —I love you."

The last words were choked with sobs. Her hands flew to her face to hide the tears pouring down her cheeks, and she sank down, bowing her shaking head over her knees.

He groped along the pew toward her like a blind man, his eyes fixed in a daze of grief. His outstretched arm encountered her shoulder, and he dropped on the cushion beside her, embracing her so that her head rested on his breast. His lower lip was quivering like a boy's who has been made to feel ashamed. He could say nothing, but he lifted her face in his two hands and kissed her wet cheeks again and again, tasting the salt of her tears.

FOUR

Love

I

AFTER THE evening service Laura walked back to the rectory alone across the dark grass. Her mother had gone to bed immediately after their early supper. She had a splitting headache, she said, and allowed Laura to fuss at her bedside until she was comfortable.

"I wonder you want to go—after all that has happened," she said to Laura, thinking that people all over town would know about the drowning, and would be eyeing her all through the service.

"I'll stay if you want me, mother," Laura said, sitting down on the bed beside her.

"No, no—it's not for me. I was thinking of you, dear," said Mrs. Macaulay, stroking her cold hand.

But Laura felt that she needed more than ever the consolation of the service, and a renewal of the mood which sometimes came to her on her knees while the choir chanted the responses or her father intoned the words of familiar prayers.

This last year or two she had lived a secluded life, seeing very few people except her pupils and the parishioners she met on her way in and out of church. Even her brief companionship with

Harry had been a part of her concentration on a life devoted to music. She had enjoyed the seclusion. The narrower it became the more intense and intimate had grown its satisfactions. She had become self-centred, self-contained—so that people had looked curiously at her, twitting her about never seeing her any more.

But suddenly last night she had been carried up from the wharf in sight of half the town. She was the survivor of a tragedy that would be talked about for weeks. Friends had called that afternoon to see how she was.

Life could not be lived without touching people. Even if her swift falling in love with Tavistock had not softened her, this happening last night, she felt, would have opened her eyes to how selfish she had become. But her love for Tavistock had changed her so completely that she felt she had lived a great many years in one night and a day. On the faces of people around her in nearby pews—people she had known all her life—she recognized for the first time the signs of what love and suffering and death had done to them. People who had seemed ugly to her—almost hateful—she could see now as the victims of frustrated love, jealousy, disappointments and the thousand petty tortures that humans bear.

Because of what she had suffered in the church that afternoon—she found in her heart a sympathy for every living thing, which surprised her by its newness and its power to make her own burden of disappointment easier to bear.

She stepped into the shadows of the biggest lilac bush at the corner of their garden. It was here that Tavistock had stood one evening, listening to her playing. She had come across the grass, walking with her head down, her wrists hanging at her sides, like a nun who has surrendered all thought of joy in this life, and looks fixedly, with rigid lips and stiff controlled body, toward some salvation in a future existence. She stood now in the shadow where Tavistock had stood, looking at the dark windows of the music-room, and trying to imagine how she had appeared to him in the glow of the candles. But she could not. All she could think of was that he would never stand there again. She might see him once more—but he had convinced her that his purpose was higher than earthly love.

During their last few minutes together he had made her see at least a glimpse of what all his life he had held as his destiny. She was no clearer than before as to the nature of the miracle—the sacrifice—he was to suffer, but he had told her enough and shown her what he had borne in anticipation of it, to convince her that some strange Gethsemane awaited him.

Once she had felt in him a power that bordered on the supernatural—as though he were possessed by a devil or an angel, whose bidding he was forced to obey. But in their last few minutes together he had shown himself wholly a man, driven to some tragic end by his passionate sympathy for humanity.

If Jesus had been sent to suffer for us, surely, too, he had been sent. She felt in him the strength, the beauty, the compassion, the purity of a soul coming straight from God as another victim—another sacrifice. She no longer had any fears for him. He was more than man and in death he would somehow triumph. Her only wish was that she could have been near to comfort him—but she knew now that he must be alone—she must wait and hear of his death at second-hand—with the certainty of it being misconstrued, misjudged; so that for years, perhaps, it would not be acknowledged a miracle. Only a few—only perhaps herself—not even her father—would know or credit his real purpose.

Standing there, she found comfort in the magnitude, the grandeur of the thought that perhaps she alone understood him—she alone, after he was gone, would interpret his sacrifice to the world—even though at present it was still not clear to her. He had sworn to her that she would understand it—that after it had happened he would appear to her, in some fashion, to make it all plain to her—and through her belief in him the world eventually would come to see what he had been sent to accomplish. She comforted herself with this thought of her own destiny, linked with his.

She moved slowly through the garden, and came to the verandah steps. Everything around her seemed changed by the exaltation of her mood. The familiar wall of the church with the stone buttresses between the windows—the little tower with its tiny blunt steeple—the dark corner of their own house where the verandah went round to the side door—the few trees—and the evening sky at that hour—the whole place, which through intimacy had grown somehow small and cosy, became drenched with a new significance. It seemed to tremble all about her as though on the eve of some event that would make it all memorable—not only to herself, but to every one. She had a vague feeling of an historic quality attaching to it, and before going in she looked about her, to fix it all in her mind, so that in the future she would have the memory of it just as it was on this portentous night.

2

She went in the side door. One light was burning downstairs—in the hall. She groped through the kitchen to it and sank into the chair beside the grandfather clock. Its loud familiar tick—a part of the curious closeness of the house—reminded her at once of her mother, and she ran softly up the stairs, calling to her as she went.

Mrs. Terry was with her, a woman who lived less than two blocks away, behind the school, and who came over often in the evenings to do her knitting with the Canon's wife. They talked little, and always of wools and silks and stitches and of the people for whom they were making things. Once in a long while they would speak of somebody in the Ladies' Aid who perhaps ought to have devoted more time to charitable work. But it never degenerated into gossip. The facts would be stated, and instead of comment Mrs. Terry and Mrs. Macaulay would glance at each other in a guarded, knowing way and go on with their work.

Mrs. Terry had a listless monotonous way of speaking, which sounded as though she never expected anyone to listen to her, but was talking simply for the sake of being companionable. She began to talk as soon as Laura showed herself, but neither Laura nor her mother felt called upon to pay much attention. They made signs to each other while Mrs. Terry rambled on. Laura gathered that her mother's headache was better, that she was all right with Mrs. Terry, and that Laura need not bother staying.

She took off her hat and coat and dropped them on the bed in her room. As she went downstairs there was a rattle of wheels outside, a familiar voice called "whoa," and before she could reach the front door Dr. Bundy stepped solidly in, closing the door behind him with more than his usual care.

Laura was standing under the light, and her hand, which had clung to the stairpost while she paused to make sure who was coming in, lingered in mid-air as though suspended by the floating quality of her thoughts. The doctor noticed it and also her pallor and the dreaminess of her eyes. She had taken off the blue silk dress before church and put on a black one, which made her look slenderer than usual. He remarked all this, and instead of the usual heartiness of his greeting he took two deliberate steps toward her and gripped her elbows tightly.

"All this has upset you badly, darling," he said.

"Yes," she said, meeting his serious, downward glance without any attempt to disguise her preoccupation with strange thoughts, "I shall never forget these two days."

"Your father's not home yet," he said, releasing her arms and glancing about.

"He'll be here any minute. Come in and sit down," she said, drawing aside the curtain over the study door. "Perhaps you can tell me something."

He put his arm about her and led her into the study, his head leaning a little toward her so that his beard almost touched her hair. She sank sideways into a chair, crossing her arms on the back of it, and sat looking fixedly into the black, empty grate. For a moment or two he stood beside her, his heavy, blond head slanted above her, his eyes rolled up under his lids—considering. His beard shook two or three times, as though he were going to speak, but he stepped back, reaching for the arms of a chair behind him, and sat down without turning his head away from her.

"It isn't only the—the drowning—that is on my mind," she said at last, shifting her abstracted glance half-way toward the doctor, crouched in his chair a few feet away.

He lifted his hand slowly and laid his curled forefinger thoughtfully against his lips.

"Something else has happened to me," said Laura, raising her voice slightly after waiting a moment for him to speak. But he made no sound.

"Why are you so quiet, uncle?" she said, taking her arms from the chair-back to face him.

"I don't seem to know you, Laura."

He said this slowly, musingly, while he searched her eyes for the girl he had known so long.

"Besides," he added, without stopping the search, "I have something on my mind, too."

She showed no interest in what it was, but pressed her long fingers together between her knees, and drooped her head in a daze, as she had in the boat the night before.

"You're not thinking of Harry?" Bundy said very quietly.

She shook her bent head slowly from side to side, and something kindled sharply in the doctor's eyes as he stared at the white parting in her hair. But before he could speak there was a sound at the door, and the Canon could be heard moving in the hall. Laura raised her head very slowly. The doctor got up.

3

"So you're here, Sturge," the Canon said, stepping into view and stopping with his hand on the drawn curtains as soon as he noticed Laura.

"I've just arrived," said the doctor.

The Canon had seen Bundy's horse and rig tied up outside. Usually on Sunday nights he stabled Minnie somewhere and spent an hour or two chatting or listening to Laura play.

"Can't you stay?" the Canon asked.

"Not long, Malcolm. I dropped in—specially. There's something I wanted to ask you. But Laura here has me worried."

A slow smile passed over Laura's face as she glanced up at her father, something like the smile of an invalid who is gently amused by the hopes of every one around her that she is going to get better.

"You're worn out," the Canon said, coming over and touching her hair lightly. "It's natural, isn't it, Sturge?" he asked the doctor in what he conceived to be a manner that would soothe her.

"She's not depressed," Bundy said.

"No," said Laura, getting up and stretching herself to her full height with her back half-turned to them.

The Canon exchanged glances with Bundy. They looked into each other's eyes earnestly and anxiously, believing they were unobserved, but Laura had turned and caught the glance. "I wish you would both tell me something," she said. Her tone was almost cold, as though she expected opposition or that they would treat her as a child.

"Sure we will," said Bundy. "Sit down, darling."

The Canon picked up his pipe from the mantelpiece and began filling it, glancing under his brows at Laura as she sat down facing the doctor.

"I'd like to know what you think about miracles," Laura said, in a tone she tried to make even and ordinary.

"Miracles," repeated the doctor, in as nearly the same tone as he could achieve.

"Yes," said Laura, speaking cautiously and as though she were anxious that the conversation should be begun in just the right way. "I'd like to know what you think about the way they happen. Are there people who have the power to perform miracles—whenever they like? Or does God choose some person at a particular moment to do what he wants done?"

"What do you mean by a miracle?" asked Bundy. He held his hands apart in the air, as though measuring off a space into which one portion of the problem could be investigated by itself, before going on to the next. "Do you mean the sort of thing that happens at Lourdes, or do you mean what Marconi does without wires?"

"A sort of miracle has happened to me," said Laura solemnly, "but not—not what one calls a miracle—really. It has made me think, though. I'm sure that all this," and she made a sweeping gesture that included not only the room but the town outside, the sky and the stars, "all this is only a sort of shadow of what really happens. We are nothing compared with the forces that flow through us. And I'm wondering if we keep these forces from working because we are not ready for them—not expecting them—and feel ourselves too weak to be of any use." She paused and looked from one to the other. "Is that it?" she asked, with the utmost earnestness. "Is it because we don't feel capable of miracles that none ever happen to us? If we believed ourselves capable, wouldn't there be a miracle for us to do, waiting to be done?"

They were not sure she was finished, but when she had been silent for some seconds the Canon said: "It's the old question of faith, after all—isn't it? If ye had faith ye could move mountains."

But he could see she didn't like it. It was something learned out of a book—a scrap of the jargon he had repeated all his life without knowing what it really meant. He knew nothing about faith of that kind. He simply believed in it. It was no more than a belief in a belief. He twisted one leg awkwardly around the other and pursed up his lips under his moustache, ashamed of his inability to understand what was going through his daughter's mind.

The doctor, meanwhile, was leaning back, his hands clasped behind his head, his glance roving excitedly over the ceiling. He wanted to ask her point-blank whether she'd been talking to the Englishman—what was his name?—Woodstock?—Lancaster? —the gloomy-looking fellow who had stood dripping behind her last night on the wharf.

Gawthorp had taken him aside, whispering in his ear in the dark an astounding story. And at her first mention of the word "miracle" he had guessed. It wasn't only the word. It was something in her face—in her voice—something that connected at once with the way Gawthorp had sounded last night. Gawthorp, of course, was scared—scared stiff—and she wasn't. This fellow —what the devil was his name?—Tadcaster, or something—had talked differently to her, no doubt. These fellows who go queer on religion are often strong for women. The two things go together. There are plenty of famous cases. And poor old Rittenhouse in the Home . . .

It was easy to see why this Englishman had been attracted to her—had spilled his mad story to her. Yet Bundy couldn't figure when they had found an opportunity to talk, unless they had met somewhere to-day. The accident last night had thrown them together, and the Englishman had grabbed at the chance of finding a sympathetic listener. Well, he'd found one, that was certain. She was perhaps the one person in town who would listen to him. He remembered her as a child—the things she had said—putting things together and deducing something from them in a way that was often more than "grown up"—finding analogies, similes, that would never occur to an adult—except to a poet, perhaps. She had lived in an imaginative world of her own, even then—a very child-like world, but dark with a profundity that had often amazed him. And lately, when he sometimes asked her why a certain thing she had played should stir him so deeply, she would turn on the stool and look at him in surprise, and say something like "Well, if you were a mother—if you were the mother of Jesus and saw them taking his body down from the cross—wouldn't you feel like that?"

At first he had asked her, almost breathlessly, "Is that the sort of thing you get out of music?—is *that* why you play as you do?" But he was over his astonishment at her now. Only last Sunday she had said to him, after playing something: "Don't you feel as though the room is full of horses?—it almost smothers me to play that thing. It feels like horses let loose—trampling people—smashing everything. Don't you feel smashed?"

Yes, she was the one person this Englishman might get to sympathize with him—in the whole town. She had a terrific sense of suffering—she could face evil—she could create it under her fingers and fill the room with it—beauty, too, of course—but Bach appealed to her more than anybody—the agonizing return, over and over again, of the same monotonous sequences of sound, dragging at a person's heart-strings . . . dragging . . . dragging . . .

This Englishman had been talking to her about his mania—

some sort of miracle that would wipe out the knowledge of good and evil. He would have liked to talk to him himself. He would like to find out what it was all about. He felt like asking her point-blank: "What sort of miracle does this Englishman expect to perform?" But it might put her on her guard.

He remembered her question: "If we believed ourselves capable, wouldn't there be a miracle for us to do, waiting to be done?" He took his hands from his neck, lowered his head and looked at her. Her glance was fastened on him. Something glowed in her always eager eyes—something new. He was abashed by it. She couldn't know she was revealing so much. He turned quickly to the Canon, who was puffing at his pipe and looking fixedly at the floor.

"Were you preaching about miracles to-night, Malcolm?," he said.

"No—no, no," said the Canon. "Laura's been talking to this man Tavistock I mentioned to you yesterday. I wish he were here."

"He may come," said Laura. "He may be here any minute."

The Canon swung one knee over the other and slouched deeper into his favourite chair. "I told him," he said, "that you'd understand him better than anybody. I asked him to drop in here to-night—and Laura tells me he's going to try to. I'd like to know what you think of his notions. Last night he stayed for a while and I thought of you and your Whitman." He smiled indulgently.

"Me and my Whitman!" echoed the doctor, with pretended petulance.

"He said something about Whitman this afternoon," Laura murmured, puckering her brows to recall what it was. "Something about eternity—something about men and women being in eternity."

"'There is eternity in men and women'—was that it?" asked Bundy.

"Yes," nodded Laura. "I thought of you at once. I told him you were *soaked* in Whitman. I hope he comes. . . ."

"It *would* be excellent to hear the two of them at it," the Canon agreed, shaking the ashes from his pipe into the dark grate.

"Well, I don't know," said the doctor doubtfully. "Whitman could be thoroughly mystical at times—but he got his mysticism out of the natural. You were talking about miracles, darling. Whitman never believed in miracles. Well, now—I shouldn't put it that way. He says in one place he had no *objection* to miracles. Characteristic, isn't it?—that word 'objection.' As I remember it, he said he had no objection to miracles because he considered a wisp of smoke or a hair on the back of his hand as curious as any miracle. So, you see, perhaps your Mr. Tavistock and I wouldn't get along at all."

The Canon leaned over the broad, yielding arm of his chair. "No, but Whitman's attitude towards good and evil," he said, "*that's* what I was thinking about. Tavistock has evidently been reading him. He says, as Whitman does, that there is no evil—and yet he grieves because man has a sense of guilt. He even seems to think that 'another Christ like man'—those are his own words—a man he thinks is the true 'Comforter'—will come to wash away our sense of guilt. Christianity, he says, is—"

"That's not Whitman!" Dr. Bundy broke in. "Whitman says the poet—the prophet type of man—never divides the righteous from the unrighteous—and *further*—'knows no possible forgiveness or deputed atonement.'" He held up his two hands, widely separated, as though one might represent Whitman and the other Tavistock. "If there is no evil," he added challengingly, "where is the need for atonement?"

"Don't ask me," said the Canon half-jocularly. "I'm just an old-fashioned parson who believes in original sin."

"It isn't atonement," said Laura positively. "He doesn't believe in the atonement, either. He says that Jesus himself realized he hadn't saved the world when he prophesied that the Comforter would follow him—'to reprove the world of sin and righteousness and judgment.'"

Laura stopped and sat perfectly still, fingering the knot of hair on her neck, as though listening to his words in her mind.

"Yes," said the Canon helplessly, and in a tone of monotonous repetition, "to reprove the world of sin and righteousness and judgment . . . yes . . ."

Dr. Bundy did not look at him. He was watching Laura. "Has Mr. Tavistock told you," he said warily, "whether he has any idea of the form this miracle is to take?"

She looked at him, and he could see that she felt the question a challenge. "He doesn't know," she said. "He simply believes it will happen. He knows it *can* happen. And he is waiting for it."

"*He* is waiting for it!" cried the Canon, grasping his knees and throwing himself forward in his chair.

Last night when the man had talked to him—here in this very room—he had believed his sadness was due to thinking of what this new Christ—this Comforter—would have to suffer. Tavistock, he felt, had taken on himself a sort of John-the-Baptist role of announcing another saviour. But this—this was the rankest blasphemy. With even more emphasis than before, he repeated: "*He* is waiting for it."

"Yes," said Laura, looking directly over his head as though she could not bear to witness the grimace of horror which she knew was distorting his face. "I hadn't intended to tell you—until after it—after it has happened. But we shan't see him again until it *has* happened—and it may be—tonight. He will come here first—afterward—if he can—if it doesn't—if it doesn't kill him."

"Ah!" ejaculated the doctor in so strange a tone that Laura flung round at him and studied the anxious knotting of his thick brows.

"What is it, Uncle?" she said.

"He thinks it may kill him," said Bundy gravely, but with deep suspicion in his tone.

"He doesn't know. He doesn't know what will happen—or how it will happen. But he believes—he *knows*—that it can and must happen—and if not through him, then through somebody else."

"And do you believe that it *must* happen," the doctor asked her.

"Yes, I do," she said. "A man couldn't have tortured himself as he has—couldn't be as *sure* as he is—unless—unless God was in him."

Dr. Bundy got up and went to the fireplace. He leaned his elbows on it with his back to the room. The Canon and his daughter avoided each other's eyes. They both stared silently at the doctor's broad back until he turned slightly and said over his shoulder to Laura: "You believe that this man is what he thinks he is himself—a new Christ! Not in the sense that Whitman was—stating the old gospel in a new way for the new world—but a man sent from God—a *son* of God—sent to perform a miracle—sent to redeem the world. You believe that—do you?"

He turned and peered at her from under heavy, frowning brows. Her eyes did not waver. "I talked to him only for a while—not long—this afternoon. But I believe there has been no one like him—since Jesus—no one so troubled by the world's sorrows—no one who . . . Tell me, Uncle—has there been *one* man who has conceived such a thing to be possible—and having conceived it, has been ready to make the sacrifice himself—prepared himself for it—given up everything for it . . . ?"

"No," said the doctor, his voice trembling with the sympathy he felt both for Tavistock and for her, "no—there have been no such men—except . . ."

He stopped and walked abruptly to the window at the end of the room, overlooking the garden.

Laura watched him, biting her teeth together in a sudden grimace of impatience. "You think—" she began, but checked herself. "Aren't there plenty of people," she cried, scarcely without a pause, "who think Whitman was mad? I believe Daddy does. But *you* don't."

He turned and saw that she was not disturbed by his doubts. She was simply disappointed that he could not follow her. He wished profoundly that it could be someone elso who should tell her—but he could not keep silent. She believed in Tavistock. It even looked as though she loved him. The sooner it was over the better.

4

He came and sat down in a chair half-facing her and took her hands as he had often done when talking intimately with her since she was a little girl.

"Laura," he said, "I've got to tell you this—and Malcolm, too. This man is—is dangerous."

"Dangerous!" cried the Canon, getting quickly up and coming to stand over them.

Laura looked up into her father's face and then back at the doctor. She looked at them both steadily, and Bundy could see that she was regarding him simply as a crank on the question of insanity.

"You don't believe me," he urged.

"Uncle!" she said, "can't *you* believe that such a man—I mean a man with such an idea—is *possible*? Say—for the moment—that he isn't the man—that the miracle won't happen to him. But he believes in it. Don't you think that faith like that means—"

"Laura, darling," exclaimed the doctor, his beard quivering with anxiety not to alarm her too suddenly, "he's told you only half the story. Men like that are always secretive. It's only in the last few days that he has talked to anybody, but he's got to the stage now where he can't contain himself. He talked to Gawthorp yesterday—to your father last night—to you to-day." He raised three fingers, one after the other, and dropped his hand on his knee. "But only in hints, darling—telling one this and another something else. Do you see . . . ?"

"What has he told other people that he didn't tell me?" Laura demanded, her slanting eyes steadily fixed in their corners, regarding him anxiously.

"He didn't tell you what the miracle would be," said Bundy solemnly.

"No," said Laura. "He told me he didn't know how—or what—would happen."

"But he told your father that this Comforter, who is to come, would do evil—innocently!—didn't he, Malcolm?"

"Yes," said the Canon, quickly clearing his throat.

"Can you imagine," asked Bundy, looking directly into Laura's eyes, "what particular act of evil he intends to commit?"

She seemed suddenly relieved, and drew her hands quickly from the doctor's grasp to gesture with, vehemently. "It isn't an *intention*!" she cried impatiently. "That's just the sort of word you would use. You think it's a mania. He isn't planning anything—or intending anything. He is simply waiting for the miracle to happen. He will be its instrument. It will be something that has been thought evil, up to now, but because of the miracle it will be known to be innocent. That's all."

The doctor shook his great head sadly. "But, darling," he said, "there seems to be no doubt that he knows the nature of the miracle—the exact kind of evil. That's the terrible part of it."

"You mean he has told somebody that?"

"Yes."

"Whom did he tell?"

"Gawthorp."

"Gawthorp!" echoed the Canon.

"Why should he tell *him*?" asked Laura suspiciously.

"I don't know," said the doctor, "but he did—in a curious, roundabout way, of course—but . . ."

"Ah!" sighed Laura, "Mr. Gawthorp has got something twisted that he said."

"I'm afraid not, Laura."

"Well—what did he say? And how did he say it?"

The doctor shifted a little deeper into his chair. "He told Gawthorp that he had some sort of presentiment—and a little later he called it knowledge—that a certain act was about to be committed which would involve him."

"Yes," said Laura. "*What* act?"

"Murder!" said the doctor in as calm a tone as he could manage.

Laura raised her hands quickly to her face, pressing her fingers against her cheek-bones. Her eyes narrowed, half in horror and half in angry impatience.

"I told you Mr. Gawthorp had got it twisted," she said. "And *you*, Uncle—because you're looking for insanity—you've got it twisted still more." She dropped her hands to her lap again and gripped them tightly together. "He probably told Mr. Gawthorp he had a presentiment—that's just what he would say. And he may have said that what was going to happen would possibly kill him. He may even have said, 'I expect to be killed'—something like that. And Mr. Gawthorp might very well think he meant murder."

The Canon was listening to her intently, and began nodding as soon as she stopped, apparently satisfied with her explanation. But the doctor was not. He got up from his chair and groped for the Canon's arm while he continued to look down gravely into Laura's lifted eyes.

"You don't think—?" said Laura hesitatingly. "You don't agree with me?"

"No," said Bundy, in a deeply convinced tone, his lower lip showing under his thick moustache as he clenched his jaw.

"You think he's mad—and—and a murderer?"

The doctor pressed his fingers into the Canon's arm, trying to keep his steady gaze levelled at her, so that she would be impressed by his conviction.

"Yes," he said. "I do. I think he plans murder. I think he's a dangerous man."

"But what makes you think it—apart from what Mr. Gawthorp said?"

The doctor stepped back a pace and settled himself solidly with his hands behind him. "Gawthorp was thoroughly scared. He came to me and the Chief last night—down there on the wharf. He was rattled—excited—and men like Gawthorp don't scare easily."

"But—it's absurd, Uncle," said Laura. "He isn't capable of an evil thought. If you knew him at all, you would know that. It's because he's incapable of evil that whatever happens to him—whatever he does—he will do innocently—a greater will than his own will direct him."

"Even if it is murder?" said the doctor doggedly.

Laura trembled from head to foot, but her eyes did not waver. "Yes," she said, "even if it is what you call murder. He will prove to you—and the whole world—that there can be no evil."

She turned to her father and regarded him anxiously, half-distrustfully. "You talked to him, Daddy," she said.

The Canon doubtfully fingered the silver cross on his watch-chain. "He's fanatical," he said softly. "He has strange ideas—but—"

There was a sudden knock at the front door that made them all jump. They were wrought up with feeling, and the knocking at the door immediately connected itself with their thoughts of murder and the supernatural.

The Canon was the first to regain his composure, his lip twisting under his moustache as he guessed that it would be the caretaker.

"It's probably Hyslop," he said, moving to the door.

"Hyslop doesn't knock like that," said Laura, getting up.

"No—that's right," the Canon said, flinging aside the curtains. His heart thumped at his side as he went through the hall to the front door.

Laura glanced quickly, nervously, at the doctor, and ran to the study door, gathering her skirts about her and standing there shaking.

It was a boy at the door—Enos Sadler's boy. He had come fast on his wheel and was breathing hard. "Is Dr. Bundy here, sir?" he asked.

"Yes," said the Canon.

"Julie sent me down to the Home for him, but they said he was out. They said he might be here—being Sunday night. Mr. Linklater is dying, sir. He may be gone by now. They want the doctor."

Bundy, hearing his name, had come out into the hall, linking his arm in Laura's and drawing her with him.

"I'll come at once," he said.

"I think I'll go with you, Sturge," said the Canon, running to the hall-rack for his hat.

"No," said Bundy, snatching up his cap from the table beside the door. "No. You stay with Laura—God knows what she's going through."

"Never mind me," said Laura, peering out of the open door in a dazed, absent-minded way.

"You're all right—are you sure?" said the Canon, touching her arm gently.

"Mother's upstairs, anyway," she said, almost impatiently.

"Come on, then, Malcolm," said the doctor, treading heavily across the verandah.

The Canon ran behind him down the steps and climbed into the buggy, while Bundy untied the rein he had fastened to a tree. They drove off quickly, waving their hands to Laura, who stood at the edge of the verandah. The moon was up, and when they were out of sight she looked at it, riding in shining isolation in the clear sky.

FIVE

Faith

I

AFTER LEAVING LAURA, late in the afternoon, Tavistock returned to his room. He went to the window and stood looking down at the swaying branches of the maples, brushing rhythmically against the high fence with a sound like slow, distant waves.

Presently he sat down, leaning forward with his elbows on the sill, his chin in his hands, so that he overlooked the church roof and the rectory garden.

In a vague way he felt that he should stay there in the room until night. He would wait for the stars. The mystery of the sky would help him.

He was ready. Laura's belief in him had melted all his doubts. He kept repeating to himself: "It is possible! It is possible!" Yet he looked forward to what was going to happen to him with a new feeling. The thought of murder was no longer in his mind.

In Laura's presence a change had come over him. It was not to deceive her that he had kept silent about the nature of the miracle he expected. Whatever happened—it would not be murder. Whatever it was—it would be an innocent act. It was useless to frighten her—or himself—with the word "murder." That is what he had been doing all this time. He had looked past the act to its consequences—to the name people would put on it. Sometimes his whole nature had revolted at it. At other times he had regarded himself as a sort of martyr—a man whose life and death would be looked back to by countless generations.

But that was all gone now. Instead of heightening his egotism, Laura's faith in him had dispelled it. While she clung to him he began to realize what it was he had always been seeking. It was nothing more or less than a sign from God. It was his mind which had continually suggested to him the nature of the sign. But his mind was quieted. He had become like a child—waiting in a mood of expectancy for a promised surprise.

He sat for a long while at the window, his forehead leaning on his crossed wrists, his eyes closed. He kept himself still, desiring nothing, not even wishing to hurry the complete surrender which he felt was near. All these years he had been forcing himself—exerting his will—trying to shame himself into action. But now he was relaxed. It would come. It was possible. He was ready.

He got up and stretched himself on the bed, lying on his back with his arms straight down by his sides, his chin raised. It struck him that he must look like a corpse. He nodded to himself. It was for that reason he had stretched himself on the bed. He wanted to *shed* his body. Words came to him—floating into his mind from the pages of Whitman:

> "O to disengage myself from those corpses of me,
> which I turn and look at where I cast them,
> To pass on (O living! always living!) and
> leave the corpses behind."

All around him stole the familiar sense of presences—angels—bearing him up. An imagined sky came close, as though he were approaching it. The stars grew, dazzling him with their brightness. It seemed to him that he could feel the pull of their attraction.

He knew why Job had spoken of the morning stars singing together—coupling them in the same breath with the sons of God shouting for joy. He knew why Blake had made of the "morning stars" his grandest design. He felt there was a kinship between the stars and the sons of God—the great souls who have known the unity of everything. His own desire had been that the earth should be like a star—single and singing!

He had risen so high in thought that the world seemed to have shifted from under him and was removed to a great distance. The experience of solidity beneath him, and the drag of gravitation, were so washed from his mind that it was as though he had never known the feel of earth under his feet or a hand on his shoulder. The world became a distant star. He seemed to hang in a web of harmony—upheld by soaring, crossing, invisible forces, which through their interlacing made an inevitable, peaceful place for—his spirit to rest.

2

A knock at the door sounded like a thunder-clap, reverberating in infinite space. He lifted his head slowly and heavily, as though he were unpractised in a world of weight, and his voice came automatically to his lips, saying sharply: "Who is there?" He heard the words issuing normally out of his mouth, but in his mind the question seemed prolonged as though he had heard himself utter it in a dream—in a world of shadows.

Yet by the time Pitts called back his name, Tavistock was alive again to his surroundings. Jumping up quickly, he surveyed the room without any sense of strangeness.

"Come in, Pitts ," he called. And when the red, coarsened face he expected was suddenly thrust into view through the half-opened door, he smiled and nodded familiarly, as though Pitts were his room-mate and might rightly be expected to drop in at any minute.

"This, too, is reality," he said to himself, watching the old man close the door behind him with extravagant carefulness, as though sealing up a secret partition.

This, too, was reality—this flesh and blood, bearing the marks of debauch and suffering in the lined forehead, the bloodshot eyes, the slack mouth, the quivering chin. Here was a man who had somehow got into the world and had suffered for it. He was real. He was perhaps eternal. He must mean something. He must be, at least, some sort of shadow or symbol—the *wrong* side of something which in eternity was living in harmony and joy.

In a tiny space of seconds there flashed through his mind the days and nights in Africa—the comings and goings of Pitts—Clara's eyes on him, and his on her—the bitterness and contempt flowing between them—the vile words he had overheard them flinging at each other—and his lust for her squinting his eyes—flaring up even the other night when they mentioned her again after years of absence—no love between them ever—on her side only panic, and on his the frankest lust.

But they were real—a man and a woman—and they had suffered—and meant something. It was impossible that they were not somehow finally good. If the web of harmony in which he had hung was real, there must be places in it for them. If not, it was not as real as they.

But it was. It was more real than seeing him come into the room, his mouth mysteriously pursed with some bursting secret.

3

These thoughts swept through his mind while Pitts was fastening the door, and came blunderingly in a great hurry across the carpet, his face twitching with excitement as his lips lolled open to speak.

"I was here this morning," he whispered, bending almost to Tavistock's ear, "but you were out some place."

"Yes," Tavistock nodded. "I went across the lake. I was away all morning."

Pitts plumped himself down on the edge of the bed and bent forward, almost double, shooting out his lips in a staccato whisper: "You're being watched."

"Eh?" Tavistock exclaimed, endeavouring to bring his mind to earth to fathom Pitts' excitement.

"You're being watched. You'd better get out of town. I've seen this sort of thing before. I knew a poor blighter in England—as decent as . . ."

"What are you talking about?" asked Tavistock more seriously. "*Who* is watching me? Are you mad?"

"No," cried Pitts, pounding his dirty fist into his palm. "No—but they think *you* are."

"They! They!" repeated Tavistock impatiently, "who are *they?*"

"Gawthorp and the Chief and Doc Bundy," belched out Pitts in a prolonged puffing breath. "Gawthorp thinks you're dangerous—I'm telling you straight. What's the use o' beating about the bush? You frightened him somehow—talking about murder—and he popped the whole thing to Bundy and the Chief—last night—after they'd taken that youngster's body away. He buttonholed 'em both right there on the wharf. I was right there myself when he told 'em. Pretty tight I was—but it sobered me up, believe me—what he told 'em."

"What *did* he tell them?" said Tavistock peremptorily.

This was something he hadn't foreseen—that he might be watched and intercepted. His need to unburden his secret to someone before his hour of destiny struck had made him talk unwisely to Gawthorp. And now, perhaps, at the moment when he was ready—after years of vacillation—at the moment of miracle—they might dash out from hiding, stop him and drag him away. This was wholly unforeseen—that out of his own mouth they might convict him of madness and put him somewhere—lock him up—so that the miracle might never happen and he would beat at the walls—crazed by the confinement—a real madman!

"What *did* he tell them?" he repeated, wrenching his thoughts away from such a picture.

"He told Doc Bundy you talked to him like—like a maniac—and you were going to murder somebody. He said you weren't safe to be loose—to be—"

"God in heaven!" cried Tavistock, raising his clenched hands above his head and springing up to his full height. He took three frantic strides to the door and back again until his brow almost struck the upper pane of the window. Already he was acting like a man caged and out of his mind.

"It is not *my* will," he said suddenly, in a deep tone that echoed faintly back from the glass.

"I'm in God's hands," he began, turning to Pitts, who sat crouched and trembling on the bed; but he broke off, regarding the old man curiously. "Tell me, Pitts, do you ever pray?"

The old man wiped his fingers awkwardly across his mouth. "Not for years," he stuttered. "Not for a good many years."

"If you were near dying," Tavistock said solemnly, lifting a hand slowly in the air between them as though to quiet the old man's fears, "if you were near dying, Pitts, you *would* probably—you might say some prayers—eh?—wouldn't you?"

Out of the past, as he stood there gazing fixedly at the old man, came a fragment from the most solemn moment of Bach's

St. Matthew *Passion*—the moment when Jesus, after crying again with a loud voice, yields up the ghost. He remembered how the chorus in sombre harmony breathed out the words:

"Be near me, Lord, when dying,
O part not thou from me !"

"Maybe I would," he heard Pitts answer.

But the words still floated in his mind, and he repeated them aloud:

"Be near me, Lord, when dying,
O part not thou from me!"

He dropped his lifted hand gently on Pitts' shoulder and looked down into the rounded, bloodshot eyes bent on him now with yearning pity.

"I'm not ill, Pitts," he said. "But if I were—if I were dying—and I asked you to pray with me . . ." His grasp tightened on Pitts' shoulder and a note of urgency came into his tone. "Kneel down and pray with me, Pitts," he said, bending closer.

The old man leaned sideways away from him, shuddering. "No—no, no," he muttered between chattering teeth.

"What?" cried Tavistock.

Pitts slid away from him off the bed, and stood up. "No," he whispered, "no—no—while my eyes were closed you would kill me!"

"What?" cried Tavistock again.

Tears rolled down the old man's cheeks. He grasped the iron railing at the foot of the bed and leaned toward Tavistock, trying to speak, but his tongue clicked helplessly against his teeth.

"You, too, are against me," Tavistock said evenly, without accusation in his tone.

"No," said Pitts hastily, "no—I'm not against you. I came to warn you. I'm afraid of—of what they . . ."

"They may come here," Tavistock said. It was not a question. He was thinking aloud.

"Yes, certainly," said the old man. "You'd better leave town. You'd better take the midnight train to-night. Eh? I'll help you down to the depot with your things. That's the best thing. Pack your things. Quick."

Tavistock leaned back against the wall near the window. His head gently knocked against the wall as he inclined it backwards and sent his glance roving over the ceiling.

"I have no *things*," he said, with contemptuous emphasis.

At that moment there was a slight noise on the stairs, and Pitts darted forward. "It may be the Chief—now," he whispered. "What'll I tell him? Can you lock the door? Where's the key? How about that window? Can you drop . . . ?"

He ran to the window and stuck his head out. Tavistock, his head leaning against the wall, did not move.

The sounds of a heavy tread came nearer as Pitts withdrew his neck from the window. He pointed to the fire rope coiled under a chair. "Look! It's easy. That's the way."

He gesticulated feverishly under Tavistock's lifted chin, but the roving eyes paid no heed. The thud of feet on the carpet of the corridor came level with the door and passed without stopping. They could hear someone rapping at a distant door and a muffled voice calling from within.

4

Pitts dropped his hands to his sides and breathed more easily. Tavistock stirred. When he stepped away from the wall, he staggered slightly with a sudden dizziness. He felt weak. It was difficult for him to make up his mind to move—to go anywhere. He seemed to have no energy. His body, as well as his brain, seemed numbed and inert. Yet he had been thinking, these last few minutes, that he must go out. It was necessary to face the idea of murder—in cold blood. He had to face it—see through it—see that it was not evil. He had to be somewhere—where it could happen. He wanted it to happen outside—under the sky. At the last moment—to gather strength—he would look at the stars. He raised his hands, curling his fingers tightly, and stared at them, thinking that he had no other weapons. He had always put aside the thought of weapons. He had never really faced the thing—pictured it—rehearsed it. He had believed all along that the moment would provide its own means.

More than once he had thought of Abraham's sacrifice—how he himself clave the wood for the offering and laid it on the back of Isaac—he himself carrying the fire and the knife—to kill his own son and burn his body on the mountain-top. Abraham had faced the sacrifice—prepared for it with weapons—and *his* miracle had happened—a ram caught in a thicket was there to substitute for his only son.

Tavistock had sometimes wondered if *his* miracle might be something like that. If he could overcome himself and surrender himself completely, it might be that the blow need never be struck. But he had always rejected the idea as a false hope. He rejected it again, now. He thought again of what Clara had said about Hamlet: "A man who cannot kill is only half a man."

It was horrible, but there was truth in it. A man who constantly examined his impulses—weighing them carefully and delaying action until he had satisfied a niggardly, bloodless intellect—such a man had cut himself off from life—despising half of it—finding half of it evil.

He had to *see* that killing could be innocent. It had seemed so for a moment the other night in Julie's shack. For a few seconds he had felt that Pitts was intended for his victim. And somehow Pitts had been affected by his thought. "It was as though I *had* died," he said. "It was like the resurrection."

Then, yesterday, in this room, facing Gawthorp there in the chair, the same thought had come. And to-day—in the church this afternoon—there had been a moment, too—only a moment —when Laura's faith in him made him feel that he could be justified in killing her, as Abraham was ready to kill his own son.

But if it was not to be his will, surely it was not for him to pick the victim. All that was demanded of him was that he should be ready. "Readiness is all," he repeated to himself.

The words, echoing in his memory, acted like a spur to his body. His eyes, which had been staring vacantly into space, became aware of Pitts standing beside the bed, stroking his thighs as though his legs were numb with cold.

"Let's go down by the lake, Pitts," he said suddenly. "It is better there."

The words had uttered themselves as swiftly as they had come into his mind—without volition—as though a voice had spoken through him. He took it for a sign. His confidence returned with the thought that he was being guided. His eyes brightened. The lines were smoothed from his forehead, and he took Pitts' arm to lead him out, as though they were going to a great feast.

Pitts offered no resistance. He did not even raise his glance to the other's eyes. He was afraid of the madness that might be in them. He went out of the door with him and along the corridor, his eyes swivelling into their corners to watch every movement Tavistock made. When they came to the head of the stairs he slipped his arm free and stepped aside to let Tavistock precede him. Tavistock looked at him meaningly—pausing a moment before he took the first downward step. "You're afraid of me, Pitts," he said, smiling pitifully.

He did not expect an answer. The old man followed him down the stairs and out into the street without a word.

5

They came to McCully's bush and Tavistock turned off into the path which ran diagonally through the wood from the magistrate's house toward the lake. They had not spoken all the way. Once or twice Tavistock had looked behind to see if they were being followed, but the streets, almost as light as day under the brilliant moon, were deserted. The usual Sunday night quiet had descended over the town.

The two men went silently along the path. The sharp, multitudinous trilling of bullfrogs along the shore, unified in one shrill, continuous chord of high-pitched sound, and growing in intensity as they approached the lake, made their footsteps in the soft earth inaudible even to themselves.

As they came in sight of the water, glittering under the moon like flowing, molten silver, Tavistock turned off the main path into one less frequented, but which he knew well.

"Where are you going?" Pitts asked in a low voice.

"I know this place," Tavistock said. "There's a fallen tree in here—in a bit of a clearing. I've been here often. There's a sort of hush that helps you to pray."

"You've got praying on the brain," said Pitts impatiently. "If you'd tell somebody what's worrying you, perhaps—"

"I'll tell you," answered Tavistock, in an indulgent tone. "We'll sit down in here and I'll tell you the whole story. And you can go back and tell them whether I'm mad or not."

They came to the tree—an old oak shriven by lightning years before—lying along the ground. Tavistock stepped over the tree and sat down, facing the shining water. Pitts shuffled through the grass around the blasted, upturned root and sat down beside him.

"I'd like to be quiet awhile first," said Tavistock, cupping his chin in his hands and leaning forward. "Go down to the lake and back—do you mind? There's the path—right there."

Pitts lifted himself heavily and moved through the trees in the direction of the shore.

Tavistock glanced at the old man's back only for a moment. Then he closed his eyes.

He strove upward—climbing in his mind—seeking freedom from his body—the merging of himself with the mightiness above and outside himself—striving to become one with the being that pours through an eternal succession of dying and re-born things.

From a height of inwardness he tried to sense unity in the world—in the world of things. He tried to draw it all together—past and present and future—in an everlasting *now*. He tried to crush into the tiny chamber of his mind the immense reaches of infinite space and the brightness of starry circlings through endless time.

The sense of *nowness* eluded him, but he became conscious of a change in his breathing. He felt his hands moving slowly, rhythmically, symmetrically—first touching his breast, which seemed to be filled with sweet, unaccountable air, drawn from an invisible dayspring—then behind his head, gently supporting his neck, which had slanted backward of itself so that his brow paralleled the pathway of the stars—and finally down, slowly, behind his back, with the slow gesture of a man disrobing himself—baring himself for a plunge into an unfathomable experience.

Each movement came of itself, easing his body to the point of losing it, so that what remained of him lay still and open, like a pool into which the downshine of heaven could pour.

And as he became unconscious of his body the web of harmony seemed to descend over him and through him, drawing together everything he had ever known or believed, so that his life became like a rose unfolding before him in a garden of perfection.

It was as though there had been before a male and a female in his soul, yearning for each other, but held apart in a vain, insatiable passion. They had come together, and now he was filled with a tenderness which he had only experienced in the presence of someone deeply loved—yet the loved one seemed to be another side of his nature, hidden for a long time, and now returned. It was like a mating of all the many sides of his nature—all the persons who lived in him—the many voices—the thousand urgings—so that he became himself like a universe—and himself the God in it—reigning in it!

He was silent and perfectly still a long time.

6

Pitts, when he came out to the road, looked toward Julie's place. It was just around the bend, so that the lighted window in the front faced down the road. Drawn up in the ditch outside the shack was a horse and buggy. The moonlight glinted brightly on the metal parts of the harness and on the newly painted spokes of the wheels.

The thought leapt immediately into Pitts' mind: "It's Doc Bundy's. They can't find Tavistock and they're after me or Julie to tell 'em where he is."

He sprang across the ditch and started to run through the underbrush, missing the path by a few yards. He ran recklessly, lashing his face against low branches hanging in his way and stumbling over roots, muttering, "God Almighty" between every snorting breath.

Through the trees he could see Tavistock sitting in the same place in the clearing, but his head was flung back in an unnatural posture, as though he had been strangled.

"He's dead! He's killed himself!" Pitts almost shouted aloud, halting and clinging to a tree to keep his balance. His legs had suddenly given way. Waves of unspeakable chill mounted his spine and attacked his brain. "He's killed himself," he said, feeling his heart freeze in his breast.

At first he was unable to move. He clung to the tree, trembling and shuddering. But in a few moments he felt himself drawn forward, taking long, stealthy steps, as though he were stalking something. The moonlight shone on Tavistock's raised jaw so that his face seemed cut off. A chaos of horrible thoughts spun in Pitts' mind as he crept up, but they were quickly dispelled. A twig cracked noisily under his foot and Tavistock sprang up, peering about him in every direction until he espied the old man a few yards away.

He came slowly along the path and Pitts—looking at him fearfully—saw his face in the full light of the moon. It was transfigured. It was like an angel's.

Pitts knelt down where he stood. He could stand no longer. He went down on his knees and waited, not knowing whether the hands outstretched as Tavistock came nearer would gently touch his head in blessing, or grasp at his throat.

When Tavistock came to a stop in front of him the terror left him. He looked up eagerly into the unearthly face.

Tavistock kept his arms lifted as though he were waiting for a flash of vision to know what to do.

In a voice that seemed to come from the air above him, he said: "Pitts—are you the man?"

As he asked this question his face changed, in the twinkling of an eye. Pitts scrambled to his feet, shouting something meaningless—a frenzied gabble that reverberated in all the trees—and began running as fast as he could toward the light in Julie's window.

SIX

Transfiguration

I

LAURA WENT back into the house and stood in the doorway of the study, looking at the empty chairs where they had been sitting. The room seemed to be full of their words—their misunderstanding—so that she did not want to go in.

It was more than misunderstanding. The air seemed heavy with suspicion—fear—even horror. The doctor believed he was dangerous. She felt his eyes on her again as he said: "You believe this man is what he thinks he is—a new Christ?"

Her eyes drooped and she swayed giddily against the doorpost. She had been through so much that her mind was aching. The effort to think—to experience anything more—caused a violent throbbing in her head. She wanted sleep. She wanted to forget.

She dragged herself wearily across the hall to the little room where she gave her lessons and sank down in a padded chair, facing the piano. It was dark in the room, but the row of keys gleamed whitely in the half-light from the hall.

The effort to hold her faith in Tavistock's "destiny," against the suspicions of the doctor and her father, had worn her out.

Their hints of madness had affected her, even while she clung staunchly to a belief in his saintliness.

The doctor's words ran again in her mind—"a man sent from God—a *son* of God!"

In his presence she had believed it. She loved him—his magnetism had captured her. She would have floated with him into the wildest dreams, believing them real if he had only whispered that they were. He could have carried her with him—wherever he went. His touch—his presence—would have been sufficient for her—anywhere. He was a man whose like she had never seen or expected. But—"a son of God!" What did it mean? The doctor, with his suspicions, had twisted and confused all her thoughts about him. She could not recover the look of exalted passion in his face—nor the deep reverberance of his voice in her heart. Even his words seemed to have faded from her mind.

"It's because I'm so tired," she told herself. "I'm too tired to think—to remember. They've taken him away from me—somehow. They've killed him. I can't get back to him."

Her thoughts were beating against the thicket of fears they had raised in her mind.

"He said nothing about being 'a son of God,'" she said to herself. "It was they who said that. They don't understand him—they don't know what he expects to happen—and they make it all seem mad. If he would come—if he would come—to-night—when they get back—"

Her mind reeled again and she pressed her fingers hard against her temples.

But the doctor wouldn't come back. He would go on to the Home from Linklater's place. And how could she expect Tavistock? He had said he might never see her again. He would come—if he could—to tell her what had happened. It might be that he would somehow *appear* to her. . . .

She flung her hands from her face on to the arms of the chair, her nails digging into the thick, worn leather, her gaze fastened across the room in a wild stare.

How could she sleep, unless he came?

"I shall never sleep to-night," she moaned to herself. "How can I rest until I know what has happened to him?"

Yet the staying awake—the waiting—the whirl of wild, fearful thoughts in her mind—how long could she stand it?

Across the room the piano keys seemed to grin at her like a row of mocking teeth. The dark shape of the piano began to assume the form of a squat, demonic, shadowy head—growing monstrously. . . .

She jumped up and almost ran into the hall.

"I'll go upstairs and sit with mother and Mrs. Terry," she said, but she did not move. She stood under the light—listening. Between the ticks of the clock she listened for some sound—some sign. Perhaps no more than a breath of air might come to her to tell her that the miracle had happened. Whatever the sign should be, she knew that when it came she would recognize it. It would be unmistakable.

Yet how could a sign come to her? By what means? By whose power?

As she continued to listen her fears returned. She felt something ominous in the approaching sign. She felt it coming toward her through space behind her head—and instead of reassuring her—satisfying her—it had now become menacing. She felt like praying that it could be stopped—that it would never reach her. If it touched her she would shriek.

She turned about quickly and cast a terrified glance behind her. The hall-rack, hung with a miscellany of hats and clothes, stood in its accustomed place.

2

She began to think that perhaps these strange fears—and the feeling that her mind could bear no more—were coming to her from Tavistock. Perhaps in his final hour he was experiencing these shudders—these shrinkings from the sign that might shatter him.

Perhaps the doctor had seen in him a type whose mind—beset by fanaticism—her father's word—might easily lose itself and break down. They were already right, perhaps. Long thinking on his destiny might have sent him mad. But was he a man who could plan murder—even in a fit of madness?

Gawthorp was convinced of it. Uncle Sturge was convinced of it.

She covered her mouth quickly to prevent herself from crying out in sudden horror.

Was the miracle he expected a murder—a murder he himself would commit? He had spoken of evil—done innocently. Was that what he meant?—that this force—whatever it was—would strike through him—would strike somebody dead—by his hand! But how—*innocently?* If it were done somehow *unconsciously* he might be innocent—but how could that affect the world?

It was all mad. This was the first opportunity she had had to think it all out since she had left him in the afternoon. All her thoughts till now had revolved around the strangeness, the exaltation, the passion of aspiration, she had felt in him. More than all she had been grieving over the loss of him—as a man—as a man who had loved her—a man she could have worshipped. He had seemed to ascend out of her life into a realm of spirit—where she could not follow.

With a pang she recognized that she had been blind—and selfish—as usual. Most of her pity—her grief—had been for herself—at the thought of losing him. She had never really entered into the state of mind which he was experiencing. If she had—if she had tried harder to understand him—sympathize with him—instead of clinging to him—trying first to persuade him that he must be wrong—and later closing her ears to what he said so that she could climb with him—emotionally—to the strange heights that seemed to be natural to him—if she had truly understood him she would have seen that he was suffering—not in renunciation of earth and love, as he himself believed—but through the melancholy of a delusion—the pains of a mind turned in upon itself to the verge of madness.

"I must find him," she said, looking quickly at the clock. It was a minute or two past nine. The clock had chimed the hour while she had been standing there near it, but her mind had been too distraught to notice the sound. She had been standing under the chandelier, rigidly upright, like a person in a trance, her hands clasped tightly together and pressed against her breast.

"I must find him," she said to herself, dropping her hands, and unconsciously gathering up her skirt. "I must find him. Perhaps Uncle Sturge is right. Perhaps he *is* dangerous. I must find him and bring him back."

Her coat and hat were upstairs, but she was too anxious to bother with them. If she went up she might be drawn into talk. Her mother or Mrs. Terry might ask questions. She didn't want them to know where she was going. Yet she might not be back for a long time. They would worry.

She went into the study and took a sheet of sermon paper from the drawer of her father's desk. Dipping his thick pen in the ink she scrawled a few words:—

DADDY.

I've gone out. I won't be long. I want to see Mr. Tavistock and find out about something. Don't worry about me.

LAURA

Beside the ink-well was a mounted buffalo-hoof which the Canon used as a paper-weight. She cleared the papers from his blotter and placed her note in the centre by itself, with the buffalo-hoof on top of it. She glanced around the room, left the light burning, and went out, closing the front door quietly behind her.

3

The moon was high in the sky. The trees, the houses, the road—everything was brilliantly lit—so that it seemed almost like day, except that the light was softer—more mysterious—and so beautiful that a sigh of yearning lifted itself heavily in Laura's throat as she tiptoed down the steps and hurried bareheaded along Charlotte Street toward the lake.

He was staying at the Manitoba Hotel. She remembered him saying so last night. But on a night like this he would not be in his room. He would be on the lake. She would hire a canoe from old Dan and go out and find him.

As soon as she was out of earshot of the house she began hurrying, her little heels thudding rapidly on the wooden sidewalk. At the corner she crossed the road and passed the magistrate's house. McCully's bush looked more mysterious than she had ever seen it, with the moon throwing dark shadows under the unmoving trees.

She came to where the path turned off, and for the first time in her life she hesitated to enter the familiar wood. For a few yards the path seemed to shine like a strip of silver between two dark banks of grass—then it was lost in a deep shadow, as black as a cave, and as chilling to her thought. A few twisted tree-trunks, half-seen in the darkness, seemed to be hiding themselves purposely—treacherously—ominously. . . .

She was too distraught to laugh at her fears. Already an electric feeling gripped her neck, sending cold shocks upward across her head. She steeled herself against the shudders creeping over her shoulders, and hurried on, keeping to the sidewalk at the edge of the bush. She could turn off by Enos Sadler's place and go on to Dan's along the lake road.

The dogs barking as she approached Sadler's added to her terror. She knew Sadler's dog—a mongrel collie—but in the night and in her present state, with another dog across the road adding his full-throated baying to the noise, she needed all her nerve to keep on and turn down to the lake road past Sadler's barn.

The growling died away behind her as she passed under the arching branches of the willows. Beyond the trees the lake lay like a sheet of silver under the moon. The sharp, familiar, jutting roof of Dan's boathouse came into sight. Separating itself from the others, jumbled along the shore, it stood out against the shining sky.

She went down the bank, sprang rapidly down the two or three steps to the wharf, and began examining the boats that were tied up there before she even looked around for Dan. He came ambling out of the tiny cupboard-like office, the blue enormous puffs of smoke from his pipe ascending straight up behind his head as he approached her. But before he spoke she had espied on the stern of one of the rowboats the name *Sigrid*.

"Mr. Tavistock is not on the lake," she said to Dan, in as normal a tone as she could manage.

"No, missie," said the Icelander, wagging his head from side to side and baring his broken teeth. "No, he not come to-night."

He swept his hand with the pipe in it widely away from his body in a gesture of negation.

Laura nodded at him a great many times, as her father might have done, and walked away from him, climbing the bank heavily, burdened with dejected thoughts.

As her foot touched the last of the steps she thought suddenly: "If old Mr. Linklater is so ill—that is where he will be. He has befriended him all this time—he will know about it—he will be there. Uncle Sturge and Daddy will be there, too."

Her heart was lightened as she stepped up on to the road and went along toward Linklater's through the dark arch of shadow the moon flung under the willows.

She felt like running. She wanted to meet them all together there—even if the old man was dying—even if he was dead. Death no longer held any horror for her. It was life that chilled her—the thought of life alone, without the man she had suddenly learned to love—the thought of what might happen to him—worse than death.

Worse than death! Death seemed good—natural—peaceful —a proper end. What she couldn't stand was the thought of madness.

Perhaps they were there, around the old man's bedside now. The doctor would be watching Tavistock. Perhaps, when they all came away they might bring him with them—talk to him—take care of him—nurse his mind back to health.

She was convinced now that he was out of his mind—or dangerously near it. Faith in his "destiny" had left her. There was no longer around his presence in her mind the aura of an archangel —a son of God. Now that it had passed she was almost glad. She could regard him again, as she had last night, as a man sick with some sort of suffering, who could be saved—restored to a normal, happy outlook.

When she remembered the passion in his eyes—last night and again this afternoon—her heart warmed with the thought that his love for her, his desire for her, would be enough to lift the cloud over his mind, if he would but surrender to love and give up his delusion of the coming miracle.

They would meet again, she felt sure, in a few minutes, at

Linklater's bedside. Seeing her again, unexpectedly, might be the turning-point. At one time, during their hour together in the afternoon, he had almost given up his mission.

"I want to live—I want to love you," he had said.

The words were sweet to her. She murmured them, almost aloud, as though she would have liked the willows and the lake to hear.

And later, after her outburst of tears, he had said: "Oh, Laura—if I belonged to earth—"

But he had not finished the sentence. The visions in his mind had obscured the shining love in his eyes.

She could see him now as she had never seen him before—the torture of suspense smoothed from his long, haggard face—his speaking eyes alight with clear, human hunger for her—his voice brightening and laughing—his whole nature responding to the warmth and colour of life—as soon as the burden of this mad sacrifice could be lifted from his mind.

Suddenly she saw him. He was coming along the road toward her, not far off, but distant enough that she recognized him only by his height, his walk, and because he was hatless, as always.

She was close to Linklater's now, but she had not been watching the road. The faint sound of a paddle dipped regularly in the water near at hand had drawn her attention to the lake. She had expected to see a canoe a few yards from shore, but there was nothing to be seen. She was puzzled and had almost stopped, to listen more carefully, when the canoe showed itself for a moment, slipping through the high reeds close to the bank. It was well ahead of her now. Whoever was paddling had passed her almost noiselessly, and for some reason was keeping out of sight in the cat-tails. She had seen the bent figure only for a second—long enough to see that it was a man.

The queerness of the occurrence was forgotten as soon as she lifted her glance to the road. There was Tavistock—in the flesh

—coming toward her. She had no sooner espied him than her fears returned. Even at a distance she could see by the pace of his walk, the hang of his arms, and his bent head, that he was more dejected than she had ever seen him.

She had barely time to recognize him before he disappeared. He was opposite Linklater's and had stepped off the high sidewalk into the garden. The growth of pig-weed hid him from view.

Without thinking, she began to run. Her mind was a chaos of new, unnameable fears. She ran blindly, the sound of her heels echoing in the willow-branches overhead. She reached the broken fence around the old man's shack and sprang down into the overgrown path. The huge leaves of the pigweed made a dark aisle through which she had to pass to reach the house.

Half-way along the path she heard a shout issuing from the open door. It brought her to a stop, her hands leaping to her face, her blood standing still as though frozen in her veins.

She had been so intent on following Tavistock that she had forgotten about her father and the doctor. If they were inside, the doctor's buggy would surely be tied in the ditch.

"Where could they have gone?" she thought.

The faint light of the lamp hardly penetrated the accumulated dirt on the front window, but its yellow glow could be seen beyond the dark edge of the half-opened door.

The strange shout had numbed her whole body, but hearing no further sounds, she drove herself forward, trembling from head to foot.

She stepped up on to the sloping floor of the old verandah, clutched at the door, which was jammed fast on a warped plank inside, and thrust her head into the shack.

Tavistock was standing straddle-legged with his back to her, facing the light. At his feet, near the old man's bed, something lay in shadow—something dark—a form—a man—the body of a man!

A groan, as though she herself were expiring, sounded in Laura's throat.

Tavistock wheeled swiftly around and cried, "Laura!" in a strange, expectant, exultant voice—a voice of triumph.

"Who is it?" Laura sobbed, clinging with both hands to the door and staring past him at the naked feet lying dead in the circle of lamplight on the floor.

"The old man—Linklater," said Tavistock, coming toward her. His face was against the light so that she couldn't tell what he looked like. She raised her hands in a gesture of horror, stopping him in the middle of a stride.

"Is he dead?" she whispered.

"Yes."

"Murdered?"

"Yes. But not—"

He stopped and looked into the air above him as though he sought words from on high.

"Great God! he *is* mad!" she breathed out in a gasp of terror.

Tavistock stretched out one hand toward her and said in a low, calm voice: "No—no, dearest—I didn't kill him."

He took another step toward her. "The miracle *did* happen," he said. "I came here—only a minute ago—only a minute before you—and the murder—was done—was *being* done."

He was mad. This was another of his dreams.

"When I came to this door," he said, "there was a man standing over his bed—strangling him. He saw me and let out a shout and ran out the back way—and the old man fell on the floor."

She took one step toward him and peered into his face. "Oh, beloved, is this true?"

He looked deeply into her eyes. "It is true. He ran out and jumped into a canoe he had there—I heard the splash as he pushed off—"

"A canoe!" exclaimed Laura.

"Yes. I heard the rattle of the paddle when he picked it up."

Laura grasped eagerly at his elbows. "I saw a man in a canoe sneaking through the cat-tails—he passed me just before I saw you. It must have been . . . Who was it? Did you know him?"

Tavistock did not speak.

"Oh, tell me," she cried. "If you knew how I've worried—how frantic I am—"

"Dearest!" he whispered. "I've tortured you so much. But I shouldn't say—I couldn't see clearly—I couldn't swear—"

"But who did you think it was? Tell me, and not another soul."

He clasped her cold hands in his and stroked them. "I thought it was that breed—what is his name?—that—"

"Jukes?"

"Yes."

She leaned nearer to him and turned him toward the light to look intently in his face.

"And you," she whispered, "what has happened to you? You look—"

"I am saved," he said.

She looked at him more searchingly than ever. "You mean that this—was your miracle?"

"Yes—perhaps it *was*—a miracle that has saved me from miracles—and madness!"

SEVEN

The Miracle

I

THE CANON and Dr. Bundy were at the door of Julie's place, coming away, when Pitts staggered up the path under the choke-cherry trees and stopped in front of them, breathless. Lamplight through the door fell on his frightened face.

The doctor, standing a step or two above him on the broad stoop, holding open the screen-door, glanced once at his staring eyes and said sharply: "What's the trouble, Pitts ?"

The old man, panting hard, pointed to the dark bush behind the house.

"Tavistock," he gasped.

The Canon, still only half-way out of the door, talking to Julie, heard the name, and turned abruptly. "What's this, Sturge?"

The doctor did not answer. He sprang down the two steps and grasped the front of the old man's coat. "What has he done?" he demanded.

"He's mad," Pitts gulped. "He was in the bush there. He was going to kill me. It sounds awful, doctor—but that's the truth. He's mad."

"What did he do?"

The old man hopped about from one foot to the other, gasping for breath after running so hard. "I ran away," he whispered. "I was scared stiff."

"Did he follow you?"

"I turned round to see—just as I came out on the road. He was going the other way—toward Linklater's."

"Were you talking to him before he threatened you?"

"Yes," said Pitts. "I went to his room. I heard what Gawthorp told you and the Chief last night—and I went—I went to see—what he was like."

The Canon had put on his hat and was standing close beside the doctor. Julie had come out on the stoop. She stood with the knob of the screen-door in her hand, bent over, listening.

"What was he like?" said the Canon.

"He—he isn't right, Canon. He's mad—I'm sure he is."

"You think he's gone over to Linklater's?" the doctor asked abruptly.

"He went that way."

"Does he know the old man is dead?"

Pitts' mouth gasped open. "Dead!" he exclaimed.

"Yes," said the doctor soberly. "He died about an hour ago. And Tavistock didn't know?"

"I'm sure he didn't. I was with him just about an hour." He paused and hung his head. "So the old man's dead. Sort of sudden, wasn't it?"

"Yes. They sent for me Julie—here sent for me—but I was at the Macaulay's—and he was dead before we could get there."

He touched the Canon's arm. "We'd better go back there, Malcolm, and see if we can find this madman. If he goes there and finds the house empty and the old man dead, it may—"

"He *will* go crazy," said the Canon fearfully.

"No," said the doctor. "It may bring him to his senses."

2

They went one behind the other through the overgrown garden—the doctor ahead, the Canon behind him. Pitts had stayed behind, gladly enough, to answer Julie's questions.

As they came up to the verandah, voices could be heard inside.

"There are two people talking," the doctor whispered over his shoulder.

They stopped. "That's Laura!" exclaimed the Canon, groping for the doctor's arm. "In God's name—what is she—?"

But Bundy had also recognized her voice, and with one stride leapt onto the verandah. He ran through the door and stopped, so that the Canon, close behind, almost collided with him.

Tavistock and Laura, startled by their sudden entry, turned and gazed at them in surprise.

"Laura!" cried the Canon, stepping quickly from behind Bundy. "What are you doing here?"

But the doctor had espied the body of the old man on the floor—the body they had left composed in the bed only a few minutes before. "What is this?" he demanded abruptly. "What has happened?"

Tavistock inhaled a long breath, and looked down at the twisted figure beside the bed. "He has been murdered," he said, in a deep tone that echoed through the bare room.

The doctor flashed a grim, meaning glance at the Canon and leaned down to his ear. "Be ready for anything," he whispered. Then he stepped forward, encircled Laura's waist with his arm and drew her away from Tavistock.

"How do you know he was murdered?" Bundy said.

"I saw it."

The doctor said to Laura: "Go with your father, darling."

But Laura slipped her waist from his grasp and stood looking at him in amazement. "What's the matter, Uncle?" she asked breathlessly.

"Don't ask me now," he said in a low voice, shaking his head warningly at her. He took a step toward Tavistock and stood still, bracing his feet firmly.

"There's a mistake here somewhere, Tavistock," he said, in a quiet, controlled voice. "Linklater died—peacefully—an hour ago."

"What?" cried Laura, glancing with sudden frenzy at her father.

"Were you here when he died?" Tavistock asked the doctor quickly.

"No," said Bundy. "Canon Macaulay and I arrived too late. But we saw him—in the bed there. I examined him. He had been dead, then, perhaps half an hour."

Tavistock looked across at Laura and was about to speak.

"How does he come to be on the floor?" asked Bundy gravely.

"It will sound strange to you—" began Tavistock, but Laura interrupted him.

"But it's true," she cried. "I saw the man myself."

The doctor glanced at her warningly, shaking his heavy head at her, frowning.

"I came," said Tavistock more hesitantly, "I came here—to see him—not knowing he was dead. I came with—but never mind that. I got to the door and looked in—and—as I thought —he was being murdered. A man stood over him with his hands at his throat. When he saw me he let the old man go and the body rolled on to the floor. The man—"

"It was Jukes—Jack Jukes," said Laura, looking excitedly from one to the other. "I saw him in a canoe—just before I got here—sneaking along very quietly, close in to shore, in the cat-tails. It was Jukes."

"He ran out the back way," added Tavistock. "I heard his paddle rap against the canoe when he jumped in—I heard a splash. Now that it isn't murder, I'll tell you—it *was* Jukes."

The Canon took a short stride toward Bundy and began nodding and wagging his head. "That's who it would be," he muttered incoherently, his mouth twisted with excitement. "He came to the magistrate's last night—while I was there—just before the drowning. He was here—cursing at old Dave—the day before. He had a notion old Dave had money hidden away here that belonged to him."

The doctor looked searchingly at Tavistock from under his heavy brows. He was on the point of saying, "You're a lucky man," but he checked himself. He was surmising that Tavistock had come there—a maniac—bent on murder. Pitts' fright had confirmed the suspicions Gawthorp had already sown in his mind. But the man seemed so thoroughly rational now. Even on his own theory, that a shock might bring him to his senses, it was difficult to believe he had ever been as dangerous as Gawthorp and Pitts had made out.

If he had come there bent on murder, the shock of seeing what would look like his own act, being enacted by another, would undoubtedly have an effect on his mania. The doctor shook his head over the mystery of events, thinking that even if Jukes had not been there, just at that moment, death had already forestalled the purpose Tavistock may have carried in his mind when he came to the shack.

He brought out his thought adroitly, turning to the Canon and saying: "Jukes was lucky. If no one had known the old man was dead already, he might have had a charge of murder against him now."

"I might have had—myself," said Tavistock.

Laura stepped away from her father toward him. "Tell them

what you started to tell me," she said eagerly. "They were even more anxious about you than I was. Tell them what happened to you."

As she spoke, the doctor noticed the exultant, ecstatic look return to Tavistock's face. "It's so new—so marvellous—I would like to tell everybody," he said simply, with an almost boyish awkwardness which surprised all three of them.

3

The quiet night outside seemed to have been made for confidences, uttered in a low tone between people sitting close together under the stars. There are nights when an expanse of starry sky, a profundity of silence and the depths of strangely shaped shadows cause people to whisper to each other of things which they have kept hidden for years, things which in daylight they would never utter.

This intimacy of feeling grew between the four of them as they came out beside the lake. They had placed Linklater's body back on the bed, and leaving the lamp burning for the undertaker, who was soon expected, they had left the house with a feeling of relief.

"Let's sit up here on the bank," Laura had suggested, pointing to a grassy spot deeply shadowed under two willows whose branches were curiously intertwined.

"Hadn't we better go home?" the Canon said. "The mosquitoes . . ."

"We'll make a smudge," said Bundy, and at once began gathering twigs and handfuls of scorched grass.

"They're not bad to-night," said Laura, helping to gather material for the fire. "And the sky is so wonderful."

"Yes, it's better here," said Tavistock.

The doctor took matches from his pocket and got the dried grass burning, while the others stood around waiting to see which way the smoke would be blown.

There was no noticeable breeze in any direction, but the smoke drifted toward the trees, and they sat down under them, the doctor lying full length near the smudge, ready to replenish it with handfuls of grass.

EIGHT

Illumination

I

"FOR YEARS NOW," said Tavistock, "I've lived for one thing."

The Canon took off his round hat and laid it down beside him in the grass. The doctor hitched himself forward and leaned more heavily on his elbow. Laura, looking up steadily at the stars, crossed her ankles and drew them under her.

"I believed," Tavistock went on, "I still believe—that there is no such thing as evil. I'm surer of it than ever. I *know* there is no evil. But for years I looked for some sort of miracle that would convince everybody—that in God's sight nothing can be evil. I believed that this—this miracle—would come through a man. I looked for such a man. I waited for years. And finally I became convinced that I was the man who—who . . ."

"Who might be 'the Comforter,'" said Bundy.

The Canon, lifting his head as though scenting something a long way off, repeated in a dreamy tone the words that had puzzled him so much: "To reprove the world of sin, and righteousness, and judgment."

"Yes," said Tavistock. "Exactly!" He fell silent, plucking at his heels, which were curled up under him.

Laura reached toward him in the dark and touched his elbow gently. "Tell them what happened—in there," she said. "You started to tell me . . ."

He covered her hand on his arm and held it there. "Yes—something happened to me," he said, and the three listeners at once recognized in his tone the same paradoxical serenity they had seen on his face in the shack. "During the moment that I stood there—watching that breed struggling with the old man—I was changed. No. A change that is instantaneous isn't a change. It was like being made—made again—made *new.*"

He lifted Laura's hand from his arm and held it in both his own, clasped together in the cool grass.

"All your old ideas were—washed away," said Bundy.

"It was like—well, it was like being born again—like being another person—and with an understanding of life that would have been inconceivable—to the person I used to be."

He paused and looked sideways at Laura, at her profile against the lighted sky. "Everybody, I imagine, has felt hints—at some time or another—of the mystery of life," he said slowly, consideringly. "Hints, I mean, not of the puzzle—but of the answer—if you know what I mean."

"Yes," nodded the doctor.

"You've had hints of the answer—have you, doctor?" Tavistock asked.

"Yes, but never mind. Go on."

"Well, in that moment," said Tavistock, with surprising boyishness, instead of the gravity they all expected, "I got the *whole* answer. I don't mean the *reason* for anything. It was a sudden seeing that there is *no* reason for anything."

"Ah!" exclaimed the doctor jubilantly.

"You're thinking, perhaps, that it was a natural fling-back from what I'd been through—is that it?"

"No, I wasn't thinking that," said Bundy softly.

"I've heard people explain experiences like this in that way," Tavistock said dispassionately. "They think that people who are *too* reasonable—people, I mean, who are always looking for reasons—always questioning and doubting—atheists or agnostics, in other words—are exactly the people who suddenly flop over into some sort of—well, conversion is usually their word for it. And these conversions, they think, are not so much a seeing of the light, as an escape—a refuge—from too much thinking, too many doubts. A surrender, if you know what I mean."

The Canon signified assent with a double grunt in his throat.

"You mean that you *did* see the light. It was a sort of illumination," the doctor said, with eager interest.

"You could call it that, I suppose," said Tavistock. He was weary of words and names. He had caught a glimpse of life after years of wandering in a fog of words and dreams. It was as though he had caught hold of something real and solid. The line of an old hymn ran through his mind: "Lay hold on life—" Yes, and what was the rest of it? "Lay hold on life and it shall be—thy joy and crown eternally." Yes, now he knew what it meant. Words like that, he felt, would now be clear to him. He had concerned himself too much with words—puzzling over them—wrestling with them—as Jacob did with the angel—trying to wring their secret from them. He said to himself: "Life has gone by while I have been worrying about the *meaning* of it. And now—it's strange—the meaning isn't any clearer—but *life* is! I'm like a blind man seeing the earth for the first time."

He felt the doctor's glance fixed on him, and said: "It wasn't like a light, but it was as though I had been blind all my life—and suddenly saw the earth for the first time. I knew a chap in Africa who had what he called an illumination. It changed his whole life. Up to that time he had been an intellectual—a cynic—a misanthrope almost. And then suddenly, he said, he became like a child. I remember questioning the value of his experience.

It seemed queer to me that such a terrific experience—that was the word he used—'terrific'—should do nothing more than restore him to the—the level, you might say—of ordinary people. And yet that's what he insisted on. 'I can see now,' he told me, 'that some terrific shock was necessary to make me like any ordinary, *simple* person.' I remember the emphasis he put on the word 'simple.' And—of course—it wasn't enough for me. I've always felt that an illumination—a mystical experience—would be something unearthly—apocalyptic—a union with God. But now it has happened to me it isn't a bit unearthly. It is here on earth. You see—"

Tavistock paused, smiled and drew a hand lingeringly across his eyes, as though wiping away the last wisp of a web of entanglement. "You see," he went on, "I realize, now, that I've always looked outwards. I've always been straining for some vision—some sign—some *answer*—that would come out of the air somehow—out of the sky."

He raised his head and actually laughed. "It's amazing, really. All this time I've been the rankest materialist. That's really it. Looking for material signs and wonders. It's simply never occurred to me that the miracle takes place inside—here—and now! I've been looking all my life for—for—*another state!* And yet I should have known. There was a chap at Cambridge, I remember, who claimed to have been converted—saved. The chaps all joshed him terribly, but one day I got him alone and asked him about it. I said to him: 'What you mean is that you have a *promise* of salvation. You will be saved—after you die. You will go to heaven—*then!*' And I can still remember how he looked at me and said, 'No, Geoff. I mean I am saved *now!*' And I said, 'But, my dear boy, you are here—talking to me. You're not in heaven.' And then—I shall never forget how he said: 'I don't have to die to be saved—to be in heaven. At this moment—at this moment—I am sitting at the right hand of God the Father Almighty!'"

Tavistock looked at the doctor and shook his head. "I didn't understand it. But I do now. God the Father—and heaven—are not a million miles away. It *is* possible to 'walk with God'—as they used to say—here—on this earth. Only—somehow—it isn't God. Not the old remote God, anyway. Perhaps it is only just a simple, natural joy in being alive—a sort of childlike trust in—in the power that brings us here. The whole point seems to be that it can't be talked about—it's too *simple* to be talked about."

Tavistock looked at the Canon, hoping that he would say something, so that he himself could remain silent. He wanted to *live* this experience he had found—not talk about it. But Laura's father had his head twisted to one side, staring abstractedly at the grass.

2

The night had deepened over them. The moon was sinking and the stars shone more brilliantly than ever in a darker blue. There was hardly a boat or a canoe left on the lake—none at all near at hand—and the four of them sitting there quietly in the shadow of the trees felt the spell of darkness and silence descending over them. The doctor was more conscious than the others of the immense blue canvas confronting them, painted with constellations. He felt the smallness of man beside the infinitely ascending wall of night, and after a brief interval he turned to Tavistock and asked, in a low voice: "Now that you've had this experience, what do you think of your—your belief in a Comforter?"

Tavistock, who had also been looking at the stars, but without seeing them, drooped his head slowly. "Ah!" he said. "When I think of that—well—I can see now that it *had* become a mania. It began with rebellion—with the thought that Christ—that God even—had not done all that could be done for suffering humanity. It was *humane* enough—to begin with. But that any man should think himself somehow superior to God—*better* than God!—what madness! And yet—that's what I was hoping to do—to be a light in a dark world. I can't imagine what has always blinded me to the sunshine. The mind, I suppose. This puny little mind of ours—fiickering like a candle in all this sunshine—and yet we *trust* it. The things we can't see by its miserable light we refuse to believe in. What madness! Roff was quite right—I thought too much. But, you—you don't think that I planned a murder of *that* kind."

Dr. Bundy unclasped his hands from behind his head and sat up straight. "Then you did plan a murder—of *some* kind?"

The old look of melancholy returned for a moment to Tavistock's face. "No," he said patiently, "I never *planned* it. I didn't want to will it. It wasn't to be my will. I felt that if I kept myself ready the miracle would use me—it would strike through me—like the lightning. Brooding on it must have sent me half out of my mind or I would never have got as near it as I did."

"But you *did* get near it," said Bundy. "Pitts told us you threatened him."

"I didn't threaten him," said Tavistock softly. "I asked him *if he was the man*. I felt in my heart that he wasn't. Yet I wanted to hear his denial. I was full of doubts, although those last two days I had felt myself drawn to . . . to . . ."

His changed face clouded over again and he plunged his fingers frenziedly through his hair.

"You mean you had decided who it was to be?" asked Bundy, in a tone that showed his sympathy with Tavistock's torture.

"It seemed to be decided for me."

"Who was it?"

Tavistock flashed a pitiful glance at the doctor. "Linklater!" he said.

"Merciful Father!" cried the Canon.

"You see," Tavistock plunged on, "I could never will it or plan it. I had no weapons and I wouldn't get any. It was to be done spontaneously and only if I could see it innocently in the moment of doing it. But gradually Linklater became mixed up with my thoughts about it. The old man was praying for death. He wanted to die."

"You really went there—then—intending . . ." the Canon began, but chokingly stopped.

"No!" cried Tavistock. "I came out of the bush—after Pitts had run away—and started down the road—as though I was being drawn. But all the time I felt that I wasn't ready. I wanted to live. And, anyway, this wasn't what I had dreamed of. Was there anything godlike in that—to kill a half-dead old man? Even to think of it sickened me. Yet all this time I was going toward his shack . . . drawn . . . fascinated . . ."

He ran his hands through his hair again, as though shaking off evil presences. "I know what hell is," he declared passionately. "It is the lowest, most damnable reach of the mind of man. No poet has ever given the least hint of its vileness, its meanness, its horrible, slow, revolving torture."

He became calmer and looked around at them enquiringly. But their heads were bent in darkness and neither of them made a sound.

"I wanted to give it up," he said, gaining command of himself. "I *gave* it up. I had given it up a dozen times just in the last two days. I gave it up—once and for all. I looked at the moon over his house and I swore to its whiteness—'I am not the man!' But voices like devils howled in my ears. 'Coward!' and 'failure!' they sneered at me. 'The new Christ!' they hissed at me. 'How can you live?—how can you live?' they jeered, 'if this is not done?' And by this time I was in the garden . . . but there was no garden, no house, no man to kill . . . only this hell in my soul. I found myself at the door. I looked in. *And it was being done*!"

The Canon scrambled to his feet, his face working like a man with a palsy. He raised his hands over his head and grasped a low-hanging willow branch to cling to, trembling.

The doctor did not move. His fingers, clenched over his forehead, were pressed against his closed, throbbing eyelids.

Laura drew her hand away and covered her face, as one shudder after another shook her.

Tavistock threw out his arms in a cross-like gesture—a gesture of complete surrender. "Suddenly I saw—I *saw*—that there was no evil. This murder I thought was being done was innocent. Any murder!" he cried, his voice mounting, "anything!—everything anyone ever thought was evil—all rushed together with the good—and I could see it—together—unified—I could see it *as the nature of God*!"

3

He stopped and looked over his shoulder at the short dark body of the Canon under the tree, the pale blur of his face half turned away.

There was something on the tip of Tavistock's tongue—one more thing he wanted to say—something he thought might hurt the Canon, and yet he felt compelled to say it. He wanted to purge himself completely of his old life. He wanted to say this one thing, so that they would know that the last trace of his mania—his mission—had been washed from his mind.

Until he had uttered it he did not want to look at Laura, or even think of her. He wanted to be finished for ever with the thought that had always poisoned him—the thought that God was a failure and that man must come to his rescue with miracles and crucifixions and resurrections from the dead. He knew at last that he could not help God—that God needs no help. He felt free—as God is free.

"You won't like this, Canon," he said, "but I want to tell you what I felt—everything I felt. . . ."

"Go on, go on," the Canon urged, in a sort of groan.

"As soon as I saw—what I saw—the perfection of everything—the harmony of good and evil—I knew that God never had any need to send a Son to this earth because of its sins. There was no need for Christ—or any new Christs. The Christ story seems to me now simply a symbol of God himself suffering—in his own body—the universe. God himself suffering everything—causing everything—enduring everything—and rejoicing in his strength—his eternal victory over death."

The Canon let go of the branch he was holding, and squatted down again in the grass, drawing his knees up tightly against his chest. A buggy came along and went rattling by on the road behind them. For a few moments the noise was deafening. When it had passed, Tavistock waited for one of the others to speak.

It surprised him that he had wanted to say so much. His perpetual need to talk, to think, to puzzle over things, had disappeared, it seemed to him, in the moment when old Linklater's head had rolled into the moonlight. He had accepted it as a murder. In a flash he had understood all murders—all deaths. He accepted death as the dark sister of life. He accepted everything. He accepted the earth.

He had told them all this only because of Laura. She had come into the shack just as his heart was bursting with this sense of a greater mystery which needed no solution. His first step across the threshold into a life *that had only to be lived*—was toward her. His own voice had awakened in him again when she came and stood in his arms. Over a dead man's body he had felt the first stirring of this new free life, when she had lifted her head and kissed him as a woman kisses who no longer fears or wonders, but has chosen and knows she has chosen and cares for nothing else.

He was eager now to be silent. He was eager to love. The shadows of his long grieving, which had made the earth seem sinister, were gone. The whiteness of the water under the moon was like an echo of what had happened within himself. The soft night—a night of bridal whiteness—seemed to have been made for the whispers of all mating things.

He turned slowly and looked at the oval of Laura's head against the shining sky.

"Now," he said to himself, "I can think of the earth."

Notes

4 Poplar Plains—Based on Portage la Prairie, Manitoba, to which Brooker's family emigrated from England in 1905 when he was seventeen years old. Numerous historical, architectural, institutional, and geographical details of the community's development up to 1907, when it officially became a city, are inscribed in the novel: its founding as a white settlement by a charismatic Anglican missionary, its railroad history, the coming of Ukrainians at the turn of the century, the building and style of the churches described in the novel as well as the Home of Incurables, the presence of Native and Métis peoples, the town "lake" and its boat rental business, and the years of boom, bust, flood, cyclone, and arson (though the order of the latter two are reversed; cf. 134). Two differences in Brooker's fictional history are notable: Firstly, Brooker is clearly sympathetic to the economic hardships and social prejudices with which Native and Métis live, but like other modern Canadian writers concerned about the immiseration of the modern Native, he is not interested in showing their own, persisting forms of social organization and historical power. (Hence Brooker's use of the term "breed" for mixed-blood Natives, which is introduced here at the outset and later applied to the sympathetic character Jukes, refers at once to a real social element and to an imaginary racialized type, that the author wants to re-value in a positive rather than derogatory way—*even* while this term marks a failure to transcend negative racial cliché in general.) Secondly, while the real missionary founder of Portage, Archdeacon Cochrane, established his settlers in 1851 and died in 1865, Brooker extends his life to the present, to provide a character whose perspective encompasses the whole story of the fictional

community's development. Ironically, a community leader did exist with such a long view: the influential Chief Yellowquill of the Saulteaux Chippewas (1832-1910). See Anne M. Collier's *A History of Portage la Prairie and Surrounding District* (Altona, Manitoba: D.W. Friesen and Sons, 1969).

4 Galicians—Immigrants from Galicia, a region in southeastern Poland and northwestern Ukraine.

5 "The Comforter will come . . ."—John 16:7-8. The coming of the Comforter is initially promised in John 14:16-17. Here as elsewhere, Brooker's biblical citations are based on the King James Version. Tavistock interprets the Comforter to refer to a kind of second Christ, that is an apocalyptic Redeemer, but a secular one, the product of human time, creation, and symbolization (unlike the orthodox Messiah of Revelations, or the Holy Ghost with whom the Comforter is traditionally identified).

30 "kind o' gentle—kind o' womanish"—Brooker is concerned to show that Tavistock's higher consciousness is androgynous (cf. 259). In his 1931 essay, "Nudes and Prudes," he suggests that sexual difference may be "the primary division of Being, the first mysterious step taken by the primal unity towards multiplicity" (74-5). As such it offers a crucial figure for the relationship between unity and multiplicity, between social closure and historical creativity, that he wishes encode in the injunction to "think of the earth."

30 His bare head . . .—The description of Tavistock's physiognomy conforms remarkably with that of the French poet, Charles Baudelaire, author of *Flowers of Evil* (1857). Dennis Reid has shown that a sculpture of Baudelaire by Raymond Duchamp-Villon, owned by Toronto collector friends, "impressed Brooker greatly," and can be seen as the basis of figures in at least two of his early paintings (12).

31 unsubstantial blueness—Throughout the novel, blue and red are contrasted with a painterly emphasis, and linked to contrasting experiences of identity and difference, that Brooker would not have thought arbitrary (e.g. Tavistock's "escape" from the "inferno" of the bloody sunset over the industrial zone, into the "cleared, blue space" of his imagination, 39). Under the title "The Blue and the Sweet," Brooker collected notes and writings on theories of colour, and on the significance of colours in literature, which he intended to publish in the form

of short stories or essays (now in the Bertram Brooker Archives at the University of Manitoba). Relevant to the concerns of this novel is Brooker's reference to the difference between blue and red described by the philosopher Alfred North Whitehead, as a both absolute and particular, hence exemplary, existential "contrast" to be comprehended in the totalizing work of *Process and Reality: an Essay in Cosmology* (1929).

32 "It is possible!"—A paradigmatic Faustian claim, in its Goethian Romantic context referring to a liberated (for good or ill) human creativity and consequent range of experience. Brooker may have invented the quotation for the novel: I have not discovered these exact words or a plausible transliteration in any version of the Faust legend.

33 Job, Psalms, Hamlet, Lear, Blake, Bach, Palestrina—The first four citations mark Brooker's commitment to an existentialist tradition which questions, from the position of a self isolated in profound agony or alienation, the order or value of one's social or cosmological world. The last three "answers" mark his interest in mysticism and music as offering emotive and formal, rather than conceptual, images of unity in and with that world (cf. 203-4). Significantly, Brooker cites not Romantic composers, but Palestrina and Bach. The first exemplary interaction between Tavistock and Laura is his secret listening to her playing Bach (37), an interaction that Laura will later replay to herself, symbolically taking over his position in the shadows (228-9). The contrapuntal layering, the dynamic complexity, and the theatrical effects of baroque music are appropriate to the theme of a struggling search for symbolic form adequate to temporal change and heterogeneity.

38 Beardsley's drawings for Wilde's *Salome*—Aubrey Beardsley produced a series of drawings (1894) for Oscar Wilde's play based on the biblical Salome (conventionally a figure of amoral sensuality, who danced before Herod in exchange for John the Baptist's head on a platter, Matthew 14:6-10).

38 "Give me the daggers"—*Macbeth* II.ii.51.

53 "To him that overcometh . . ."—Revelations 2:17.

56 The misery that will not let us rest—Reference to John Keats' unfinished poem, "The Fall of Hyperion: a Dream" (1819), lines 148-9. The poem is more extensively qtd. 91-92. Curiously, a contemporary

reviewer of the novel considered this "a good theme for a country in the making" (*Evening Telegram*, Toronto, Oct. 9, 1937; Bertram Brooker Archives). Grace discusses the poem in greater detail in her 1989 article (68-70).

59 "Judge not lest ye be judged"—Matthew 7.1.

60 "That is in Romans"—Tavistock has drawn upon the subtle argument of Paul's Epistle to the Romans, regarding the dialectical dependence upon each other of sin (or morality) and the commandments (or law). Here Paul appears to idealize the Edenic innocence of knowledge of good and evil, as a figure for the metaphysical redemption offered in the present through internalization of grace in love rather than externalized deference to law. The Canon's reply, "For all have sinned . . .", is Romans 3:23; to which Tavistock responds with "The law speaks only . . .", 3:19.

61 "That they may be made perfect in one"—John 17:23. "Be ye therefore perfect!" is Matthew 5:48.

62 "God is light . . ."—1 John 1:5-7.

71 Sigrid—A violent, powerful, and pagan queen of Denmark, c. 1000.

76 There was a man sent from God—John 1:6.

96 "I'll be thirty-three"—That is, the paradigmatic age of the lost pilgrim Dante at the opening of the *Inferno*, and of the archetype behind this figure, Jesus Christ in his final days.

96 "Makes you think of the plagues of Egypt"—That is, when all the waters of Egypt turn to blood, as a sign of its crimes, Exodus 7:19-21. The insistent repetition of this blood imagery throughout, and of the "plagues of Egypt" reference specifically (159), suggests the dark side of Brooker's national allegory.

100 "Another Terry"—Dame Ellen Terry, a famous English actress known especially for her Shakespearian roles, and for her partnership with the equally famous actor Sir Henry Irving, whose career was founded upon his portrayal of Hamlet. Tavistock is supposed to have begun as an actor in Irving's Lyceum company (33).

103 "I wouldn't will anything"—This statement marks an important difference in Tavistock's thought, at this narrative moment, from that

of Nietzsche, despite his "obsession" with Nietzsche's transvaluation of all values. Tavistock wants impartially to symbolize his world, to create an adequate sign for it. He therefore wishes to renounce his individual will except insofar as it is a will to sympathy—a purely reflective or aesthetic ideal which Nietzsche's predecessor, Arthur Schopenhauer, discussed in *The World as Will and Representation* (1819). This ideal is also the subject of a poem by Brooker, "the doctor" (Sproxton 62-3).

111 "There is an eternity in men and women"—Reference to phrases from Walt Whitman's Preface to *Leaves of Grass* (1855), repeated as a verse in his poem, "By Blue Ontario's Shore" (1856 edition). References to Blake and Goethe are general rather than specific, but Brooker's explicit intertexts for this novel are respectively, *The Marriage of Heaven and Hell* (1793) and *Faust* (1808/1832).

112 revolution of 1905—The period of strikes and riots all over Russia, in opposition to the obstinacy of a conservative tsar and the failure of significant liberal reforms. The first duma was a representative assembly whose powers were limited almost entirely to a consultative function.

123 "the greatest good of the greatest number"—The formula of utilitarianism, as conceived by Jeremy Bentham and popularized as such by John Stuart Mill.

124 "a murder, let us say . . ." A very similar argument is the seed of Raskolnikov's murder in Fyodor Dostoevsky's *Crime and Punishment* (1866).

125 Pascal—Blaise Pascal, French religious philosopher, best known for the notes and fragments collected under the title *Pensées* (1658), from which these arguments are drawn. The example of the one-eyed man is from fragment 409 of the standard, Brunschvicg edition.

143 South African veteran—Of the South African war (1899-1902) between the British Empire and the Orange Free State and Transvaal Republic.

186 "Nothing is overcome . . ."—Virgil, *Aeneid* V:710.

190 "Surely he hath borne our griefs . . ."—Isaiah 53:4.

191 "He became as we are . . ."—Reference to 1 Corinthians 9:20-22.

198 "Jesus among the Doctors in the Temple"—Luke 2:46.

211 Jacob's ladder—Genesis 28:12. This is another image through which Brooker endeavours to show the complementarity of contrasting truths (heavenward and earthward, idealist and historicist).

234 Lourdes—The French pilgrimage site of the cult of Our Lady of Lourdes, where miraculous healing is supposed to occur.

234 Marconi—Marchese Guglielmo Marconi, inventor of wireless telegraphy and pioneer of global radio communications.

238 "knows no possible forgiveness . . ."—Walt Whitman, Preface to *Leaves of Grass* (1855).

248 "O to disengage myself"—Walt Whitman, "O Living Always, Always Dying," published first as a section of *Calamus* in *Leaves of Grass* (1860 edition).

249 Job had spoken of the morning stars singing together—Reference to Job 38:7. Blake devoted one of his series of drawings to this theme, in which God speaks to Job of Creation, in his *Illustrations of the Book of Job* (1821).

255 Abraham's sacrifice—Genesis 22.

256 "Readiness is all"—*Hamlet* V.ii.195.

286 "like a candle in all this sunshine"—Reference to William Blake's *Marriage of Heaven and Hell*, Plate 22. Brooker once considered entitling the novel "Candle in Sunshine," with Blake's text quoted in an epigraph.

Selected Bibliography

The following annotated list of publications by Brooker and his critics is far from exhaustive, and is intended only to provide a useful introduction to Brooker's writing for the reader new to it. Works selected either provide a general understanding of his artistic activities and interests, or pertain especially to his writing.

Primary

——. "Conrad's View of Life." *Canadian Forum* 5.55 (Apr. 1925): 207, 208, 210. This attack on Conrad's "pessimism" reveals Brooker's extensive reading of Conrad, and his struggle to affirm Conrad's poetic gifts and historical insights, while rejecting his resignation to modernity as an unchanging and unchangeable fate. Given the strong elements of resignation in the endings to Brooker's own *Think of the Earth* and *Within*, it is tempting to read this essay as an expression of a conflict in his own work.

——. Ed. *Yearbook of the Arts in Canada, 1928-1929*. Toronto: Macmillan, 1929. This volume brings together many of the influential voices in the arts of its time. Brooker's introduction, "When We Awake!" develops an analysis of Canadian historical diversity as opposed to an ideal of unity, and the related role of the artist.

——. *Elijah*. New York: William Edwin Rudge, 1929. A series of graphic illustrations for texts from 1 and 2 Kings.

——. [under pseud. Richard Surrey.] *Layout Technique in Advertising*. New York: McGraw-Hill, 1929. A grammar of visual design, applying the formal qualities of high art to commercial ends.

——. [under pseud. Richard Surrey.] *Copy Technique in Advertising*. New York: McGraw-Hill, 1930. The rhetorical forms and elements of advertising texts, normally with reference to literary models, with digressions into literary analysis.

——. "Idolaters of Brevity." *Sewanee Review* 39 (Jul.-Sep. 1931): 263-8. An unremarkable essay which mixes an analysis of the economic basis of modern "brevity" in literary form, with an attack on Naturalist writers. Of interest is Brooker's ambivalent appraisals of a range of writers, as against his call for idealist historical narratives that reach, at least implicitly, from the past *through* the present to the future.

——. "Nudes and Prudes." 1931. *Documents in Canadian Art*, ed. Douglas Fetherling (Peterborough: Broadview, 1987): 66-75. A discussion of censorship, aesthetic theory, education, and sexuality.

——. *Within*. 1935. *The Dragon: A Parable of Illusion and Disillusion*. 1936. Two experimental plays published together, ed. Sherrill E. Grace. *Canadian Drama* 11.1 (1985): 251-79.

——. "Mrs. Hungerford's Milk." 1936. *Voices of Discord: Canadian Short Stories from the 1930s*, ed. Donna Phillips, introduction by Kenneth J. Hughes (Toronto: New Hogtown, 1979): 92-100. Hughes offers an interesting political-economic analysis of Brooker's story, 24-27.

——. [under pseud. Huxley Herne.] *Tangled Miracle*. London: Thomas Nelson and Sons, 1936. A pulp detective novel. Brooker's turns his profounder struggle for an idealism that will yet "think of the earth" into a playful form: a crime takes place among a mystical cult that believes in the *physical* ascension of the soul.

——. *Think of the Earth*. Toronto: Thomas Nelson, 1936. The novel was simultaneously published in England by Jonathan Cape, receiving numerous reviews in Britain and Canada—positive, negative, and mixed.

——. Ed. *Yearbook of the Arts in Canada, 1936*. Toronto: Macmillan, 1936. The delayed sequel to Brooker's *Yearbook* of 1929. His introduction, "Art and Society," is an extraordinary summa of his view of art and life, original not in its individual parts but in their synthesis. It promotes Keats' negative capability, understood as prophetic crisis and the chameleonic nature of the artistic self open to experience, as well as the importance (somewhat paradoxically) of inutility, alienation, and novelty in modern art. It concludes with an exemplary statement of the post-Nietzschean unity in disunity, or perfection in change, which Brooker sought to idealize in art.

——. "The Future of the Novel in Canada." 1938. *Canadian Novelists and the Novel*, ed. Douglas Daymond and Leslie Monkman (Ottawa: Borealis, 1981): 150-53. Brooker's observations on the state of the Canadian novel and its audience. It is especially interesting for its call for Canadian historical novels, against its perception of modern Canada as the vanguard in a global "levelling process . . . which threatens a rather grey, equalized, regimented scene for the future novelist."

——. *The Robber: A Tale of the Time of the Herods*. Toronto: Collins, 1949. Historical fiction that takes Jesus' contemporary, Barabbus as its protagonist, representing him as a grass roots rebel leader with his own parallel political and spiritual trajectory. It was the most widely disseminated of Brooker's novels.

——. *Sounds Assembling: The Poetry of Bertram Brooker*. Ed. and introduction by Birk Sproxton. Winnipeg: Turnstone, 1980. A selection of Brooker's published and unpublished poetry, together with a few prose reflections and short essays. Of the latter, "The Poetry of E.E. Cummings" (1930), is revealing for its influence by modernist writers such as T.S. Eliot he elsewhere sharply criticizes (see Arnason 82), specifically the importance of the English metaphysical poets and their relevance to modern art.

Secondary

Arnason, David. "Reluctant Modernist." *Provincial Essays* 7 (1989): 77-85. A study of Brooker's critical writings, nicely mapping out his ambivalent relationship to modernism.

Bennett, Richard E. *Register of the Bertram Brooker Collection*. Winnipeg: Elizabeth Dafoe Library, University of Manitoba, 1981. Provides a useful biography and a lucid guide to the substantial number of unpublished writings and other artefacts in this invaluable archive.

Grace, Sherrill. "Figures in a Ground: The Craft of Fiction." *Provincial Essays* 7 (1989): 63-76. A sustained and subtle analysis of *Think of the Earth* and *The Robber*, with an evaluation of Brooker's political and aesthetic ideals in relation to modernism.

——. "'The Living Soul of Man': Bertram Brooker and Expressionist Theatre." *Theatre History in Canada* 6.1 (1985): 3-22. A seminal essay on Brooker's dramatic writing. Some of this argument also appears in her *Regression and Apocalypse: Studies in North American Literary Expressionism* (Toronto: University of Toronto, 1989).

Reid, Dennis. *Bertram Brooker*. Canadian Artists Series: 1. Ottawa: National Gallery of Canada, 1979. The best introduction to Brooker as a visual artist, including a chronology of his exhibitions and a selected bibliography. The National Gallery also has a selection of writings by and about Brooker, many drawn from periodicals, in three microfiches devoted to him in its Canadian Art Microdocuments.

St. Pierre, Paul Matthew. "Bertram Brooker." *Dictionary of Literary Biography 88: Canadian Writers, 1920-1959, 2nd Series*, ed. W.H. New (Detroit: Gale Research, 1989): 32-36. The most thorough biographical overview for literary purposes.

Sproxton, Birk. "'The Subjective Underground': The Stream of Consciousness." *Provincial Essays* 7 (1989): 52-62. A persuasive analysis of a modernist technique and a modern as opposed to romantic sensibility in Brooker's poetry.

Tippett, Maria. "'Shape' as an Attention Compeller." *Provincial Essays* 7 (1989): 86-88. Together with Mavor Moore's remarks (89-90), a very suggestive look at the significance of Brooker's writing on advertising.

Wagner, Anton. "'God Crucified Upside-Down': The Plays." *Provincial Essays* 7 (1989): 38-51. A response to Grace's article of 1985, which debates the genre of Brooker's plays in relation to his philosophical and political ideas and to expressionism, with fascinating reference to plays and essays not previously commented upon.

AGMV Marquis
MEMBER OF THE SCABRINI GROUP
Quebec, Canada
2000